I0831392

DOOMSDAY: Haven

The Doomsday Series

Book Two

by

Bobby Akart

Copyright Information

Other Works by Amazon Top 50 Author, Bobby Akart

The Doomsday Series

Apocalypse

Haven

Anarchy

Minutemen

The Yellowstone Series

Hellfire

Inferno

Fallout

Survival

The Lone Star Series

Axis of Evil

Beyond Borders

Lines in the Sand

Texas Strong

Fifth Column

Suicide Six

The Pandemic Series

Beginnings

The Innocents

Level 6

Quietus

The Blackout Series

36 Hours

Zero Hour

Turning Point

Shiloh Ranch

Hornet's Nest

Devil's Homecoming

The Boston Brahmin Series

The Loyal Nine

Cyber Attack

Martial Law

False Flag

The Mechanics

Choose Freedom

Patriot's Farewell

Seeds of Liberty (Companion Guide)

The Prepping for Tomorrow Series

Cyber Warfare

EMP: Electromagnetic Pulse

Economic Collapse

DEDICATIONS

For many years, I have lived by the following premise:

Because you never know when the day before is the day before, prepare for tomorrow.

My friends, I study and write about the threats we face, not only to both entertain and inform you, but because I am constantly learning how to prepare for the benefit of my family as well. There is nothing more important on this planet than my darling wife, Dani, and our two girls, Bullie and Boom. One day, doomsday will come, and I'll be damned if I'm gonna let it stand in the way of our life together.

The Doomsday series is dedicated to the love and support of my family. I will always protect you from anything that threatens us.

ACKNOWLEDGEMENTS

Writing a book that is both informative and entertaining requires a tremendous team effort. Writing is the easy part. For their efforts in making the Doomsday series a reality, I would like to thank Hristo Argirov Kovatliev for his incredible cover art, Pauline Nolet for her editorial prowess, Stef Mcdaid for making this manuscript decipherable in so many formats, Chris Abernathy for his memorable performance in narrating this novel, and the Team—Denise, Joe, Jim, and Shirley—whose advice, friendship and attention to detail is priceless.

In addition, my loyal readers who interact with me on social media know that Dani and I have been fans of the television reality show *Big Brother* since it began broadcasting on CBS in the summer of 2000. The program was one of the greatest social experiments ever imagined. Each season, more than a dozen contestants compete for a half-million-dollar cash prize.

During the months-long airing of the program, the houseguests are isolated from the outside world, but we, the viewers, get to watch their every move via more than a hundred cameras and microphones. The opportunity to study how people interact under these unusual stressful circumstances has allowed me to create diverse and interesting characters for you, dear readers.

Over the years, we've been fortunate to meet several of the past *Big Brother* contestants, and this year, for the second time (the first being our friend Judd Daugherty, who was a doctor in the Boston Brahmin series), I've actually written four of them into the characters through the use of their first name and unique character attributes.

During the airing of season twenty during the summer of 2018, early on in the show, an alliance formed between a group of six who controlled the game from start to finish. You can imagine the high fives Dani and I exchanged when they named their alliance *Level 6*, the title of book three in my Pandemic series released in the summer of 2017.

To season twenty winner, Kaycee Clark; our favorite *showmance* of all time, Angela Rummans and Tyler Crispen; and to one of the funniest, most real people I've ever seen on television, "JC" Mounduix—thank you for inspiring the Rankin family in the Doomsday series!

Thank you all!
Choose Freedom and Godspeed, Patriots!

About the Author

Bobby Akart

Author Bobby Akart has been ranked by Amazon as #55 in its Top 100 list of most popular, bestselling authors. He has achieved #1 bestselling Horror Author, #2 bestselling Science Fiction Author, #3 bestselling Religion & Spirituality Author, #5 bestselling Action & Adventure Author, and #7 bestselling Historical Author.

He has written over twenty international bestsellers, in nearly fifty fiction and nonfiction genres, including the chart-busting Yellowstone series, the reader-favorite Lone Star series, the critically acclaimed Boston Brahmin series, the bestselling Blackout series, the frighteningly realistic Pandemic series, his highly cited nonfiction Prepping for Tomorrow series, and his latest project—the Doomsday series, seen by many as the horrifying future of our nation if we can't find a way to come together.

His novel *Yellowstone: Fallout* reached #50 on the Amazon bestsellers list and earned him two Kindle All-Star awards for most pages read in a month and most pages read as an author. The Yellowstone series vaulted him to the #1 best selling horror author on Amazon, and the #2 best selling science fiction author.

Bobby has provided his readers a diverse range of topics that are both informative and entertaining. His attention to detail and impeccable research have allowed him to capture the imaginations of his readers through his fictional works and bring them valuable knowledge through his nonfiction books.

SIGN UP for Bobby Akart's mailing list to receive special offers, bonus content, and you'll be the first to receive news about new releases in the Doomsday series.

VISIT Amazon.com/BobbyAkart, a dedicated feature page created by Amazon for his work, to view more information on his thriller fiction novels and post-apocalyptic book series, as well as his nonfiction Prepping for Tomorrow series. Visit Bobby Akart's website for informative blog entries on preparedness, writing, and a behind-the-scenes look into his novels.

BobbyAkart.com

Author's Introduction to the Doomsday Series

November 8, 2018
Are we on the brink of destroying ourselves?

Some argue that our nation is deeply divided, with each side condemning the other as the enemy of America. By way of example, one can point to the events leading up to the Civil War in the latter part of the 1850s, right up until the first cannon fire rained upon Fort Sumter in Charleston, South Carolina. It's happened before, and it could happen again.

The war of words has intensified over the last several decades, and now deranged people on the fringe of society have taken matters into their own hands. Ranging from pipe-bomb packages mailed to political leaders and supporters, to a gunman shooting congressmen at a softball practice, words are being replaced with deadly, violent acts.

To be sure, we've experienced violence and intense social strife in this country as a result of political differences. The Civil War was one example. The assassination of Martin Luther King Jr., followed by the raging street battles over civil rights and the Vietnam War, is another.

This moment in America's history feels worse because we are growing much more divisive. Our shared values are being forgotten, and a breakdown is occurring between us and our government, and between us and the office of the presidency.

Our ability to find common ground is gradually disappearing. We shout at the television or quit watching altogether. Social media has become anything but *social.* We unfollow friends or write things in a post that we'd never dream of saying to someone's face.

Friends and family avoid one another at gatherings because they fear political discussions will result in an uncomfortable, even hostile exchange. Many in our nation no longer look at their fellow Americans as being from a different race or religion but, rather, as supporting one political party or another.

This is where America is today, and it is far different from the months leading up to the Civil War. Liberal historians label the conflict as a battle over slavery, while conservative historians tend to argue the issue was over states' rights. At the time, the only thing agreed upon was the field of battle—farms and open country from Pennsylvania to Georgia.

Today, there are many battlefronts. Media—news, entertainment, and social—is a major battlefield. The halls of Congress and within the inner workings of governments at all levels is another. Between everyday Americans—based upon class warfare, cultural distinctions, and race-religion-gender—highlighting our differences pervades every aspect of our lives.

Make no mistake, on both sides of the political spectrum, a new generation of leaders has emerged who've made fueling our divisions their political modus operandi. I remember the bipartisan efforts of Ronald Reagan and Tip O'Neill in the eighties. Also, Bill Clinton and Newt Gingrich in the mid-nineties. The turn of the century hasn't provided us the types of bipartisan working relationships that those leaders of the recent past have generated.

So, here we are at each other's throats. What stops the political rancor and division? The answer to this question results in even more partisan arguments and finger-pointing.

Which leads me to the purpose of the Doomsday series. The term *doomsday* evokes images of the end of times, the day the world ends, or a time when something terrible or dangerous will happen. Sounds dramatic, but everything is relative.

I've repeated this often, and I will again for those who haven't heard it.

All empires collapse eventually. Their reign ends when they are either defeated by a larger and more powerful enemy, or when their financing runs out. America will be no exception.

Now, couple this theory with the words often attributed to President Abraham Lincoln in an 1838 speech interpreted as follows:

America will never be destroyed from the outside. If we falter and lose our freedoms, it will be because we destroyed ourselves.

The Doomsday series depicts an America hell-bent upon destroying itself. It is a dystopian look at what will happen if we don't find a way to deescalate the attacks upon one another. Both sides will shoulder the blame for what will happen when the war of words becomes increasingly more violent to the point where one side brings out the *big guns.*

That's when an ideological battle will result in the bloodshed of innocent Americans caught in the crossfire. Truly, for the future of our nation, doomsday would be upon us.

Thank you for reading with an open mind and not through the lens of political glasses. I hope we can come together for the sake of our families and our nation. God bless America.

Now, couple this theory with the words often attributed to President Abraham Lincoln in an 1838 speech interpreted as follows:

America will never be destroyed from the outside. If we falter and lose our freedoms, it will be because we destroyed ourselves.

The Doomsday series depicts an America hell-bent upon destroying itself. It is a dystopian look at what will happen if we don't find a way to deescalate the attacks upon one another. Both sides will shoulder the blame for what will happen when the war of words becomes increasingly more violent to the point where one side brings out the *big guns.*

That's when an ideological battle will result in bloodshed of innocent Americans caught in the crossfire. Truly, for the future of our nation, doomsday would be upon us.

Thank you for reading with an open mind and not through the lens of political glasses. I hope we can come together for the sake of our families and our nation. God bless America.

Epigraph

"Strategy without tactics is the slowest route to victory.
Tactics without strategy is the noise before defeat."
~ Sun Tzu: *The Art of War*
*****

The real rulers, you'll never see.
~ Anonymous
*****

The Tree of Liberty must be refreshed from time to time
with the blood of patriots and tyrants.
~ Thomas Jefferson
*****

If they bring a knife to a fight, we bring a gun.
~ President Barack Obama, 2008
*****

Either you control destiny, or destiny controls you.
~ George Trowbridge in *Doomsday: Apocalypse*

PREVIOUSLY IN THE DOOMSDAY SERIES

Dramatis Personae

PRIMARY CHARACTERS

George Trowbridge — A wealthy, powerful Washington insider. Lives on his estate in East Haven, Connecticut. Yale graduate. Suffers from kidney failure. Father of Meredith Cortland.

The Sheltons — Tom is retired from the United States Navy and is a former commander at Joint Base Charleston. Married to his wife of forty years, Donna. They have two daughters. Tommie, single, is with Naval Intelligence and stationed on a spy ship in the Persian Gulf. Their oldest daughter, Willa, is married with two young children. The family lives north of Las Vegas. Willa is a captain at Creech Air Force Base, where she serves as a drone pilot. Tom and Donna reside in downtown Charleston.

The Rankin Family — Formerly of Hilton Head, South Carolina, now residing in Richmond, Virginia. Dr. Angela Rankin is a critical care physician at Virginia Commonwealth Medical Center in Richmond. Her husband, Tyler, is a firefighter and a trained emergency medical technician. He was formerly a lifeguard. They have two children. Their daughter, Kaycee, age eleven, nearly died in a helicopter crash as a child. Their youngest child, J.C., age eight, loves history and is a devoted student of America's founding.

The Cortland Family — Michael *Cort* Cortland is chief of staff to a prominent United States Senator from Alabama. His wife, Meredith, is a teacher and the daughter of George Trowbridge. The couple met while they attended Yale University. They have one child, twelve-year-old daughter Hannah. They live in Cort's hometown of Mobile, Alabama. They have an English bulldog named after Yale's mascot, Handsome Dan.

The Hightower Family — Will Hightower is retired from the Philadelphia Police Department and in his mid-forties. After he left Philly SWAT, he got divorced from his wife, Karen. He moved to Atlanta to work for Mercedes-Benz security, only seeing his children—Ethan, age fifteen, and daughter Skylar, age eleven—periodically. Will also has a second job as *Delta.*

Hayden Blount — Born in North Carolina, but now resides in the Washington, DC, area. She is an attorney with a powerful law firm that represents the president in front of the Supreme Court. She formerly clerked for Justice Samuel Alito, a Yale graduate. Single, she lives alone with her Maine coon cat, Prowler.

Book One: *Doomsday: Apocalypse*

It was the beginning of great internal strife, neighbor versus neighbor, warrior versus warrior. The fuse was lit with a simple message, understood by a select few, but impacting the lives of all Americans. It read:

> On the day of the feast of Saint Sylvester,
> Tear down locked,
> Green light burning.
> Love, MM

And so it begins …

In *Doomsday: Apocalypse*, all events occur on New Year's Eve

New York City

It was New Year's Eve, and New York City was the center of the annual celebration's universe. Over a million people had crowded into Times Square to bid a collective farewell to the old year and to express hope and joy for the year ahead.

There were some, however, who had other plans for the night's festivities. A clandestine meeting atop the newly constructed One World Trade Center, ground zero for the most heinous terrorist attack on the United States in history, revealed that another attack was afoot. One that sprang from a meeting in a remote farmhouse in Maryland and was perpetrated by a shadowy group.

In New York, Tom and Donna Shelton, retirees from Charleston, South Carolina, belatedly celebrated their fortieth anniversary atop the Hyatt Centric Hotel overlooking Times Square. Caught up in the moment, they made the fateful decision to join the revelers on the streets for a once-in-a-lifetime opportunity to be part of the famous ball drop and countdown to New Year's.

However, terror reared its ugly head as a squadron of quadcopter drones descended upon Midtown Manhattan, detonating bombs over Times Square and other major landmarks in the city. Chaos ensued and the Sheltons found themselves fighting for their lives.

After an injury to Donna, the couple made their way back to their hotel room, where they thought they were safe. However, Tom received a mysterious text, one that he was afraid to reveal to his wife. It came from a sender whom he considered a part of his distant past. It was an ominous warning that weighed heavily on his mind.

The text message read:

The real danger on the ocean, as well as the land, is people.
Fare thee well and Godspeed, Patriot!
MM

Six Flags Great Adventure, New Jersey

Dr. Angela Rankin and her husband, Tyler, were in the second leg of their educational vacation with their two children, Kaycee and J.C., although the New Year's Eve portion of the trip was supposed to be the fun part. They had arrived at Six Flags Great Adventure, the self-proclaimed scariest theme park on the planet.

Following a trip to Boston to visit historic sites related to our nation's founding, they were headed home to Richmond, Virginia, with planned stops in Philadelphia and Washington to see more landmarks. The planned stop at Six Flags was to be a highlight of the trip for the kids.

The night was full of thrills and chills as they rode one roller coaster after another. Young J.C., their son, wanted to save the *wildest, gut-wrenchingest* roller coaster for last—Kingda Ka. The tallest roller coaster in America, Kingda Ka, in just a matter of seconds, shot its coaster up a four-hundred-fifty-six-foot track until the riders reached the top, where they were suspended for a moment, only to be sent down the other side. Except on New Year's Eve, some of them never made it down, on the coaster, that is.

When the Rankin family hit the top of the Kingda Ka ride, an electromagnetic pulse attack struck the area around Philadelphia, which included a part of the Mid-Atlantic states stretching from Wilmington, Delaware, into northern New Jersey. The devastating EMP destroyed electronics, power grids, and the computers used to operate modern vehicles.

It also brought Kingda Ka to a standstill with the Sheltons and others suspended facedown at the apex of the ride. At first, the riders avoided panicking. To be sure, they were all frightened, but they felt safe thanks to Tyler's reassurances, and they waited to be rescued.

However, one man became impatient and felt sure he and his wife could make their way to safety. On his four-seat coaster car, with the assistance of a college-age man, they broke loose the safety bar in order to crawl out of the coaster. This turned out to be a bad idea. The young man immediately flew head over heels, four hundred feet to his death.

The man who came up with the self-rescue plan and his wife attempted to shimmy down a support post to a safety platform within Kingda Ka but lost their grip. Both of them plunged to their deaths.

Safety personnel finally arrived on the scene, and they began the arduous task of rescuing the remaining passengers, leaving the Rankins for last since they were at the front of the string of coaster cars. Unfortunately, as the safety bar was lifted, J.C. fell out of the car, only to be retrained by a safety harness that had been affixed to his body.

Despite the fact that he was suspended twenty feet below the coaster, held by only a rope, the family worked together to hoist him to safety and an eventual rescue. But their night was not done.

The Rankins made their way to the parking lot, where their 1974 Bronco awaited them. Tyler pulled Angela aside, retrieved his handgun that was hidden under the chassis of the truck, and explained. The EMP had disabled almost all of the vehicles around them. Thousands of people were milling about. Most likely, they had the only operating vehicle for miles. And the moment they started it, everyone would either want a ride or would want to take their truck. When they decided to leave, it would be mayhem. So they waited for the most opportune time—daylight.

Mobile, Alabama

Michael Cortland split his time between his home in Mobile—with wife, Meredith, and daughter, Hannah—and Washington, DC, where he served as the chief of staff to powerful United States Senator Hugh McNeil. Congress had remained in session during what would ordinarily be the Christmas recess due to the political wranglings concerning the President of the United States and attempts to have him removed from office. But that was not the reason Cort, as he was called by his friends and family, was taking the late evening flight home.

He had been summoned by his father-in-law, George Trowbridge, to his East Haven, Connecticut, estate. Trowbridge was considered one of the most powerful people in Washington despite the fact he'd never held public office. Cort was the son Trowbridge never had, and as a result, he had been taken under the patriarch's wing and groomed for great things.

The conversation was a difficult one, as the old man was bedridden and permanently connected to dialysis. However, as they conversed, Cort was left with these ominous words:

Either you control destiny, or destiny controls you.

Cort was consumed by what his father-in-law meant as he waited for a connecting flight from Atlanta, Georgia, to Mobile, Alabama. The flight that should have been routine was anything but. On final approach to Mobile, the plane suffered a total blackout of power. Nothing worked on board the aircraft, including battery backups, warning lights, or communications.

The pilots made every effort to ditch the plane in the Gulf of Mexico, but the impact on the water caused the fuselage to break in two before it sank towards the sandy bottom of the gulf.

Cort leapt into action to help save his surrounding passengers, including an important Alabama congressman from the other side of the aisle. His Good Samaritan efforts almost killed him. He almost drowned on that evening and was fortunate to be rescued and delivered to the emergency room in Mobile.

After a visit from Meredith and Hannah, Cort began to assess the devastating events around the country and then hearkened back to the words of his father-in-law regarding destiny. Deep down, he knew there was a connection.

Atlanta, Georgia

On the surface, Will Hightower appeared to be a man down on his luck although some might argue that he'd made his own bed, now he had to sleep in it, as the saying goes.

Will's life had changed dramatically in the course of two years since a single inartful use of words during a stressful situation caused his family's world to come crashing down. He had been a respected member of Philly SWAT, one of the most renowned special weapons and tactics teams in the nation. Until one night he lost that respect.

During the investigation and media firestorm, his ex-wife, Karen, turned to the arms of another man, one of his partners. His son, Ethan, and daughter, Skylar, were berated in school and alienated from him by their mother. And Will made the decision to leave Philadelphia to provide his family a respite from the continuous attacks from the media and groups who demanded Will be removed from the police force.

With a new start in Atlanta as part of the security team at Mercedes-Benz Stadium, Will looked forward to a new life in a new city, where his children could visit far away from his past. Ethan and Skylar arrived in Atlanta for a long New Year's weekend that was to begin with a concert, featuring Beyoncé and Jay-Z, at the stadium.

A poor choice by his son landed the kids on the field level of the concert in front of the stage, and then the lights went out. Saboteurs had infiltrated the stadium and caused all power to be disconnected. The thousands of concertgoers panicked, and the kids were in peril.

Will was able to find an injured Ethan and frightened Skylar. He whisked them away to the safety of his home; however, their evening was not over. Will was able to pick up on the tragic events occurring around the country. The collapse he'd feared was on the brink of occurring manifested itself.

Then he received a text. Four simple words that meant so much to his future and the safety of his children. It read:

Time to come home. H.

He'd been asked to come home. But not in the sense most would think. His home was not back in Philadelphia with an ex-wife who'd made his life miserable. It was in another place that he'd become a part of since he left the City of Brotherly Love.

It was time for him to go to the Haven, where he was simply

known as Delta.

Washington, DC

Hayden Blount was young, attractive, and a brilliant attorney. She also represented the President of the United States as he fought to protect his presidency. After winning reelection, the president came under attack again, but this time, it was from his own side of the aisle.

Making history, his vice president and members of his cabinet invoked a little-known clause of the Twenty-Fifth Amendment to the Constitution to remove him from office because they deemed him unfit for the job.

Using Hayden's law firm to represent him, the president counterpunched by firing all of the signers of the letter and installing a new cabinet. This created chaos within Washington, and many considered the machinations to have created a constitutional crisis.

The matter was now before the Supreme Court, where Hayden once clerked, and she was putting the final touches on a brief that had to be filed before midnight on New Year's Eve. After a conversation with the senior partner who spearheaded the president's representation, and a brief appearance at the firm's year-end soiree, Hayden left for home.

Trouble seemed to be on the horizon for the young woman when she got stuck on the building's elevator for a brief time. After enduring two drunken carousers, the elevator was fixed, and she happily headed for the subway trains, which carried people around metropolitan Washington, DC.

She was headed south of the city toward Congress Heights when suddenly, just as the train was at its lowest point in a tunnel under the Anacostia River, the lights went out, and so did all power to the train.

A carefully orchestrated cyber attack had been used to shut down all transportation in Washington, DC, including the trains, public buses, and the airports. The city was brought to a standstill, and Hayden was stuck in the subway, in the dark, with a predator stalking her.

She got away from the man who would do her harm, using her survival skills and Krav Maga training. Then she helped some women and children to safety by climbing up a ladder and through a ventilation duct.

Once at home with her beloved Maine coon cat, Prowler, Hayden began to learn of the attacks around the country. She was shocked to learn the Washington transportation outage wasn't the lead story. It was far from it.

Monocacy Farm, South of Frederick, Maryland

The story ended as it began. The people who had initiated these attacks came together for a toast at the Civil War–era farmhouse overlooking the river. They weren't politicians or elected officials. They were spooks, spies, and soldiers. Government officials and bureaucrats—accountable to no one but themselves.

They shared a glass of champagne and cheered on their successes of the evening, hurtful as they were to their fellow Americans. They acknowledged their task had just begun. Standing before them, the host of the gathering closed the meeting with the following words:

"One man's luck is often generated by another man's misfortunes. I, for one, believe that we can make our own luck. It will be necessary to achieve our goals as laid out in our carefully crafted plans.

"With this New Year's toast, I urge all of you to trust the plan. Know that a storm is coming. It will be a storm upon which the blood of patriots and tyrants will spill."

He raised his champagne glass into the air, and everyone in the room followed suit.

"Godspeed, Patriots!"

And so it began …

Doomsday: Haven begins now …

Prologue

October 2018
Orlando, Florida

Ryan Smart crouched down next to his bed and listened. At night, in the darkness, his home was eerily quiet, but he sensed a presence in the living room. He turned to the two sets of eyes that he could barely make out in the ambient light. They eagerly awaited his instructions.

He put his arms on their shoulders and whispered, "Girls, we have to make a break for the front door. You have to run as fast as you can to keep up with your daddy. Can you do that?"

Unable to fully comprehend the situation, they didn't respond, but Ryan sensed they would follow his lead. He slowly rose from his crouch and steadied his nerves.

"Run, girls! Run!"

He bolted out of the bedroom and raced down the long hallway toward the front door. Behind him, the sounds of the girls' feet digging at the floor in an effort to keep up grabbed the attention of the figure lurking in the dark.

"Hey!" the voice shouted as Ryan raced by.

Now the girls had a new sense of urgency as they ran to keep up. His oldest twin, by all of a minute, was quickly by his side while his other girl, who was slightly overweight, lagged behind like the chubby kid in the horror flicks who always got caught by the ghoul or the demon.

"This way, girls!"

Ryan rounded the banister of the stairwell and darted into the library, with his girls hot on his heels. They circled the antler chandelier that hung from the ceiling, its candelabra bulbs dimmed to a low orangish glow.

The trio had eluded the ghostly apparition that had appeared out of nowhere, and now they had run full circle through the house until they reached the family room.

That was when Ryan collided head-on with the dark figure dressed in a black cloak and a matching pointed hat.

The Blair Witch.

"Gotcha!" she exclaimed, the word coming out with a gravelly, evil hiss.

Ryan tried to dodge the witch and rolled over the back of the L-shaped sectional sofa until he was tangled up with half a dozen pillows. Within seconds, the girls leapt on top of his back, doing a victory dance as they panted for air.

"Hide, girls! She'll put us in her cauldron and boil us for supper!"

"I've got you now, my pretties!" The Blair Witch swung her cape and cackled.

Blair Smart, his wife, dressed as a ghoulish witch, circled the end of the sectional and piled on Ryan, too. The Smart family, Ryan, Blair and their two English bulldogs, Chubby and The Roo, had become a tangled pile of people and pup.

"Get off me, you monsters!"

The Roo barked several times and then smothered her daddy with wet, sloppy bulldog kisses. Chubby, whose name was appropriately bestowed upon her from the day she was born, was the first to leave the scrum and plop on the cold tile floor of the kitchen, panting for air.

"Ouch!" exclaimed Ryan as he rolled over in pain. The Roo had spun around and pushed off his nether regions in order to join her sister on the floor. Using his best English accent, he complained, "You guys gotta stop crackin' me clackers. I might need them someday."

Blair swatted at him and kissed him on the cheek. "No, sir. You won't."

Ryan pushed himself up on the sofa and pulled the witch close to him. "Hey, baby, you wanna get ghoulish with me?"

"You're weird," she replied with a laugh. "No, we need to feed the girls. The cats are probably staring in the windows, looking for yummies. And I have no idea what we're gonna eat for dinner."

Ryan pouted and held her hand as she rose to go into the kitchen. He stretched behind the sofa and reached for the remote to turn on the television. Orlando's local news channel filled the screen, and he turned down the volume.

If it bleeds, it leads—was a phrase often used by *New York* magazine in the eighties, referring to fear-based media. Over the years, Ryan had learned a newscast was no different than any other business. It had to make money. In order to make a profit, the station had to sell advertising time. The more viewers the station could boast, the higher the demand. It was basic supply and demand economics.

A report was showing scenes of a violent attack in downtown Orlando at the Dr. Phillips Center, a performing arts complex that frequently hosted concerts, comedy and theatrical events.

Following a comedy show featuring Kathy Griffin and Chelsea Handler, the attendees filed out of the facility only to be greeted by protesters angry with the duo for their stance on political issues. The verbal assaults had erupted into a barrage of fisticuffs, leaving several people badly injured. In today's age of digital imagery courtesy of the smartphone, every punch that drew blood was replayed on the family's big-screen television.

"What happened?" asked Blair as she set the girls' food down on their place mats. Chubby stuck her head in the bowl and began to chomp at her kibbles mixed with strained pumpkin before Blair could set the bowl down.

"Same old, same old. Another day, another riot, or protest, or whatever has managed to piss someone off."

Ryan didn't like to watch the news anymore. It angered him more than it informed him. Plus, he'd become keenly aware that the television news media fed him what they wanted him to see. The nation had become hyper-politicized. It didn't matter what interaction Ryan and Blair had with the outside world, somebody's political agenda or point of view slipped into their consciousness. They tried to avoid it by watching less television, to no avail, as tonight's newscast proved.

He was about to turn off the monitor when Blair stopped him. "Wait. Check out the Mega Millions payout. One-point-six billion dollars. Maybe we should play?"

Ryan chuckled. "The lottery is a scam. It's a tax on poor people by giving them hope to hit it big, but really they're pissin' their money away."

Blair slugged him. "You're such a pessimist sometimes."

He shrugged and then mumbled, "I guess the news is getting to me."

Blair tried to cheer him up. "Come on. I have an idea. Let's play a ticket. It's only a dollar, for Pete's sake."

It was a Friday evening and the drawing was to take place that night. Ryan didn't want to go out just to buy a lottery ticket, but he wouldn't mind going to Publix to pick up something to eat that didn't require his bride to cook.

"Okay, deal. But we have to get some Boar's Head meats and cheeses with some of that thick Sara Lee Artesano bread, okay?"

"Fine by me," Blair replied. "Let's pick our numbers. There are five regular numbers and then the sixth number works as a multiplier. If we hit the winning numbers, we can cash in on the one-point-six billion bucks!"

Ryan laughed and pulled his wife to sit down next to him again. He turned off the television and retrieved his phone off the sofa table. "Okay, let me put our numbers on the notepad app; then we'll head for the store. Whadya wanna play?"

"No, we'll do it together," she replied. "Like this. I'll pick a number, and then you pick a number. Right?"

Ryan smiled and readied himself for the first pick. "Go ahead, Blair Witch. What's the first number?"

"Four. There are four Smarts, so we should pick four."

"Um, okay. I pick eight."

"Why eight?"

Ryan quickly replied, "It's my birthday."

"Everybody does that," she said, shaking her head. She thought of her next number. "I pick eleven. One is a powerful number. Combining it with another one makes the number eleven, one-one, creating a master number."

"You're joking, right?"

"Nope," said Blair, who was very serious. "In numerology, the number eleven is said to have powerful forces that can guide you toward change and opportunity."

Ryan shook his head and laughed. "All-righty, then. I choose twenty-two. There are two of us and we're a team. Two times eleven is twenty-two."

"Good grief," said Blair with an accompanying eye roll. "Well, lucky for you, despite your logic, twenty-two is also a master number."

"Hey, I'm gettin' the hang of this stuff."

Ryan just earned another eye roll. Blair summarized. "So we have four, eight, eleven, twenty-two, and we need one more. I choose one because we only need one set of numbers to win one billion dollars."

Ryan cocked his head. "Wait, the jackpot is one-point-six billion."

"I know, but after the government sucks the taxes out of our winnings, we'll only get a billion."

"Oh, yeah. Damn government!" Ryan genuinely lamented the thought of paying nearly half his winnings in taxes. He immediately began to think of ways to minimize his tax bite. It was the American way.

"All right," continued Blair. "We've picked out five main numbers. Let's add them all together. When we have that number, since it's a multi-digit number, we'll add it together to make our last number."

"Huh?"

"Just trust me on this. I am the Blair Witch."

The two of them reiterated their numbers. One. Four. Eight. Eleven. Twenty-two. The total was forty-six.

"Now what?" asked Ryan.

"Okay, forty-six is a multi-digit number, so we'll add four plus six to equal ten. Ten is our Megaball number."

"Why don't we add together eleven and twenty-two?"

"They're master numbers."

"I'm so confused."

"Relax, Mr. Smart, I've got this," said Blair with a smile. "One, four, eight, eleven, twenty-two, and the gold Megaball number is ten. I feel like a winner, how about you?"

Ryan laughed and gave his wife a high five. The two fed the cats on the way out to their garage and talked during the short drive to Publix about how they'd spend their winnings. Blair was first with her wish list.

"I'm a simple girl. You can just buy me baubles and bags. How about you? Do you still wanna build your dream beach house?"

Ryan thought for a moment. Florida had just experienced two years of back-to-back devastation at the hands of Hurricane Irma and then Michael. He wasn't sure if he wanted to deal with the storms that might come their way someday.

"Actually, I was thinking the mountains."

"Tennessee?"

Ryan shook his head and replied, "Nah, been there, done that. Twice. North Carolina, maybe. I love the Smokies, or even the foothills that would be within a couple of hours of the coast. Ever since I was a kid skiing around Banner Elk, I liked the concept of owning property in a secluded spot. You know, on a lake or maybe a river."

"Sounds heavenly," cooed Blair as they pulled into the Publix parking lot, which was teeming with shoppers, or lottery ticket buyers.

Ryan screeched on the brakes. "Watch out!"

Blair used the dashboard to brace herself as their truck screeched to a halt. A homeless man pushed a shopping cart between two cars into the middle of the parking lot without looking. Ryan had seen him at the last second.

Blair let out a sigh. "Jeez, Louise. We've got ya, buddy."

"No kidding," added Ryan as he found a parking spot and the two exited the vehicle.

Inside, the store was full, as fellow *lottery winners* worked their way around the customer service desk. A line of twenty people wrapped their way around the kiosk and into the floral department, waiting their turn to make a play for the Mega Millions jackpot.

Blair sighed. "Honey, we can skip it. It's pie in the sky anyway."

"No, I've got a feeling. You wait in line. I'll hit the deli counter and pick up the bread. By the time I make the rounds, you'll be near the front."

"Sounds good." Blair squeezed her husband's hand, and Ryan was off to gather up their dinner. By the time he got back, she was the next in line.

He was slightly out of breath from his shopping. "Good, I'm glad I caught you before you got to the front. I have an idea."

"What is it?"

"Let's both play the same numbers."

"Why? We'll just split the winnings."

"Exactly," Ryan responded. "I'll take a lump sum and deal with the tax hit. We'll have plenty of money left over to build a new house or whatever. You take the cash payout over thirty years. That'll give you a guaranteed income for life, pretty much."

At the time, Blair was forty-five and Ryan was fifty-eight. They never spoke about it, but longevity generally favored women, and their thirteen-year age difference would leave Blair to support herself for many years after Ryan passed away. His logic was solid.

She shrugged. "Um, you're the boss. Makes sense to me."

"Wait, what was that?" he asked with a big grin.

"Makes sense to me," she repeated.

"No, before that. You know, the *boss* part."

"Shut up. It was a slip of the tongue in a moment of weakness. Give me a dollar. I might just keep my winnings for myself."

Ryan pulled out a dollar, and the two of them approached Carlos the customer service agent. His robotic actions didn't allow him to notice that both of the Smarts played the same numbers.

1 – 4 – 8 – 11 – 22 with a Megaball Number of 10.

As they exited the kiosk, Blair pulled Ryan in front of the lottery ticket dispensing machine. "Wait, I wanna take a snap for Instagram. Hold your ticket next to mine."

They positioned their hands under the pink flamingo emblazoned below the Florida Lottery logo on the side of the machine. Blair took a couple of pictures and scrolled to her Instagram app.

"No, you can't post it on the 'Gram," Ryan admonished. "Then everybody and their brother will know we won. They'll be on our doorstep in the morning with their paws out."

"But—" began Blair before he interrupted her.

"No, here's what we'll do. When we win, we'll tell no one. We'll hire one of those attorneys in Tallahassee specializing in lottery trusts to hide the identities of the winners from the public. Then we'll systematically call all of our friends and family."

"But you said we can't tell anyone," interjected Blair.

"No, not to tell them about winning. Instead, we're gonna ask, no, beg for a loan. We'll make it something big, like five thousand dollars. They're all gonna say no. Right? So when we win, if we do tell them and they come around looking for their slice of the pie, we can say '*remember back when I needed the five grand?*' My answer's the same. N-O, no."

Blair shoved her ticket into her shorts pocket and escorted Ryan out of the store. "You're so rude, husband."

PART ONE

NEW YEAR'S EVE

Two years later …

CHAPTER 1

Early Morning
New Year's Eve

Ryan Smart awoke before dawn on New Year's Eve. It didn't matter that a four-day-long holiday weekend was upon them. There were still things to attend to, and he had a couple of appointments scheduled throughout the day.

He quietly kissed Chubby and The Roo on the top of their heads, then made his way to Blair, where he nuzzled up against her neck and whispered, "I love you." A slight smile came across her face and she mouthed the words back to him. At this hour, that was as much as he'd get from his wife of nearly twenty-five years.

She typically slept for a couple of hours past when he got up for the day. To balance things out, she always stayed up a few hours later at night. It was one of those compromises made in marriage that allowed a couple to have their *alone time* without having to take nights out with the girls or play in Friday night poker games with the guys.

Ryan made his way into the bathroom and closed the door behind him so as not to disturb the girls. He hopped on the scales, as he'd done every day since the summer of 2018. Earlier that year, he'd become concerned about his heart. Hypertension and the threat of Type-II diabetes had raised alarms that he'd kept hidden from the love of his life. His doctor started him on medications, but Ryan was encouraged to do his part.

He coupled a better diet with weight training and exercise at the local gym. By year's end, he'd lost nearly fifty pounds and was in the best shape of his life. He vowed not to go back to his previously chubby self, a promise he made to himself, and for the benefit of

Blair. It was selfish, he'd often thought to himself, to get so big in the first place.

Turning sixty hadn't caused him to place one foot in the grave, as they say. He looked in the mirror and a young man looked back, at least in Ryan's eyes. To be sure, the graying hair wasn't what he liked to see, but hey, at least it was all still there.

His two-day beard came out gray, something he could deal with. What drove him nuts were all the squirrely hairs that emerged around his eyebrows, ears, and nose. Over the last several years, he'd become a proficient plucker, even watching YouTube videos to master the art.

Then Blair warned him that at some point, his eyebrows might stop growing, so he took to trimming them. He wasn't sure if she was pulling his leg, as images of Larry Hagman, J.R. of Dallas fame, and his bushy brows would pop into his mind. He returned to plucking anyway and was pleased to see the Hagman-brow theory was spot on. They sure enough came back, whenever and in whatever length they felt like.

Ryan got dressed and made his way to the kitchen. As he got older, he found himself adopting an established routine that included fixing an insulated cup with a mixture of iced decaffeinated coffee and Fairlife low-fat chocolate milk. He'd started avoiding the caffeine to fight the hypertension years ago, not that he needed the stimulant to get the juices flowing in the morning, so to speak. He was always full of energy when he woke up.

He poured a bowl of cereal and sliced up a banana for extra flavor. Ryan leaned against the counter as he turned on FoxNews to see if the world had gone to hell in a handbasket overnight. As he watched the news reports from New York City, where they were setting up security for the big New Year's Eve festivities in Times Square, his mind wandered to the state of the nation.

Over the last two years, the country had become even more polarized as the presidential campaigns heated up. The president had brought America's economy to life in his first two years in office. Every demographic saw record employment and wage numbers. He began his campaign on the premise that he'd made promises to the American people and he'd kept them.

But then the primary season began two years ago, and the rhetoric turned increasingly ugly. The president's economic accomplishments immediately became a target for his political opponents. A constant barrage in the media began to take a toll on the American psyche. Despite stellar economic numbers to the contrary, politicians effectively began to convince the public that all was not as it seemed.

When the Federal Reserve surprisingly raised interest rates in October just before the election, the stock market came tumbling down. The sell-offs became so large that program trading kicked in, virtually erasing all of the profits investors had earned in the past four years. This was seen as the potential death blow to the president's reelection efforts, but his popularity remained firm with his base, and he managed a win in November.

The protests in major cities had grown out of control after the election. The allegations of ballot tampering, foreign meddling, and cyber attacks on voting machines once again called the election results into question. Without any tangible proof that the president was reelected with the benefit of these alleged misdeeds, people took to the streets from coast to coast, expressing their anger by destroying businesses and others' personal property.

The National Guard had been called in to contain riots in Seattle, Portland, and San Francisco. Angry mobs stormed government buildings in Chicago, Detroit, and New York, demanding recounts and justice. The situation became so bad that local municipalities declared early evening curfews to keep the mobs off the streets, to no avail. There simply weren't enough members of law enforcement to quell the uprisings. It was an anger that hadn't been seen since the Vietnam War, and now it was relentless.

Ryan watched as the reporting switched to the White House, where the president and his family were leaving for Florida to Mar-a-Lago in Palm Beach, Florida. The camera panned out to the protective iron fencing that surrounded the White House grounds, separating the beautifully manicured lawn from the many thousands of protestors holding up signs and chanting, "Hell no, we won't go."

Ryan finished his cereal and chuckled. "Thank God for iron fences." He rinsed his bowl out and placed it in the sink. After topping off his iced coffee drink, he headed for the front door. Before he left, he paused to look at the framed collage Blair had created two years ago. She'd displayed the photograph of their Mega Millions lottery tickets that she took. Underneath the image, the numbers 1 – 4 – 8 – 11 – 22 – 10 were written on the canvas with a black Sharpie.

She'd also included a newspaper clipping from the *Orlando Sentinel.* He read the headline and the accompanying byline aloud. "Two local winners in one-point-six billion Mega Millions payout. Anonymous winners purchased tickets back-to-back at local Publix."

Ryan put on his jacket and wrapped a wool scarf around his neck. Then he smiled and said, "Thank you," as he walked out into the icy cold North Carolina morning.

CHAPTER 2

Morning
New Year's Eve
North Carolina

Ryan climbed into his new Ranger Crew XP 1000 NorthStar four-wheeler and fired the motor. The enclosed cab with climate control was a feature not found on any other off-road utility vehicle. Heck, at the twenty-eight-thousand-dollar price tag, he could've purchased a new midsized sport utility vehicle. But then, that wouldn't befit the Ranger's purpose.

With the heat beginning to warm his feet and the morning sun revealing a smattering of snowflakes falling from the sky, Ryan took off for the barn and his morning meeting with his guys.

It was understood by the regulars who lived on the property that every day was a workday, to an extent. To be sure, if somebody got hurt or had a matter to attend to off-property, they could certainly take the time they needed. However, they were expected back as soon as possible because they all shared a common mindset. You just never knew when a catastrophe might strike.

Ryan drove along the gravel road that led away from the main house toward the always-locked front gate. On the few occasions when guests arrived, they had access to a telephone that rang in the main house first and then in his destination, the large barn that had been erected in the center of the property, designated HB-1.

When he arrived at the barn that contained a large foreman's office, his two main guys, *his right arm and left arm*, stood outside with mugs of hot coffee in their hands, allowing the steam to float into the air as they spoke.

Ryan's number one, who'd been there since he and Blair had purchased the property almost two years ago, was a hulk of a man. Standing six feet four, his tall frame was perfectly proportioned with his chiseled physique. Genetics favored him early in life, but working in the lumber industry following his stint in the military had hardened him into head-to-toe muscle.

Known as Alpha, he was part of the crew who had assembled the post and beam barn that was the first modern structure added by the Smarts after they purchased the property. The company he worked for, Vermont Frames, had assembled the timber frame structure in Vermont and shipped it on a flatbed trailer to the Smarts in North Carolina.

Alpha was the head of the assembly crew, and during the construction of the barn, he and Ryan quickly became friends. His actual name was Roger, last name unknown, but that didn't matter to Ryan. He hadn't called him anything other than his nickname, Alpha, since the beginning.

A former combat soldier in the United States Army, Alpha had proudly served his country during multiple tours in the Middle East. He'd trained with the Special Forces Operational Detachment at Fort Bragg and always enjoyed his time in North Carolina. When Ryan made him an offer to stay that included a home and an opportunity to be a part of something special, Alpha didn't hesitate to accept.

"Good morning, fellas," Ryan greeted cheerfully as he exited the Ranger. "Snow might be coming."

"They got a foot in Vermont overnight," said Alpha in his deep, baritone voice. "I don't miss it at all."

"Same here," said the older man who stood next to Alpha. "The damp cold gets into your bones."

"Echo, for a farmer, you sure do squall a lot about the weather," quipped Ryan as he slapped the older man on the back. He pointed toward the barn door and suggested they go inside.

As he did, Echo, born Justin Echols, responded, "Here's the thing. When you're farmin', you hope for sunny blue skies and mild weather."

"God doesn't make perfect weather," joked Ryan.

The former tobacco farmer continued in his crusty voice. "True, but he doesn't have to make it so doggone inhospitable sometimes. I remember in the winter of oh-nine, the dadgum jet stream dipped down so low that the temperatures around Boone and Banner Elk never got above freezin'."

Echo, the title bestowed upon him by Ryan when he was brought on board to manage the property's farming and livestock operation, had had a burgeoning tobacco farm until America's penchant for smoking waned and the Federal Tobacco Quota Program was phased out years ago.

He and his wife had tried to hold onto their business, but eventually the larger corporate farms that exceeded a hundred acres squeezed out the little guys like the Echols. The maxim that the only thing more lucrative than an acre of tobacco was another acre of tobacco held true. Eventually, the larger agribusiness companies like Cargill and the Koch brothers moved in and purchased up farms that were barely making ends meet.

Ryan had met Echo at a nearby farmers' co-op one day, and the two struck up a casual conversation. He invited the now-retired couple to the house for dinner, and they immediately hit it off. Throughout the evening, Blair and Ryan learned more about the valuable skills the Echols could offer and immediately convinced them to join the team.

Ryan recalled how he'd brought Alpha and Echo on board as the three men settled into the chairs around a hand-built wooden table in the center of the foreman's office. Over the past two years, the three of them, along with Blair, had expanded upon the Smarts' dream for the property.

They'd constructed numerous small homes and outbuildings with the aid of outside construction workers brought down from Vermont, New Hampshire, and Maine during the winter months. Over time, families were accepted into their community. Others purchased property, and still more built small homes that would be just large enough to suit their needs.

The Smarts also brought new life to the dozens of original structures that dotted the landscape of the two-hundred-acre property stretching along the meandering Henry River in Central North Carolina. These abandoned older structures had fallen into disrepair until Hollywood came knocking.

Once the set of the *Hunger Games* movie franchise, the Henry River Mill Village was now owned by Ryan and Blair Smart, and it had taken on a new name—*Haven.*

CHAPTER 3

Morning
New Year's Eve
The Haven

Western ghost towns have always been a tourist destination. Travelers enjoyed visiting the dusty remnants of old mining towns left over from the glory days of the Gold Rush era, now abandoned but still filled with iconic tumbleweeds and decrepit horse troughs.

In the Eastern U.S., there was another financial boom in the early twentieth century that resulted in small towns and villages springing up in support of what became known as the Industrial Revolution.

New innovations in manufacturing and automation swept the nation like wildfire, with small towns and villages being constructed to support the workers who came from rural America seeking work. Often situated along rivers or near shipping ports, these new manufacturing facilities took advantage of the easy transportation and the unlimited free power the steady flow of a river could provide.

As a result, the quintessential mill town was born, with the iconic image of a riverfront factory attached to a large waterwheel. It was a scene that emerged all along the East Coast and became just as prevalent as any horse-drawn carriage.

One such town had been established along the Henry River thirty minutes outside Hickory, North Carolina, one of the leading furniture industry centers in the state. The mill town, known as Henry River Mill Village, was established in 1905 and, like so many gold-panning towns of the Western U.S., promises of employment and high wages lured new residents.

For a while, the new mill town delivered on those promises. In a short period of time, as interest in the town grew, more structures were constructed until thirty-five small homes, a two-story boardinghouse, and numerous outbuildings supported the population, who worked almost exclusively at the mill.

For decades, the mill produced miles upon miles of fine yarn. However, like the boomtowns that rose out of the crusty dirt during the Gold Rush, this mill town was destined to go bust.

Eventually, industry found its way into larger population centers, using energy resources far more efficient than waterwheels, and the appetite for fine yarns began to lessen. The Henry River Mill shut down in 1973.

Sadly, the town began to die. People moved away, seeking work or a better life for their families in large cities like Charlotte and Raleigh-Durham. The town was totally abandoned by 1987 when its last resident found work elsewhere and left. All that remained was a ghost town, a throwback to the industrial age from the turn of the early 1900s.

The property changed hands as each owner fought vandals and mischievous teens. Then a totally unexpected thing happened to this quiet, desolate part of North Carolina. Hollywood came knocking.

The *Hunger Games* movie team needed a location that exuded a dystopian feel in a post-apocalyptic world. The structures that remained were in remarkably good condition considering their age of over a hundred years. The producers agreed the abandoned town would serve as the ideal setting for the fictional District 12 that appeared in the first movie of the series.

During the filming of the movie, the actors and production crew began to have an unusual feeling about Henry Mill Village. Very subtly, it became apparent that the property might be haunted. Several unusual sightings occurred, especially at night along the banks of the Henry River as well as in the main house, the largest of the structures on the property, where sounds of breaking glass and large objects striking walls could be heard.

After the filming ended and the team pulled out, the town was returned to its abandoned state, but the rumors of the hauntings persisted. Since the filming ended, a family purchased the property and began to conduct historic tours on the property, focusing on the *Hunger Games* film and the property's hauntings.

When Ryan learned that Henry River Mill Village was discreetly on the market, as soon as he and Blair settled their Mega Millions lottery winnings with the state of Florida, they made an offer and closed thirty days later.

The Haven was born.

CHAPTER 4

Morning
New Year's Eve
The Haven

"What's on tap for today, fellas?" asked Ryan as he fiddled with a pencil and a notepad on top of the table. His mind was still on the events he'd seen on the news earlier. Sometimes he hated when he was right.

"Well, all the boys are still up north for the holidays," began Alpha. "It was good of ya to allow them the whole week between Christmas and New Year's weekend."

Ryan sipped his coffee through a straw and nodded. "We got an early start because winter hit them early and shut their building sites down. Plus, now that we're in our second winter of remodeling the old worker homes, we've become more efficient."

"Storing the building materials in HB-2 helped," said Alpha.

"Well, it made sense to have them bring another barn with them from Vermont when they came south in October. We've got all the lumber we need to do our renovations and frame up several more homes. The window and door packages in the shipping containers, coupled with the roofing materials, just about give us four new tiny homes for the right buyer."

Echo added to the conversation. "Speaking of which, Miss Blair said you have two sets of prospects coming in today. That's kind of odd for a holiday, isn't it?"

Ryan shrugged and sat back in his chair. "Not if you watch the news. The country's fallin' apart, boys."

"Just like you said it would," added Alpha. "I've got buddies who went into the Guard after they left the Army. They're being deployed all over the place, from the Mexican border to the big cities. The president keeps adding more guardsmen because the media argued he was violating *Posse Comitatus* with his use of regular military."

The Posse Comitatus Act was passed by Congress in 1878. The law prohibits the use of the military for law enforcement purposes. The act allows, however, the president to mobilize the National Guard in a state with the governor's consent, and usually upon the state's request. This carved out an exception to the act in which the National Guard could be used under state authority or by executive order of the president.

"From what I've seen on the news in the last week or so, we're gonna need to double the size of the Guard," said Ryan. "Either way, interest in the Haven has grown substantially over the last six months, and we're now at the point we can be very selective."

"Based upon what you have in place, what kind of people are you still looking for?" asked Echo.

Ryan stood and wandered around the spacious foreman's office. "You know, Echo, we've always treated this like a business, but it's not about money. You guys know what happened that enabled us to cut the check for this place. We have a much larger purpose, as you know, that will benefit all of us. Toward that end, the selection of the people whom we sell to is the most important role I have."

"It's a people business," added Alpha.

"Exactly," said Ryan as he walked past his right-hand man. "With every home or parcel we sell, it's not about the money but, rather, whether this person is a good fit for our community. They have to be like-minded thinkers, committed to what we believe in. But they also have to offer something of value.

"Security was first and foremost, and we've filled those slots with very capable folks. We've also made arrangements with our security team that ensures they'll be here when the time comes.

"Initially, we needed guys who were handy with tools, both from a construction standpoint and the ability to maintain anything mechanical around here. Even in a grid-down scenario, with our solar arrays and accompanying power generators, our machinery will be a luxury that must be maintained to last for many years."

"Farmers too, right, boss?" asked Echo.

"You bet, my friend. Farmers, hunters, expert canners, and even survivalists. We never know if a situation might arise in which we'll need to send a team outside the Haven on a run of some sort. We need people who can go beyond the gates, live off the land if necessary, and get back here alive."

Alpha asked, "How do you feel about your medical personnel?"

"Weak. The ones we do have on board are absentee owners. There's no guarantee they'll make it here if a catastrophic event occurs. Sure, we have several of us who know how to bandage up wounds and deal with minor breaks. Blair has made sure our Armageddon Hospital is well equipped and stocked with supplies. But we need more people capable of treating sickness and injuries."

Alpha finished his coffee and looked at the snow flurries that were beginning to land on the windows. "If this stuff sticks, you might have cancellations."

Ryan walked over to see for himself. He pulled out his phone, which beeped, indicating he had a text message from Blair. She was awake.

"Well, the first guy is a communications specialist. During our background check, we confirmed he had ample knowledge of different radio systems and off-grid communications methods. Heck, the guy even claims he can set up what he called a *Bob Ware* phone system."

"Huh?" asked Alpha. "You mean barbwire?"

Ryan laughed as he finished off his coffee. "You heard me right the first time. I said Bob Ware, like it was some fella's name. The guy coming this morning was born and raised in Texas. He's an avid hunter and fisherman. He's got the comms skills and—"

"Hang on, boss," interrupted Echo. "You gotta help me out here. What's a Bob Ware phone system?"

Ryan smiled and explained what he'd learned online. "The guy brought it up during our second phone interview and promised to give me the details when he comes by this morning. Here's what I learned. Back in the day, especially on large ranches in Texas, barbed wire was used to encircle their property and keep the cattle in. In order to communicate with the ranch house, or a barn like HB-1, they hooked up store-bought telephones to the barbed-wire fencing."

"No way," said Alpha.

"Yeah, true story," continued Ryan. "They'd run a thin wire from the house to the barbed wire. The telephone signal would follow the length of the wire and transfer down the line along the barbed wire to the other phone's location."

"Well, I'll be dogged," said Echo. "I've had a farm and I've never heard of such."

Ryan patted his friend on the back and made his way toward the door. "Well, I hope we'll never need such a crazy way of communicating, but this new guy has the mindset to create one if, or shall I say when, the time comes."

Leaving that ominous thought hanging in the air, Ryan took off for the newest building on the property, Haven House, designated HH.

CHAPTER 5

Midmorning
New Year's Eve
Haven House

"Where are they? Where are my girls?" Ryan announced as he quickly closed the heavy wood-carved front door in an attempt to keep the cold wind from blowing the moist air into the Smarts' home. The winter storm that had been predicted days ago was showing itself, prompting hazardous-driving warnings and causing air travel to descend into chaos due to cancellations.

"They're in here, Daddy, eating their brunch like good girls," Blair replied on behalf of the girls, whose faces were buried in a bowl of kibbles and boiled egg. Rarely did Chubby and The Roo come up for air when it was time to eat. Chubby, naturally, knocked her yummies out first. Then she'd hover over her sister's bowl until she finished. At the first opening, she'd sneak in and lick The Roo's bowl. The poor child never seemed to get enough to eat.

Ryan entered the kitchen and kissed Blair on the cheek.

"Your lips are cold!" she playfully protested.

"Yeah, but your cheeks are warm. Thanks for thawing me out."

She swatted at him with a kitchen towel and turned back to the stove. "I'm gonna invite Alpha, Echo, and his missus over for lunch. I've got chili simmering, and corn bread is next on my to-do list. Whadya think?"

"For sure. I've got that interview at eleven. After that?"

"Yeah, I'll let them know," replied Blair. She continued mixing the corn bread recipe from her Aunt Sissy's cookbook while Ryan scooped up the girls' empty bowls and set them in the sink. Then

Blair turned to business. "Are you still a hundred percent on the new guy?"

Ryan opened the refrigerator and stared inside. He surveyed his choices on something to munch on, much like a bear who'd just entered a campsite and was faced with too many options. He opened the deli drawer and pulled out a pack of sliced Swiss cheese to satisfy his craving.

"You know how it is," he began. "We seek these people out, or they're referred to us. Then we scour the web and social media to see what we can learn about them. They have no idea we're even interested in pitching the Haven to them. Yet we know they're open to the prospect based upon their Facebook posts."

"I know," interjected Blair. "Our whole approach is weird, but we can't just open the Haven up to anybody. We have to be able to trust these people to have our backs, and everyone else's who lives here. You build a team through recruitment, not an open or revolving door."

Ryan put away the cheese and munched on a slice as he spoke. "Well, this fella fills a void we have in the communications aspect of the Haven. When the time comes, knowledge will be power, or in our case, information will help us secure the place. Whether it's within the confines of our fences and walls, or keeping abreast of events around the country, we can better protect ourselves from outsiders by keeping up with their activities."

"His paperwork looks good, too," added Blair.

When the Smarts came up with the concept of the Haven, they decided to be very selective in whom they sell property to. Because of their financial windfall by winning the lottery, they didn't need the money from prospective entrants into their secretive community. However, they felt it was necessary to charge their new residents something so they had a financial stake in the Haven—*skin in the game*, as they say.

If a prospective resident had a strong résumé, which meant having useful skills, a verifiable background, and a like-minded approach to preparedness, but were unable financially to make a purchase with cash, the Smarts would finance the property with only ten percent down and low payments thereafter.

Ryan grabbed a bottle of water from the refrigerator and drank half of it down. He rummaged through the junk drawer, as they called it. It was a catchall for everything from pens and notepads to scissors and Ryan's pillbox for his daily medications. Despite his excellent conditioning, now that he was in his sixties, his doctor suggested he continue his blood pressure and cholesterol medications daily.

He checked his watch. "Do you wanna meet him?"

She brushed past him and touched her hand to his shoulder. "Nah, I trust your judgment. The vetting part passed my test."

"All your PI training paid off," added Ryan. When he and Blair met, she'd maintained a private investigator's license, during which time she became adept at conducting background investigations. With the explosion of information on the internet, her duties in vetting prospective buyers online was much easier.

"Somewhat, but you're the best judge of character. Size him up, and if you're not sure, introduce him to Alpha. He doesn't like many people, so if he approves, then I say bring him on board."

"He wants to buy an existing place. He's into the rustic feel of the Haven."

Blair laughed. "Good, sell him H13 down by the old mill site on the river. It's got plenty of ghosts to satisfy his rustic feel."

Ryan hit the bathroom before going back out into the cold and stopped to check the news headlines on his iPad. A lot of the focus in Washington was on the briefs being submitted to the Supreme Court in advance of next week's big court hearing. He read part of the story to himself.

The justices called for more briefs in the president's attempts to shut down the Twenty-Fifth Amendment action taken against him by his cabinet. They seem to be singularly focused on the propriety of the attempt, so the Court granted review of the lower court decisions to determine if the overall case had merit.

There have been several amicus curiae, friends of the court, briefs filed by nonparties to the action from all sides of the political spectrum. One Court commentator referred to these additional briefs as noise, claiming they were purposefully designed to confuse the Court as to the real matter at hand.

All eyes will be on the president's legal team, led by Pat Cipollone and Hayden Blount, a former clerk to Justice Samuel Alito. Court watchers believe Blount has a unique perspective into the minds of the justices that could tip the scales of justice in favor of the president.

Ryan closed his iPad and smiled.

"You go, Foxy!"

CHAPTER 6

Late Morning
New Year's Eve
The Haven

"I'm impressed with your security," said the young man as he extended his hand to greet Ryan. "Eugene O'Reilly. Nice to meet you, sir."

Ryan tucked his cell phone back into his pocket and removed his glove in order to shake hands with their visitor. "Ryan Smart, and sir is not necessary. It just makes me feel old."

The two shared a laugh and O'Reilly continued. "Well, I have to say it wasn't a bad drive from St. Louis. After I passed Knoxville and got off the interstate, it was a little bit over the river and through the woods, but not too bad."

Ryan looked at O'Reilly's transportation. It was a newer model GMC conversion van with an enclosed trailer attached to its hitch. The jet-black ensemble had a mysterious look about it that raised Ryan's curiosity. "That's quite a rig. I guess, um, I expected you to fly in to Charlotte and rent a car."

O'Reilly kicked sheepishly at the gravel beneath his feet. He rolled his head on his neck to relieve some of the tension built up during his long drive. Then he explained, "Nope, that's all I've got. I mean, sir, um, Ryan, I don't want to be presumptuous, but in a way, I guess I am. I'm here to stay. I've sold my condo in St. Louis. I've packed up everything I want or need. Your wife indicated that you have a box truck that I could use to pick up some furniture in Hickory, or even Charlotte, if necessary. Most importantly, I've come with two forms of payment—gold or junk silver."

Ryan chuckled and looked back at O'Reilly's vehicles. They were like new and most likely filled with the man's earthly possessions. He and Blair had verbally agreed to accept him into the Haven if he passed Ryan's sniff test. Not that Ryan was gonna sniff the man's armpits, or his butt, like the girls were prone to do. Ryan just needed to get a feel for O'Reilly to make sure he was going to be a good fit and, most importantly, trustworthy. Once a new arrival became a resident of the Haven, the lives of their neighbors would be just as important as their own.

"Eugene," started Ryan as he motioned for the man to join him in the Ranger, "or should I call you Gene?"

"Actually, I go by the nickname given to me by my grandfather, Eugene O'Reilly Sr. I'm technically the third."

"Yeah, I remember that from your paperwork," interjected Ryan.

O'Reilly was about to continue when a pickup truck approached containing Alpha and Echo. They pulled to an abrupt stop. Alpha and Echo jumped out of the truck and joined them.

Alpha addressed Ryan without looking at the visitor. "We're about to run to the back forty and feed the cattle. Blair said you wanted to see me?"

Ryan replied, "Yeah, just for a minute. I want you to meet Eugene O'Reilly. He's come to see us from St. Louis."

Alpha and O'Reilly shook hands.

Then Echo stepped forward to shake and began to laugh. "Did you say your name was Eugene O'Reilly? As in Radar?"

"Um, yeah," replied the shy young man. "I was about to explain to Ryan about my nickname. You see, a bit of trivia here, but my name is the same as the character on the old television show *MASH*. In fact, my grandfather was stationed at Joint Base Charleston in the 628th Mission Support Group as part of the communications squadron."

"Nice pedigree," Alpha added.

"Yes. Well, anyway, his nickname became Radar. My father was a professor, and because he didn't go into the military, gramps didn't give him a nickname. When I was a kid, he nicknamed me X-Ray because I was into the X-Men comic books. Long story short, nobody calls me Eugene or Gene. I've always been known as X-Ray."

"Well, alrighty then," said Ryan, his favorite response to a long-winded explanation. "Whadya think, boys? We've got a communications whiz with a comparable name to a famous television military guy, and his chosen name is already part of the military phonetic alphabet."

Alpha was still unconvinced. "Can you shoot a gun?"

"I can hit the mark," X-Ray replied confidently. Then he pointed his thumb over his shoulder at the trailer. "I've got a Hornady progressive press plus dies, powder, etcetera. Everything you need for multiple calibers."

"I didn't know this," said Ryan.

"I was saving it. You know, just in case you didn't think I was a good fit."

Ryan shrugged and glanced at Alpha. His eyelids lowered like he was a wolf stalking his prey. Ryan knew his friend of two years very well. They had become, for all intents and purposes, brothers.

Alpha began to pepper X-Ray with questions. "Defense weapon of choice?"

"Mossberg 590."

"Sidearm?"

"S & W, forty cal."

"Battle rifle?"

"AR-15, full auto."

"How?"

"I bought an eighty percent lower and milled it myself."

Alpha stopped and smiled at Ryan. "Come on, Echo, we've got mouths to feed."

The two men nodded to X-Ray and left without another word. Ryan patted the young man on the back, who was somewhat taken aback by Alpha's approach during the conversation.

As the two piled into the Ranger, X-Ray spoke first. "I don't think he likes me."

"No, you're wrong about that. Alpha never wants new people to know what he thinks. It's just his way. He's very guarded. He was that way with me at first."

Ryan drove up the gravel road and turned onto a trail that led downhill through a tree-canopied stretch of woods. "You two will get along fine."

"Does that mean I'm in?"

Ryan hesitated before responding, allowing him time to enter the clearing overlooking the Henry River. A lone cabin stood on the banks of the swiftly moving water. The location of the old mill was clearly defined to their right, as the ruins following the fire of forty-plus years ago had never been removed.

"That's why we've come here first, X-Ray. Welcome home."

CHAPTER 7

Early Afternoon
New Year's Eve
Haven House

"Come on in and take a load off!" shouted Ryan from the dining room. He was setting out pitchers of sweet tea and lemonade for lunch. He'd already put out bowls, spoons, and a variety of toppings for the chili, ranging from shredded cheddar cheese to onions.

"I brought dessert, if we have room for it," said Echo's wife, Charlotte. She allowed her husband to hold the Reese's peanut butter pie while she removed her wool coat and matching gloves. Charlotte and Echo had married straight out of high school and were still very much in love. They had one child, a daughter who was killed in the line of duty. She had been a sheriff's deputy for St. Louis County. During a routine traffic stop on Interstate 270, on the southside of Florissant, she was shot in the chest by the driver and ultimately died during surgery.

It broke her parents' hearts, as this occurred about the time they were having difficulty making ends meet on their tobacco farm. The culmination of events led them to choose a new direction for their life, and that led them to the Haven.

"Why don't you set it on the table in here, Charlotte?" asked Ryan. "I'm about to bring out the chili, and the corn bread will be right behind it."

Blair emerged from the kitchen with two baskets covered with white cloth napkins. Steam emerged from the hot corn bread, filling the room with a scrumptious aroma as she walked past the group.

"Hi, guys," greeted Blair cheerfully. "Grab a seat and get prepared to be stuffed. I've made two crocks full!"

"Great!" exclaimed Alpha, who was single and a man known for speaking in single-word sentences.

Within minutes, the table was full of food and everyone was passing it around before digging in. After their mouths were full with a taste of chili, corn bread, and hot peppers from the garden, Blair started the conversation, talking about X-Ray.

"Alpha, whadya think about the new guy?"

He quickly chewed down an oversized spoonful of chili and nodded. "Seems okay to me. We didn't talk about his communications capabilities, but I guess you guys covered that before he got here."

Ryan chimed in. "We did, but I also made him open up his trailer before I accepted his payment. The back of the thing looked like a mobile command center of some type. Frankly, his whole rig appeared to be designed for surviving on the road. The conversion van gave him ample sleeping and cooking capabilities. The trailer was tricked out with ham radio equipment, CB radios, and portable satellite dishes enabling him to access the internet from anywhere."

"Impressive," added Echo.

"Yeah, and there's more," continued Ryan. "He'd created a sealing system that made the trailer into a rolling Faraday cage. Once the doors are closed, an airlock-type device seals the edges so radio waves can't enter."

"Like a microwave oven?" asked Echo.

"Exactly. I was skeptical at first, so he had me get inside the trailer while he locked me in. It kinda gave me the heebie-jeebies, you know? Anyway, once sealed inside, my cell phone couldn't receive a signal. He'd given me a crank emergency radio to turn on. I tried to find a station. Nothing but static."

"He's a geek," mumbled Alpha between bites.

Ryan took a sip of tea and decided to tease his number one. "True, but geeks can fit in here, too. There can only be one alpha, right?"

Alpha sat a little taller in his chair and grinned. He lifted his glass and lowered his voice to his deepest baritone level. "Damn straight!"

"Plus, his gun capabilities help, too," added Blair. "I can't believe I missed that part."

Ryan wiped his mouth and took a long drink of his Arnold Palmer, a fifty-fifty mixture of sweet tea and lemonade that had been his favorite drink since he played golf in high school in the seventies. "He explained that oversight, as I'll call it. First, he never talked about his guns or interest in gunsmithing on social media. He simply has a belief that the government is always watching."

"Paranoid much?" asked Charlotte jokingly.

"Can't say as I blame him, honey," Echo responded. "During those congressional hearings, they've practically admitted that they're in cahoots with the feds."

Ryan continued. "He also said he'd never purchased a weapon through a licensed firearms dealer."

"That explains why I couldn't find any purchase information on him when I used my license to access the ATF database," added Blair.

"Right," continued Ryan. "He bought everything he has from private sellers either through Armslist or at gun shows."

"What about the powder for his ammunition?"

"Black market," Ryan replied. "He told me it's easier than you'd think if you accessed the right 4chan boards or subreddits." Ryan referred to the chat boards frequented by anti-government users and many conspiracy theorists.

"Wow," said Charlotte. "I think I'll stick to canning and sorting heirloom seeds. I'll leave 4chan and subreddits to the youngsters."

The group laughed and made small talk as they finished up their meals. Alpha and Echo were going down to the recently completed schoolhouse to finish up a few things that afternoon, and then everyone was going to settle in for the New Year's Eve festivities on television.

After Ryan and Blair cleared the table and brought in fresh plates for Charlotte's peanut butter pie, the conversation turned philosophical.

Charlotte asked, "Ryan, do you have any predictions for the new year?"

"You know, I'd love to say something profound like I'm praying for world peace, a cure for cancer, and I'd like everyone to hold hands while they sing 'Kumbaya.' That's not gonna happen."

Blair reached over and touched her husband's hand. "You're the eternal pessimist." This drew a laugh from the group because in most every aspect of his life, Ryan tended to be overly optimistic. Over the years, he'd become soured on the course of the country he loved so much.

"I'm sorry, y'all, but I can't help it. I've tried to block out the signs of a society descending into the abyss. Most of it is cultural, and you have no idea how many times I look in the mirror to say 'you're just old-fashioned.' A relic. A dinosaur who doesn't understand young people."

"Boss, you're not ancient, like me," said Echo jokingly, who was only four years older, but appeared to be a decade apart.

Ryan lifted his forkful of pie in Echo's direction and nodded his appreciation. "I guess I consider myself a throwback. It's just that I have a genuine concern for the direction of our country and the events following the election." Ryan's voice trailed off as his voice got somewhat emotional. Blair squeezed his hand, offering him encouragement to continue, which he did.

"Let's just say that my doomsday clock has ticked a little closer toward the apocalypse. I honestly believe that we're one bad news story away from societal collapse. It could be a catastrophic event that triggers mayhem. Or, as we've seen, it could be political unrest that pits one side of the nation against the other."

"Like a civil war?" asked Charlotte, whose family had roots dating back to the war between the states.

"That's the thing, Charlotte," replied Ryan. "And it's complicated. Back in the 1800s, the two sides of the war could be clearly defined by geographic boundaries that necessarily made it easier to determine who was a Southerner and who was from the north. Today, it's different. Despite certain states voting either red or blue during an election cycle, we're really a nation full of purple."

"With no specific boundaries to contain one side or the other?" added Alpha inquisitively.

"Right," Ryan replied. "A civil war in the sense of what happened a hundred sixty years ago couldn't happen today. Now it would be more brutal because weapons are more powerful, and there would be more innocent people caught in the crossfire."

"A lot of innocent people," added Blair. "Think about it. I consider everyone at the Haven politically astute and knowledgeable. You have to remember, however, that half of Americans don't give a crap about politics. Less than sixty percent vote in presidential elections and even fewer during midterms. Those apathetic voters are *the innocents* that Ryan refers to."

"Exactly, darling," said Ryan. "When you watch the news and see people lying down in the middle of the highway or occupying Wall Street or some such, they're not representative of America. They are only a rabble-rousing few. Likewise, when everyone screams about white supremacy as taking a foothold just because once in a while a group of idiots with white hoods over their heads run around a town square in Pulaski, Tennessee, doesn't mean all of us are racists. Painting folks with a broad brush is unfair."

"Yet here we are," interjected Alpha.

Echo agreed. "That's true."

Ryan looked to Charlotte. "Going back to your question. Despite the apathy, as Blair put it, there is sufficient anger on both sides that eventually the trains are gonna collide head-on in a tunnel. In my opinion, the actions taken by the vice president and the other members of the president's cabinet were the functional equivalent of a bus accelerating to run over the man while he wasn't looking.

"Listen, I get that a lot of people don't like our president. I didn't like the last one, but he was duly elected. But elections have consequences, and he's won twice. Do I wish he'd stay off Twitter? Absolutely. At first, I thought it was entertaining because he constantly tweaked the media. Now every tweet is used against him, and it makes his already difficult job of governing even more so.

"However, I never imagined his own people turning on him like this. For two years, he endured a never-ending supply of subpoenas and congressional investigations after he lost the House in the last midterm."

Ryan paused and shook his head. Then he added, "He managed to get reelected only to be attacked from within."

The table had grown solemn as Ryan had said aloud what all of them had been thinking since November.

Finally, Blair broke the silence. "The question is, where does it end?"

Ryan leaned back in his chair and set his napkin on the table. He fiddled with it until it was folded neatly. His response was prophetic.

"I'm afraid a storm is coming."

CHAPTER 8

Afternoon
New Year's Eve
The Haven

By later that afternoon, the overcast skies took over, and any hope of warmer temperatures was dashed. The second interview of the day, a family of four from Trenton, New Jersey, was an interesting bunch. The father was a holistic healer who had co-authored a book with a well-known sustainable-living expert on how to produce their own food and medicine.

As the preparedness movement gained steam in the early part of the century following the Y2K scare, homesteaders and survivalists combined into a new segment of society known as preppers. Living a preparedness lifestyle was predicated on principles of self-reliance and an honest belief that the potential for catastrophic events was real.

A catastrophic event, to families like the Smarts and the others who lived at the Haven, generally included some type of collapse event that caused a long-term loss of electricity, a deadly pandemic, a collapse of the global financial system, or the societal collapse that necessarily followed.

The worst-case scenario envisioned by most preppers was a total collapse of the power grid. The world was wired, interconnected through technology, and completely reliant on the use of electricity. Gone were the days of the nineteenth century when a family could hunt, fish, and grow their own food. Today, most American cupboards barely had enough food for a week. They relied upon just-in-time inventories at grocery stores to keep them supplied, not realizing that in a catastrophic event, those grocery store shelves would be emptied in days, if not hours.

This new potential addition to the Haven filled two key holes for Ryan—holistic healing methods and a trauma nurse. The diametrically opposed careers of the husband and wife were intriguing to Ryan.

How could a couple, one who made a career of modern medicine and the other who focused on natural healing agents, coexist? In Ryan's mind, it was akin to a leftist being married to a far-right conservative. He was certain the conversations about their respective days over dinner were interesting to say the least.

Alpha escorted the family up the gravel driveway to where Ryan customarily met his prospective residents, the circle drive around the water feature lined with stone, built in the 1800s. In a throwback to the Old South, the three-tiered fountain pumped water up through the center, and then it trickled out of a pineapple, only to be recirculated again. The pineapple was symbolic of Southern hospitality, which was generally the Smarts' approach to every visitor. At least, thus far.

"Good afternoon, everybody," he greeted as he pulled the scarf a little higher on his neck. "I'm Ryan Smart. Welcome to the Haven."

The father approached Ryan first, and the two men shook hands. His wife stepped forward and she exchanged small talk with Ryan about the beautiful entry to the property. The oak-lined driveway had an air of mystery about it as the centuries-old trees created a tunnel-like canopy over the gravel. The leafless branches swayed in the wind like ghostly arms threatening to scoop up an unsuspecting passerby.

Ryan was pleased with his initial impressions although he wasn't too thrilled to see they were driving a Subaru. Blair had admonished him many times not to judge a book by its cover, and just because someone drove a Subaru didn't mean they were a tree-hugger from the *left coast.* He promised her that he would keep an open mind without reminding her that he'd been right every time. He couldn't put his finger on it, but there was something about Subarus.

"Let me take y'all on the nickel tour," he began as they piled into his truck. With the temperatures dropping and the group of four in tow, he decided to park the Ranger. The Chevy Suburban was the oldest-running vehicle nameplate in America and a favorite of law enforcement and U.S. Special Forces. His Z71 Midnight Edition package gave the large SUV a sinister look, complete with black-painted wheels, a black mesh grille, and black roof rack crossrails. It befitted the mystery behind the iron fence that surrounded the Haven.

Ryan casually inquired about the husband's background in holistic healing methods and the family's level of preparedness. His interview process always centered around questions, slyly incorporated into the conversation, to elicit a truthful response as to whether they were committed preppers.

A prospect's skills were very important to the prequalifying process, but their commitment to leading a preparedness lifestyle was tantamount when determining whether a long-term relationship could be established.

Ryan pointed out the highlights as they drove slowly through the Haven. "All of these saltbox-style homes have a distinct purpose. Some are occupied with families, as you can see, while others make up all the essentials of our own town."

He was interrupted by the family's oldest daughter, a girl of ten. "We wanna see where Katniss lived!"

"Yeah," added the youngest girl. "Tell us all about District 12!"

Ryan looked up in the rearview and forced a smile as the girls' mother told them to wait until later for the *Hunger Games* tour.

Tour? Ryan bristled. He was not a tour guide for the *Hunger Games*, but he shook it off. It had happened before, so he continued. "The Haven was designed to be self-reliant and separate from the outside world in a time of crisis. It's a place to take refuge in times of turmoil and to protect your family when chaos strikes during a catastrophic event. Here, you surround yourself with like-minded people who have a common goal—protect those you love using the unique skills each of us has. It's a place where you can find safety in a storm and a feeling of community at the same time."

The husband, who rode next to Ryan in the front of the Suburban, nodded as Ryan spoke. "We wholeheartedly agree, don't we, honey?"

"Sure," the wife replied unemotionally.

Ryan slowed and pointed to his right. "Here on the right is our Armageddon Hospital, as we like to call it. Ma'am, it may not have the quantity of medical equipment you're accustomed to in the hospital where you work, but you'll find we are remarkably well equipped. Why don't we pull in here and let you take a look?"

He slowed the truck and eased off the road in front of the building, and she replied, "No, I'm sure it's fine, Ryan. Listen, would it be possible to show the girls the places where the movie was filmed, or at least point them out along the way? You know, Peeta's bakery, the Everdeen home, and maybe even some of the places where they practiced their archery?"

Ryan sat silently for a moment, allowing the Suburban to idle and his blood to stop boiling. "I'd love to, but it is getting late in the day, and the weather is getting worse. I'm afraid we'll have to save that for your second visit."

The husband questioned Ryan's statement. "But we're ready to make a decision, aren't we, honey?"

"Um, well, I don't know," she replied. "Ryan, our children are young, and they haven't been exposed to things like we adults have. I have to ask you something."

Ryan put the truck in drive and continued down the road toward the schoolhouse. He anticipated she might ask about furthering the education of their children, a common question from parents. "Sure, go ahead."

"Well, um, I noticed your assistant was carrying a weapon."

"Yes, he was. We all do while we're on the property."

She sat up in the backseat and glanced at her husband. "Um, you mean you're carrying a weapon now?"

"Yes, two, actually. One on my hip and another around my ankle. In addition, there's one in the console under your husband's elbow."

Ryan stifled a chuckle, but smiled as the man jerked his arm off the armrest, recoiling as if a rattlesnake had revealed itself.

"Oh," she said in a concerned tone. "Why is that necessary? I mean, right now, anyway. Is something happening?"

"Ma'am, you never know when the day before is the day before. In other words, a collapse event can, and most likely will, happen when you least expect it. It's a good habit we've adopted, and we expect everyone who lives here to do the same."

Ryan's mind tried to recall the extensive pre-interview file Blair had created on the family. They represented they were pro-Second Amendment and were comfortable handling firearms. Additional training would be provided once they became full-time residents, although they were encouraged to practice with their own weapons in their hometowns. The wife's hesitation regarding the presence of firearms didn't mesh with their prescreening.

He pulled up to the school, where Alpha and Echo stood on ladders, erecting a sign that read *Little Red Schoolhouse*, a name that accurately described the barn-red-painted building surrounded by a stand of white pine trees.

"This is our newly constructed schoolhouse. We have several educators, who will teach children of all ages when the time comes. Would you kids like to take a look?"

"Yeah!" replied the youngest.

"Um, okay," the other equivocated and then bargained, "After this, Mom, can we see the Everdeen home?"

"Yes, honey, I'm sure Mr. Smart won't mind taking us around to see all the buildings."

Not a chance, Ryan thought to himself.

He left the truck running, and the family emptied out and approached the schoolhouse. Ryan introduced Echo, the more patient of his two guys and the least likely to offend a new prospect. Alpha was not a people person.

While Echo showed them around, Ryan sent Blair a text.

Ryan: The wife is gun-shy. Scared is more like it. Maybe the husband too?

Blair: What? I spoke to them about it during the phone interview.

Ryan: When?

Blair: Last summer.

Ryan: That was before the Delaware Valley school shooting.

Blair: Yeah, so?

Ryan: They also want a Hunger Games tour.

Blair: NO! Give them the boot.

Ryan: Their resumes are strong and they fill a void.

Blair: Doesn't matter. If they're a pain in the ass from the start, they're always gonna be a pain in the ass. Boot them!

Ryan: OK. Love.

Blair: Love you.

The group emerged from the school, and Ryan heard the mother promising their much-awaited *Hunger Games* tour that wasn't going to happen.

"Folks, I'm afraid that something has come up, and we're gonna have to adjourn this for a second interview at a later date."

The husband looked puzzled and glanced at his wife. "But there's more to see, right?"

"Well, of course, but you've got the gist of what we do," Ryan replied. He wasn't going to disclose anything else to them, especially the location within the Haven of their food storage and armory. "Let me have Alpha drive you back to your car."

Ryan purposefully bailed out of the interview and turned the family over to Alpha. If they peppered him with questions, he'd just stare back in response. He politely thanked them for coming and sent them on their way.

Not everyone was a good fit for the Haven, regardless of potential.

CHAPTER 9

Early Evening
New Year's Eve
Haven House

The onset of evening, coupled with a light snow, had engulfed the Haven as Ryan returned home for a New Year's party with Blair and the girls. Blair was baking potatoes to be smothered in leftover chili, sour cream, and cheddar cheese, a meal that would clog the best of the human body's arteries, which was why she only dished it up on special occasions like holidays.

"How long until the bakers are ready?" asked Ryan. "I wanna take the girls out for a romp in the snow."

Blair adopted a motherly tone, showing a vulnerable, soft side that only applied to Ryan and their bulldogs. "Twenty minutes, but no longer. It's dark outside and I'm worried about snakes."

"Snakes? Darling, the snakes have been hibernating for months."

"It's not hibernation, it's called brumation for rattlers. And they do move around, even during the winter months sometimes."

"Brumation? What?"

Blair walked up to Ryan and whispered in his ear, "Do not get my children hurt or lose one of them in the dark. If you do, you'll see what happens when rattlesnakes bite."

Ryan chuckled. "Yes, ma'am."

He put the girls in their matching camouflage harnesses and attached them to a six-foot-long matching leash. The Roo, a name that was a derivative of Scamper-Roo, was appropriate for a sixty-two-pound bulldog who could run like the wind. If she got the slightest inkling that something in the woods was interesting enough to investigate, she'd be gone in a flash. Chubby, on the other hand, would stand by and watch.

While her children, big and small, went out to play in the snow, Blair stoked the fire and turned on the news. Once again, the screen was filled with thousands of protesters who'd encircled the White House. The screen switched to a replay of the president's remarks as he boarded *Marine One* earlier. A reporter had shouted a question to him about allegations of corruption within his administration. Leaving his wife and son standing alone, the president turned and addressed the issue.

"*All too often, we think of corruption as a low-level problem within government. We've all heard stories of the cop who accepts a bribe to let someone off or the bureaucrat who demands an extra tip before granting a permit.*

"*What has been brought to my attention is a level of corruption that goes far beyond a few individual bad apples within government. I've seen nation-states around the world that exist mostly to enrich the rulers and the tiny circles of political cronies at the top of the food chain.*

"*I was astonished, as many of you were, to learn that some of the former members of my cabinet who rose up against me with this bogus Twenty-Fifth Amendment claim are also alleged to have committed corruption while they held a position of trust within my administration. I find this unconscionable, and I've asked Attorney General Christie to look into the allegations thoroughly.*"

The president turned to rejoin his family, and then he suddenly stopped. He returned to the press gaggle and added the following thoughts.

"*One more thing. There are those who claim my requests to investigate these matters are a way to gain revenge or at least discredit my former cabinet members. That simply is not true. Combating corruption is not just about eliciting trust in government, it's about maintaining peace and security as well.*

"*Historically, the pattern is clear for anyone to see. Corruption spurs revolutions, enabling extremist groups and, ultimately, fueling civil wars. Do you think America is immune to this possibility? I don't.*

"*When people come together to protest in other countries, we need to pay attention. That's because, as we've all seen, the ramifications can be vast, and regime change can come much faster than anyone expects.*

"The same holds true in this country. In America, the right to peaceful protest is a given. So is the right to vote. When the will of the people is spoken at the ballot box, it should be respected. What was done back in November by these corrupt individuals amounted to an attempted coup d'état. We can't have that in America.

"Many countries prefer not to shed light on their corruption for fear of losing the confidence of their people in the government. I'm not afraid to do that. By uncovering the actions of these corrupt individuals and holding them to account, we can ensure they get the punishment they deserve.

"It's imperative we recognize that government corruption and the insecurity of those governed go hand in hand. The more effective we are at addressing these issues, the more effective we'll be in both ending conflicts and stopping violence before it breaks out in the first place."

She'd heard enough. Blair turned off the television and returned to the kitchen. In her mind, the whole bunch in Washington was corrupt. They lied to get elected, and then they spent their years in office manipulating voters and donors to stay there. Needless to say, she was a big supporter of term limits. In her mind, it seemed to work pretty well for presidents.

As she passed through the foyer, she caught a glimpse of herself in the mirror. The move to the Haven had been good for her in many ways. She often withheld the truth from Ryan because the way she felt about their home in Florida was not his fault. It was her idea to move there, and he'd give her anything she wanted if he could.

No, it had been the culture shock and the cramped surroundings that brought on the fits of anxiety she'd begun to experience not long after their initial move to Orlando. There was never any silence in their neighborhood, even at night. During the day, cars and people scurried about. Kids playing outside, shrieking at the top of their lungs, became an annoyance.

The nonstop roar of lawn equipment was a constant irritation. At night, the blare of sirens or police helicopters pursuing bad guys interrupted their attempts to relax. Even as she fell asleep, all she could think about was the fact the next morning, it would all crank up again. There simply was no respite.

Their lottery win was a miracle in so many ways. What excited her most was not the prospect of buying things. She never really cared about stuff, although she frequently teased Ryan about it. What she really sought was peace and serenity.

Blair prepared the girls' dinner of kibbles and strained pumpkin, designed to assist their digestive system. They had just turned eleven, which was remarkable. The two sisters were loved and well cared for. Age was just a number to those two, as they still considered themselves to be puppies. Kinda like their parents.

As Ryan returned with the snow-covered, wet pups, Blair paused to smile and admire her home and family. There was nothing more important in the world than their being together and safe.

CHAPTER 10

Late Evening
New Year's Eve
Haven House

Blair had turned the volume down on the television an hour before. As predicted, Ryan had drifted off to sleep with The Roo piled on top of his lap. To her right, Chubby's tongue stuck out over her signature English bulldog underbite. She too was in a deep sleep as the three of them snored blissfully.

She had one eye on the festivities in Times Square as one unknown performing artist after another lip-synced their way through a song. Nothing but smiling faces braved the icy cold weather of New York City, as a sea of blue Nivea hats and foam wands waved happily to the music.

Once in a while, the cable news networks would switch to celebrations around the world. Christmas Island and Samoa were the first places to welcome the new year, but Sydney, Australia, was the world's first major city to put on a real performance for the big event, one that overshadowed New York City with its firework displays.

Ryan made her promise to wake him at 11:30 if, as he put it, he happened to fall asleep early. Every family had traditions around holidays. Waking Ryan up at 11:30 was one of the Smarts'.

"Ryan, it's almost New Year's." She started the arduous process. "Wake up. I wanna go in the media room so we can watch all the network coverage at once."

He tried to shake himself out of his fog. "What? Um, I'm awake. I was just resting my eyes."

"Yeah, *resting your eyes* for two hours," said Blair with a chuckle as she wrapped a blanket over Chubby to keep her in a slumber. They'd wake the girls to go to bed after midnight.

"Did I miss anything?" asked Ryan as he straightened up in his chair and slid The Roo off his lap. She managed a big stretch and grumbled at the rude intrusion on her sleep.

"Nope, but let's go into the media room and watch. You fire up the TVs while I get the bubbly."

"Why can't we just watch from here?" protested Ryan as he stood to stretch his legs and pop his back.

"I wanna see all the angles in Times Square," replied Blair. "Plus, they're gonna include Vegas too."

Ryan grumbled, "I don't understand why we even have the media room and all those televisions. I hate television. Why would anyone want more than one TV?"

Blair ignored his complaining and gathered up their iPads and reading glasses. Both were tools that were constantly by their sides when at home.

"Here, grumpy," began Blair. She handed Ryan the devices. "Take these, please. I'll be right there."

Ryan was fully awake now, but still in a grumpy mood. He didn't like being awakened from a deep sleep. "Seriously, Blair, the media room is like polygamy. The same thing applies to wives. I don't get these polygamists. Why in the heck would any man want more than one?"

Blair, who was halfway to the kitchen, stopped in her tracks and swung around. She set her jaw, and her eyes closed to a slant—*her death stare*. "Whadya have against wives, mister?"

"Nothing. I'm just saying we don't need all of these TVs." Ryan tried to backtrack. He knew the look. His attempts to defend and retreat didn't work.

"No, it sounded to me like you were equating televisions with wives. Are you saying I'm like a TV, something to be available only when you want it. To turn on and off as you please?"

Blair had started walking toward him, causing Ryan to freeze. "Um, no, no, no. Seriously, darling. I didn't mean that at all. I—"

She was right in his face now. He glanced around to see if he had a place to run to, but he was trapped against the sofa. He backed up, waiting to get pummeled.

Blair burst out laughing, as she'd gotten him again. She was the consummate practical joker, frequently teasing Ryan to keep him on his toes. She couldn't resist this time, despite his half-sleepy rant being harmless.

She leaned up and kissed him on the cheek. "Come on, grumpy. But get it together. If I miss something, I'll be really pissed!"

CHAPTER 11

Late Evening
New Year's Eve
Haven House

"Blair!" Ryan shouted her name from the media room. The tone of his voice raised alarms in the half-sleeping girls, who scrambled out from under their blankets and came running into the media room.

When Blair arrived, champagne and glasses in hand, she stopped in the middle of the doorway, astonished. "What kind of fresh hell is this?"

"Shh. I don't know where to start. A plane crash in Alabama. The transportation systems in DC are at a standstill. A concert was evacuated in Atlanta. And now they're reporting a massive power outage stretching from parts of New Jersey into Philadelphia and Wilmington, Delaware."

Blair set the bottle and glasses on a sofa table and walked around the massive sectional to approach the televisions. She glanced at her watch. It was less than ten minutes until midnight. "Ryan, this has to be coordinated. Jeez, all of this happened since I went to the kitchen? It's been two minutes."

"The plane crash showed up on the chyron of CNN first. Then the DC airports reported computer issues. I'm most concerned about the power outage."

Blair pointed at the FoxNews channel. "Turn this up. They're talking about it now."

"At approximately 11:45, only a few minutes ago, reports came from Philadelphia that power plants had failed suddenly throughout the PECO Energy Company system. PECO operates primarily in southeastern

Pennsylvania, covering all of Philadelphia and Delaware County.

"However, new reports are coming in that the power outage is much more widespread. PSE & G, the power company servicing much of New Jersey, including the state capital of Trenton, has reported a similar incident at the exact same moment. Reports coming out of Wilmington, Delaware, are similar.

"Because these events have just occurred, we haven't been able to reach Homeland Security for comment. As you can see on your screen, we are covering both the ball drop in New York City and this power outage simultaneously to keep you abreast of the latest."

Blair was pacing the floor, periodically walking close to the sixty-inch monitors to get a closer look. She suddenly pointed to the ABC broadcast of *Dick Clark's New Year's Rockin' Eve.* "Ryan, look! Turn up this one!"

The screen that had been split between coverage of the Beyoncé concert evacuation and Times Square suddenly enlarged to New York, where chaos ensued. As he increased the volume, a harried Ryan Seacrest was screaming into his microphone over the panicked revelers.

"I don't know what's happening, but everyone is running for their lives. Explosions have rocked Times Square in the last minute. The famous ball was the first target, and the crystals shattered into millions of pieces and began raining down on thousands of people below. Shards of glass struck their faces, embedding like tiny knives in their skin. Our production crew scrambled for cover on our elevated stage, and currently, I'm hiding under a tarp used to protect our cameras from the wet weather.

"My producers are telling me to leave. To get out. But to where? Now that the glass has stopped falling, I can catch a glimpse of what is happening around our stage, and it isn't pretty. The panic has caused people to push and shove, knocking one another to be used as a springboard to flee from the attack.

"And make no mistake, this is an attack. It is nothing short of a war zone down here. I've heard more than a dozen explosions, maybe two dozen. I've lost count. Some of the bombs struck targets while others seemed to detonate in midair. I don't have any idea where they're coming from or how they got here, but they were clearly airborne. I've not heard anything resembling an explosion near the ground. All of it came from above."

Ryan's phone rang, so he handed the remote to Blair. She continued to turn up the volume on the televisions as they reported from the various locations under siege around the country.

"Yeah, Alpha." She could overhear Ryan's side of the conversation. "We're watching too. Wait, what? Detroit, Chicago, Los Angeles too? How? How do you know this?"

Ryan hesitated and stared at the monitors. Blair turned the volume down momentarily to listen in. They both shook their heads in disbelief.

"Okay, okay. Keep those lines of communication open. Gather up Echo and head over to the house now.

"No, not the new guy just yet. We need to assess this situation between the four of us. The decisions we're about to make will impact a lot of lives. Hurry!"

Ryan disconnected the call and glanced at the time. It was just after midnight. He noticed his hands were shaking, but not out of fear.

"What about the other cities? There's nothing on the news about—"

Ryan interrupted her. "Coordinated attacks. Alpha called his guy at the FBI as soon as this happened. The agency is freaking out, he said. All of these events occurred within fifteen minutes of each other, with the attack on Times Square coming last."

Blair turned around and studied the televisions again. Most of the networks were focused on Times Square because that was being viewed by hundreds of millions of people around the world. The chyrons scrolled at a furious pace as news broke of the attacks around the country. The FoxNews production team was in such a frenzy they didn't bother spellchecking what they inserted onto the constant feed.

It didn't matter, as what was happening was clear to all. An attack on the United States, and it affected Americans from coast to coast.

Chapter 12

After Midnight
New Year's Day
Haven House

"Champagne?" asked Blair with a chuckle as she raised the bottle and glasses in the air.

"Yeah, right." Ryan sighed and rolled his eyes. "It's happening. I don't know by whom or from where. But one thing is certain. It's hitting the fan right before our eyes."

Blair motioned for Ryan to sit on the sofa. "Keep watching while I put this away. Red Bull?"

Ryan laughed. "You know me so well. Better make it a double."

Blair kissed her husband on the top of the head and left. Ryan alternated between the four large televisions mounted on the wall, muting three of the networks and focusing on CNN, which always did the best job of covering catastrophic events when they occurred around the world.

"*Information continues to come into CNN's newsroom as our reporters make every effort to assemble and cover this breaking story for you. The White House has issued a statement that the president is being kept advised of these events, but other than that, they were unable to comment further at this time.*

"*The perpetrator of these heinous acts is unknown, as no group has claimed responsibility. What we do know is that they were carefully orchestrated to have a maximum terror-like effect on each of the targets. The plane crash outside Mobile, Alabama, may be an anomaly, a simple coincidence unrelated to the much larger scale attacks around the country.*"

The sound of the Red Bull can popping open announced Blair's return to the media room. Ryan, who allowed himself a minute to rest and gather his thoughts, stood and began pacing the floor, as he often did when he was brainstorming. He was simply incapable of sitting still.

Blair handed him his can, and then she held his hand for a moment. "Listen to me. We've got this. We built this place for a reason, and this is it. No worries, hubs."

Ryan relaxed his body and took a long gulp of his favorite beverage. "First, two things. Happy New Year." He bent over and kissed his wife to ring in the new year.

"What's the other thing?" she asked.

"White rabbit. White rabbit," he replied, generating a hearty laugh between them. For years, they'd followed the custom to bring them good luck throughout the month.

"Oh, yeah, white rabbit, white rabbit," Blair repeated. "We're gonna need it."

Blair removed a three-ring binder that was tucked under her arm. "I brought *the book*."

After winning the Mega Millions jackpot two years ago, the Smarts had begun to brainstorm their plans for a place like the Haven. They searched around the country for locations ranging from the Mountain West to Texas and even the Cumberland Plateau in Tennessee.

Once they settled on Henry River Mill Village, Blair was charged with the task of creating a set of rules, policies, and procedures for the Haven that applied to pre-collapse living as well as what to do when the proverbial crap hit the fan.

Her organizational skills were incomparable. Blair had a knack for anticipating issues that might arise and established a detailed response to each. While Ryan used his background in real estate development to create a solid foundation for the Haven in the form of buildings and infrastructure, Blair created *the book*, a detailed guide to ensure the Haven withstood the storm, no matter how bad it was.

They pulled the ottoman closer to the sectional sofa and opened the binder to the operational guidelines section.

Ryan glanced up at the news networks, which continued to be

transfixed on the events in Times Square. "Blair, I know we don't have time to be philosophical, but I have to ask. Did you ever think we'd be at this point? I mean, look at the news. We're smack-dab in the middle of everything we've talked about for years."

She leaned back against the sofa cushions and grimaced. "Okay, all honesty right now."

"Yeah."

"At first, when you started talking about prepping, I went along with it because it seemed important to you. You weren't going overboard buying nuclear fallout shelters or escape pods that would jettison us out of our home on a moment's notice. Everything you did was common sense."

"We couldn't afford the escape pod, or I would've bought one," Ryan interjected with a laugh.

"No doubt, but listen to me," Blair continued. "Everything you purchased—from extra food to gallon jugs of water, to medical supplies—could always be used at some point. However, the last ten years really opened my eyes to how the fabric of our society is crumbling. I liked the concept of the Haven for many reasons, both personal and as to what was best for our family."

"Me too," added Ryan.

Blair leaned forward and pointed at the monitors. "But this. This kinda stuff here. No way. I never thought something like this would happen. I know you did, but honestly, not me. I love you for believing in the worst-case scenario, because our planning and the Haven will hopefully keep us all safe."

"*All* is the operative word, too. We've created a community here that's only half full. There are others out there, many of whom are directly impacted by what's happening on those TVs. I feel responsible for them also."

They both turned as Alpha's unmistakable knock came on the front door. The hard pounding was reminiscent of every cop's method of demanding someone open up. Before Ryan could push himself off the sofa, Alpha and Echo entered the foyer. Both girls, who'd sprawled out in front of the fire, shot up off the floor and greeted the men. Their exuberance was refreshing as their butts wiggled, causing them to slip on the snow-covered entry. After getting the requisite attention from the guys, they moseyed back to their spots to watch the activity.

"TEOTWAWKI, right, Ryan?" asked Echo as he entered the media room first. He often used the acronym TEOTWAWKI, the end of the world as we know it, when referring to a post-collapse way of life.

"Come on in, guys," replied Ryan. "I don't know, but it sure looks like the start of something."

"My buddy with the FBI agrees," added Alpha, his voice deep and ominous. "He was real honest with me. There are a lot of agents shocked that we were caught with our pants down on this one. With our abilities to monitor every aspect of communication in this country, he can't believe they didn't have a whiff of these attacks."

"Nothing at all?" asked Blair.

"Well, he did tell me a FISA warrant was obtained today, but they thought it was related to Islamic terrorists. In his opinion, some group with more lethal capabilities than those radicals are behind this."

"Why do you say that?" asked Ryan.

Alpha walked up to the wall of televisions and paused. He spoke with his back to the group. "The feds' gut reaction based upon the coordination and the methods used suggested a foreign government. Russia, maybe China. Heck, even North Korea is a possibility."

"Methods?" asked Ryan.

"The power outage in the Mid-Atlantic region was more than just the grid. It included vehicles and other equipment."

"EMP," mumbled Blair.

"Yes," continued Alpha. "In DC, the attacks were on several forms of transportation, including the DC Metrorail system, the airports, and mass transit systems like the buses."

"That doesn't sound like an EMP," said Ryan. "They were targeted."

Alpha turned and nodded. "Yeah. The FBI's initial assessment points to a cyber attack."

The room fell silent for a moment as the news networks were switching from one catastrophic event to another. All of the screens depicted a common scene—panic, chaos, and mayhem.

Ryan stood and paused all the monitors. He casually set the universal remote on the ottoman next to the binder. Then he spoke. "Our first job is to prevent that madness from infiltrating the Haven. Security is job number one. Alpha?"

"Our protocols are simple. We have sectors of the perimeter assigned to all residents. Everybody has a two-way radio and knows the drill. Sidearms and rifles are mandatory."

"Do the residents know?"

Alpha held up his iPhone to reveal the display to the group. "I muted the phone. I've had a dozen calls and twice as many text messages. They know, and they're all waiting on me to direct them."

Ryan smiled and patted his friend on the back. "Don't let me hold you up. Get your perimeter security established."

Echo stepped forward. "What do you want me to do?"

"First, go see our newest resident. Explain the situation and tell him to be on standby. I haven't decided what role to place him in just yet. Blair and I will figure that out. Does he have one of our radios?"

"Not yet," replied Echo. "I'll take him one. Do I issue him weapons?"

"No. He's got his own, trust me," replied Ryan. "Tell him to monitor our emergency frequency on the radio. Based upon what's happening, I expect the cell service to crash at some point."

"What else?" asked Echo.

Ryan thought for a moment. "This might be premature, but I'd feel better if we moved the livestock away from the fences on the back forty and center them in the Haven. I don't want some foolish hunter taking potshots at our meat and dairy."

"It'll be the last shots they take," said Alpha.

Ryan chuckled. "I get it, but we also don't want to get the sheriff on us either. This thing is just now unfolding. For the time being, the rule of law is still in place."

"Okay, boss, I'll get on it as soon as the sun rises," said Echo, who immediately started toward the door.

Alpha followed him, and as the men were about to exit, Echo turned and looked at the Smarts. "Boss, thank you."

Simple words, sincerely delivered.

PART TWO

NEW YEAR'S DAY

CHAPTER 13

After Midnight
New Year's Day
Haven House

For the next hour, Blair and Ryan made copious notes of what needed to be done as they kept a watchful eye on the news. Since midnight, no other attacks had transpired, but the wake of the first wave was being felt by many. The northeast from Washington, DC, to New York took the brunt of the complex blitz that systematically collapsed power grids, halted air travel around the nation, and caused hundreds of casualties as panic spread through Times Square.

"We have to recall the rest of Alpha's team—Bravo, Charlie, Delta, and Foxtrot," said Blair as she thumbed through the security personnel section of the book.

"Foxtrot will have the greatest difficulty," added Ryan in response. "She's in DC, and air transportation in the entire region has come to a halt. Honestly, I'm not even sure if she has a car."

Blair shook her head. "I'll message her anyway. We can count on her, right?"

"Yeah, she's solid. You know she's in the middle of this Supreme Court thing for the president. She might be delayed."

"We'll see," mumbled Blair. Ryan didn't need to press the issue. Blair had voiced concerns about Hayden Blount from the beginning. She had skills that the Haven needed. Most importantly, she was single without family ties to cloud her judgment or decision-making. Blair had suspected all along that her new position with the law firm representing the president would require her to stay in Washington.

"Bravo and Charlie?" asked Ryan.

"I'll message them to return home, but knowing them, they're on their way already. Bravo is probably half a case into your beloved Red Bull, and Charlie probably ditched her date without so much as a goodbye."

Ryan laughed. "Those two are hard-core. Alpha did well recruiting them from Academi."

Academi was a private military contractor that provided security to dignitaries and businessmen on foreign soil. They were also used extensively by the government to handle missions that had to be disavowed by Washington if something went awry.

Originally established in the late 1990s by former Navy SEAL officer Erik Prince, his company, Blackwater, had undergone a change in branding over the years as the private contractor was tied to several scandalous operations overseas.

To recruit Bravo and Charlie, Alpha contacted his network of operatives within the military and put out feelers. He sought covert agents and former military personnel who'd been *sheep-dipped*. Sheep-dipping was the process of taking someone who'd been in public service in the military or intelligence community and replacing their documented life with one that was created out of thin air in order for them to serve as covert agents of the government.

It was important to have one or two members of this caliber on the team in order to gain information or undertake operations on behalf of the Haven against the U.S. government. The level of training undertaken by Bravo and Charlie at Academi exceeded his own. Depending on how hard society collapsed, with these two operators by his side, they could take on all threats.

"What about the off-site residents?" asked Blair before adding, "We committed to notifying them of a potential long-term event."

"I can't imagine that they're not glued to their TVs," replied Ryan. "Do your best to reach out to them, but don't spend a lot of time convincing them. Our job is to make them aware. They have to decide whether the threat is real."

"I'm gonna focus on those who have their homes built or renovated first. And I'm gonna tell them not to come empty-handed.

Beans, Band-Aids, and bullets. They know what to do."

Ryan took a deep breath and exhaled. "That brings us to the land owners who haven't built yet. We promised to contact them as well."

Blair flipped over to the section of the book that identified families who were accepted into the Haven but didn't have a place to live yet. Ryan had modified the original bakery building as seen in the *Hunger Games* movie into a dormitory-style residential structure. It was not meant to be a long-term housing option, but was only for those who hadn't built yet but needed a place to go.

"Are we still under sixteen?" asked Ryan, who'd only installed sixteen bunks surrounded by small cubicles to provide a sense of privacy. Lockers had been built to help store their belongings. Also, the bakery building had a small kitchen, showers, and a shared bath.

Blair thumbed through the dossiers generated on each of the residents. She spoke under her breath as she did. "There are some valuable assets here. No kids. We've got enough of those already."

"Alpha has a plan for the kids," Ryan interjected.

"The oven, like in 'Hansel and Gretel'?" joked the Blair Witch.

"Nope. You'll see. Focus, darling. Are there less than sixteen?"

"We're right at it. We'd have a full house if they all show up."

Ryan nodded and stood. "We've gotta contact them all and make the offer. That was our agreement. They'll have sanctuary here until the dust settles. If this is going to be a long-term situation, we have enough building materials to add three more homes."

"We can make that work," said Blair. "Where are you going?"

"I need to see X-Ray."

CHAPTER 14

New Year's Day
The Haven

Ryan bundled up and took the Ranger along the gravel road that was now covered with a slight accumulation of snow. He turned down the path through the woods toward the cabin assigned to X-Ray. He felt like it was important to give X-Ray instructions in person and to provide him a sense of what was expected of him at the Haven.

As Ryan approached, he noticed all the lights were on in the cabin and X-Ray was carrying pieces of equipment from the trailer into the house. As Ryan arrived, X-Ray paused for a moment, nodded his acknowledgment, and then continued inside.

Ryan stomped the snow off his feet before entering X-Ray's cabin. He was amazed at how quickly the man had turned one of their smallest residences with only spartan furnishings into a warm, cozy home—complete with computer stations, ham radio transceivers, a variety of handheld scanners, and a CB base unit.

"Looks like you're getting settled in," announced Ryan as he walked inside.

"Oh, yeah. I planned on unloading my communications gear tomorrow, but, well, things have changed drastically, haven't they?"

Ryan shrugged and continue to survey his equipment. "Yeah, it seems like your timing was perfect. Heck, if I didn't know better, I might think you knew this was coming."

X-Ray unconsciously froze for a moment, just long enough for Ryan to notice, and then continued shuffling the equipment around on top of the picnic table that served as a dinette set.

The young man turned but didn't make eye contact. "Uh-huh. I'll be right back." He brushed past Ryan and hustled outside to his trailer to bring in another load.

Ryan's curiosity was piqued even more so. He didn't want to say anything to Blair, and certainly not to Alpha, both of whom had a tendency to be overly skeptical of people's intentions. But Ryan's antennae received a number of warning signals concerning their new arrival.

He was very eager to enter the Haven. That was fine. He paid in silver and gold. That had never happened before. Most importantly, he came with everything he needed to bug out permanently. He couldn't possibly know that he'd be accepted into the Haven. It just struck Ryan as odd that the young man had sold or given away all of his earthly belongings before coming there, and then hours later, the nation was under attack.

"Sorry, Ryan," said X-Ray as he dropped the gear and hustled back outside, shouting over his shoulder as he went, "I'm not much for small talk right now."

Ryan followed him outside and offered to help. "What can I do?"

X-Ray was shuffling around inside his trailer, which swayed back and forth from the man's movements. "Nothing, actually. I need to get out the Faraday cages and get them set up first thing."

A Faraday cage is a container of any shape or size that's designed to block electromagnetic fields. The conducting materials are usually made of wire mesh or metal plates that protect the contents from external electric fields. In the event of a large electromagnetic pulse event, whether naturally occurring, like a geomagnetic storm from the sun, or man-made in the form of a nuclear detonation of any size, the Faraday cage prevents the highly charged particles from destroying the electronic components of the contents.

He emerged from the back of the trailer with two sets of panels under each arm. Ryan stepped to the side as the young man walked with purpose into the cabin.

"You have portable Faraday cages?" asked Ryan.

"Yessir. Simple construction, actually."

X-Ray began to assemble the panels, which had been constructed by creating a frame out of wood and wrapping it with fine steel mesh. He quickly assembled the pieces into a box and then inserted one of the receivers along with a battery backup system.

Within the available space, he stored several handheld ham radio units, portable two-way radios, and other small electronics like GPS devices, a cell phone, and an iPad.

He quickly set the top of the Faraday cage in place and screwed it down. Lastly, he wrapped all the seams with two-inch-wide aluminum foil tape. Satisfied, he scurried outside once again, leaving Ryan in awe of the man's planning.

"Just one more, okay?"

"Uh, sure," said Ryan, who was fascinated by the young man's organizational skills in creating his post-collapse communications system. Just as he and Blair had done over the last two years in preparing the Haven for this moment, it appeared X-Ray had undertaken the same meticulous planning and practiced for this moment.

Ten minutes later, the trailer was emptied, the communications equipment was secured and fully functional, and X-Ray flopped on the sofa in front of the fire, exhausted.

Ryan spoke first, still intent on learning more about their newest resident. "I notice you don't have a television set up. We have a DirecTV antenna on the roof."

"Yessir, I know. But, um, no, thanks. I get all the news I need from the internet."

"Me too. So, X-Ray, what do you think about all of this?"

"I absolutely love it here, Ryan. Naturally, I spent the day getting oriented. I met a few of my neighbors from down the river. Nice people. Echo came and checked on me a little while ago and brought me a radio. It's all good, you know."

Ryan smiled. He hadn't spent a lot of time around the twentysomethings. They had a different energy about them, almost manic. X-Ray appeared nervous, far more so than the relatively calm demeanor he'd exhibited earlier in the day.

Initially, Ryan had come to the cabin to ask the young man to make a run for supplies at 6:00 a.m. when Walmart reopened in nearby Hickory. After speaking with him further and seeing his reaction to Ryan's subtle comment about X-Ray's knowledge of the events that were occurring, he elected to keep him closer to home.

He also determined that X-Ray should be kept under the watchful eye of Echo. The older man was very astute and had a heckuva BS meter. Echo would make sure he kept on top of X-Ray's activities without tipping his hand. Alpha had his hands full with security matters, and if he sensed X-Ray was a problem, the young man would end up floating facedown in the Henry River.

"Well, I just wanted to stop by and see how you were coming along," said Ryan. "For the time being, you'll be reporting to Echo. I imagine that'll be okay with you."

"Um, sure. I also plan on monitoring the news, ham transmissions, and military frequencies."

"Military?"

"Absolutely. Between military movements and FEMA activity, we can keep abreast of the areas of the country that are considered hot spots by the government."

"What made you think of doing that?" asked Ryan.

"Well, sir. I believe that knowledge is power. My communications apparatus is designed to tap into all available sources of information so we can be a step ahead of everyone else."

"Good to know, X-Ray."

"Sir, I want you to rest assured that I am a team player, one hundred percent. A storm is coming, and we need to be ready."

A storm is coming. A phrase Ryan had used earlier in the day, but somehow, to their newest addition to the Haven, it seemed to take on a more profound meaning.

CHAPTER 15

New Year's Day
Haven House

"How are things?" asked Blair as Ryan entered the dining room. He'd shed his winter gear and kicked off his signature L.L.Bean duck boots. He walked behind her and began to rub her shoulders as she continued to thumb through the three-ring binder.

"Darling, you must be exhausted," he began to reply. "At least I caught a few winks before the drama hit the news. You haven't slept at all. Let me take over for you."

"Nah. I've already made my phone contacts, and now I'm working on emails. The phone calls are a pain because everybody wants to talk about what's going on. After rehashing what we know, which is only slightly more than what the news is reporting now, a call was taking fifteen minutes. Now, that's exhausting."

"Are they coming?"

"Yes, at least the ones I spoke with. I have text messages and emails that I'm about to go through. Listen, I have to tell you something."

Ryan sensed the concerned tone in Blair's voice, so he immediately pulled out a chair and sat down next to her. "What is it?"

"Ryan, the plane crash in Mobile—Michael Cortland was on that flight."

"Good God, no. Is he alive? Was he with his family?"

"Yes, and alone, as he was returning from Washington," she replied. "He's being treated at the intensive care unit in a Mobile hospital. I found out through a news report."

Ryan had a puzzled look on his face. "Cort has an important job on the Hill, but he's certainly not newsworthy. Why would they mention him?"

"There's more," replied Blair. "One of the passengers who didn't make it was Johnson Pratt."

"Oh man. He's the chairman of the House Judiciary Committee. That's the guy who'll be leading the impeachment proceedings against the president."

"Well, he's dead now. Anyway, because Pratt was a high-profile congressman, I guess Cort being on board was also newsworthy."

Ryan leaned back in his chair and clasped his fingers behind his head as he stared at the ceiling. "Blair, this whole thing stinks."

"You mean about Cort?"

"No, all of it. The attacks. The way they were carried out. The targets. They all seem random, yet …" Ryan's voice trailed off as he received a text message.

"Who is it?" asked Blair.

"Delta just arrived."

"Oh, good."

"Yeah, but he brought his kids."

Blair began to thumb through the binder to locate Delta's profile. She located the highlights and read them aloud. "Will Hightower. Ex-cop. Philly SWAT. Security guard in Atlanta. Everything is current. I don't see any mention of children living with him."

Ryan interrupted. "I know he's divorced with a wife up in Philadelphia. He's got two kids, but he told us they wouldn't be coming to the Haven with him due to a nasty custody arrangement."

"Well, they're here now," said Blair, who appeared somewhat annoyed by the additional responsibility the two children placed upon the community.

"How old are they?" asked Ryan.

Blair looked through Delta's profile and responded, "Daughter, Skylar, is age eleven. Son, Ethan, is about to turn sixteen."

Ryan stood and walked toward the front door. "Not too bad. They're old enough to take care of themselves to an extent. Remember, Delta is being counted on for an important security role on Alpha's team. He doesn't have time to watch over kids."

"Are you leaving again?" asked Blair. Ryan had a lot of nervous energy.

"No," he muttered as he fired off a text. "I told Alpha to get Delta settled and have him report to HB-1 at 8:00 a.m. for our regular briefing."

He stood in front of the bay window that looked out over the front yard, down the tree-covered drive and toward the front gate. The sun was now rising over the treetops and a new year was beginning. As he reflected on the task ahead of them, Ryan received another task. At first, he ignored it, assuming it was just Alpha acknowledging his instructions. Then his phone dinged again, reminding him that the message hadn't been read yet.

He pulled the iPhone out of his pocket and hit the green-and-white message icon. He didn't recognize the number. In fact, it wasn't a name or a phone number. The sender of the message came across on the display as *322-MM*. The message itself was short.

This is just the beginning.

Godspeed, Patriot.

Blair stood and approached Ryan. "Honey, what is it? Who is it from?"

Ryan shook his head. "I have no idea."

CHAPTER 16

New Year's Day
The Haven

There comes a day when a person realizes they have the opportunity to turn the page on their life's story. As they do, the feeling can be exhilarating, or simply a relief as you put the broken pieces of yesterday behind you. It's a point when one feels there's so much more to life than the years you've left behind. When Will Hightower arrived at the front gate of the Haven and Alpha greeted him with the words *welcome home, Delta*, a page had turned, and a new day presented itself.

"How's it going, Alpha?" asked Delta as he left his old life behind and transitioned into his new one as an integral part of the Haven's security team.

"Good to see you, bud," replied Alpha in his typical, unemotional way. "Listen, I hate to do this to you, but with the situation as it is, I need you and …" Alpha's voice trailed off as he stuck his head slightly into the window and scrutinized the kids in the backseat.

Delta picked up on Alpha's hesitation. "That's my daughter, Skylar, and this is my son, Ethan. They were staying with me for the New Year's weekend until, well, you know."

"Right. Right. Anyway, I need you guys to exit the vehicle for a moment while we give it the once-over. Nothin' personal. Just protocol."

Delta nodded. "I know."

He unlocked the door and slowly exited the vehicle. Alpha was accompanied by two other residents, who were armed with AR-15s, full combat kits, and sidearms secured inside their chest rigs. When

Alpha created his security unit, he made sure they were outfitted as close to military police specifications as he legally could.

One of the residents was holding a German shepherd on a leash; the dog was pacing back and forth with his nose in the air.

Delta pointed at the dog. "New addition?"

"Yeah, he's from Paws and Stripes, a nonprofit that provides service dogs to ex-military personnel. Sometimes they're assigned to soldiers with PTSD. Other times, through some strings being pulled, they are allowed to retire when their handlers are discharged from service. This is Captain, and his training is in illegal drugs and bomb-making materials."

Delta waved at the resident and in Captain's direction. "Well, he certainly is well trained, although slightly agitated."

"All of us are a little on edge," replied Alpha dryly. "I need your kids to exit the vehicle, too."

Delta opened the back door and asked the kids to come out. Both of them protested due to the cold, and then they began to pepper their dad with questions.

Ethan was first. "Dad, what is this place?"

"Why are we here, Daddy?" asked Skylar.

Delta quickly wrapped his arms around both kids and led them away from the truck. "I'll explain everything when we get to my cabin."

"You have a cabin here? Why?" asked Ethan.

"In a moment, son. First things first."

One of Alpha's men led Captain around the truck. He was swiftly wagging his tail as he did his duty. After a couple of peeks inside, he came to the Hightowers and spent an inordinate amount of time sniffing Ethan. Then he stopped and barked several times at Ethan and Skylar.

Alpha stepped in and motioned for Captain's handler to lead the dog away. "Delta, let's step over here." The two men walked away, leaving the kids standing alone, perplexed and confused.

"I think I can explain," began Delta when they were out of earshot.

"I'm listening," said Alpha with a gruff.

"As you know, I work security at Mercedes-Benz Stadium in Atlanta. I had a shift last night for a concert and took the kids with me. They wandered down to the field level, in front of the stage. There was a lot of marijuana floating around, and I'm sure their clothes still smell like it."

"Did they smoke it?" asked Alpha. The use of drugs was strictly prohibited within the Haven, and only the Smarts' home had alcohol. Drugs, drinking, and weapons don't mix.

"No," Delta lied. "You know how these concerts can be. After the chaos, we had a heckuva time getting out of there. Ethan hit his head, and Skylar was really shaken up. Both of them went straight to bed at my place without taking a shower. When I got Blair's text, I loaded them up and hauled our cookies up here."

Alpha glanced over Delta's shoulder and studied Ethan. The boy didn't leave the best impression on those who met him for the first time. Delta knew this, but there wasn't anything he could do about at it this point. They lived in a world in which young people focused on their *individuality* rather than the impressions they made on others.

In a society that emphasized selfies on social media platforms like Instagram and Snapchat, it was hard to tell a teenage boy he needed to get a haircut and get rid of the earrings. They were more likely to flip you off and run away than comply with your suggestions.

Alpha nodded to the guards on duty and motioned for them to open the gates. "All right, Delta. Again, sorry for the inconvenience. Get your family settled and be at HB-1 for our morning briefing—oh eight hundred. We'll bring you up to speed then."

"Thanks, Alpha. By the way, am I the first to arrive?"

"Echo is here full-time, as you know. Charlie arrived an hour ago, and Bravo is en route."

Delta turned and loaded the children back into the car. After he shut the door behind them, he returned to Alpha and spoke.

"It's good to be home, brother."

CHAPTER 17

New Year's Day
Delta's Cabin
The Haven

"Dad, are you gonna tell us what's going on?" asked Ethan, barely waiting for his father to pull away from the front gate. The icy snow crunched under the weight of the SUV as he drove up the hill, with Haven House in full view up ahead. Delta drove around the circle drive that surrounded the water fountain. He turned left toward a long row of cabins that stretched half a mile along the gravel driveway.

"Son, it's a long, kind of complicated story. Here's what I want us to do. Our place is up here on the left. Let's get unloaded, get a fire going, and whip up some hot chocolate. I've got about an hour before I have to report to work."

"Daddy, do you work here, too?" asked Skylar.

"Yes, baby girl. It's an unusual job, but it's very beneficial to all of us right now. You'll see what I mean when I explain everything. Okay?"

"Okay, Daddy. I kinda like it here. It's, um, woodsy."

Delta admired his daughter in the rearview mirror. She was so innocent despite the turmoil his family had been put through. He wished he could insulate her from the madness. Maybe the Haven would give him that opportunity.

"Here we are," he proudly announced as he pulled up to the front of a nondescript, saltbox-style cabin that looked like all the others on the road. This one differed in that it had an old tire swing tied to a massive oak tree's low-hanging branch.

Back in early summer, Delta had come up to the Haven on two successive weekends to help the residents clear twenty acres to generate more pasture for the beef cattle Ryan had purchased at auction that spring. Everyone had pitched in to clear underbrush and cut down trees before sowing seed for the pasture.

Delta had brought a cord of wood to his cabin and stacked it inside a lean-to shed in the back. After eight months, the mixture of hickory and oak was well seasoned at this point. It was a valuable commodity to be used in the wood-burning stove that performed double duty as a cooktop and a source of heat. While Ethan fetched the wood, Delta unpacked and got the kids settled in the small bedroom.

On another trip to the Haven last summer, Delta had borrowed the Haven's box truck and drove down to Charlotte, where he shopped at IKEA. Their furniture, and the low prices, fit Delta's needs perfectly. When he'd outfitted the second bedroom with the bunk beds, he never imagined a scenario in which the kids would be with him. Now, with trepidation, he wondered if it would last.

"Okay, you guys, let's grab a seat and I'll explain," began Delta after glancing at his watch. He had an hour before he left for the morning briefing.

"Dad, what's happening?" Ethan started the conversation.

"Okay, first, let me tell you about the Haven. When I moved to Atlanta, I interviewed for several jobs. I put my résumé on websites, I networked on social media, and I put feelers out to people who knew about my track record in law enforcement. One of the opportunities that came my way was the Haven."

"Do you have two jobs, Daddy?" asked Skylar.

"Sort of, baby girl, although now it's most likely just one. This one."

"Did you get fired because of us?" His daughter was genuinely concerned by the fact that her brother had disobeyed their father's orders at the concert the night before.

"No, Sky. Nothing like that. It's just that, well, um, things have changed in the world."

"Is that why you wouldn't let us turn on the radio, and made us pee outside?" Ethan was a smart kid and very observant.

Delta was apologetic. "Yes, and I'm sorry about that. I wanted the opportunity to explain what's happening without a bunch of noise coming at you both from the news media."

He paused and gathered his thoughts. There wasn't a need to hit them with all of it, as they were both too young to understand. He continued. "Several things have taken place around the country that the police are still trying to sort out. New York City, Washington, Detroit, and, um, others have been subjected to, um …" Will paused as he tried to find the words.

"Daddy? Just spill it," said Skylar with conviction, causing Delta to laugh. Kids don't need to be coddled. They need to be exposed to the world gently, but truthfully.

"Okay, I will," he replied. "The news reports indicate parts of the country are under attack. Some of it is serious; other events are more of a nuisance, we think. Either way, I needed to get you guys to a safe place where we won't be exposed to the craziness."

"Was the concert attacked last night?" asked Ethan.

"Yes, son, I believe it was. I have no idea why, but it was."

"So why do you have a job here?" he asked.

"Son, I've seen a lot of horrible things in my career with the police. I believe our society is very fragile, and that one mistake, or an intentional act, could cause people to get angry or even violent. I wanted a place to keep my family safe in the event things got out of hand."

"You mean like these attacks?" asked Ethan.

Delta sighed and walked over to the wood-burning stove to add a couple of chunks of hickory. "Yes, that's exactly what I had in mind. I couldn't afford to purchase the place on my own because my priority has always been to provide for you two the best I could. So I made a deal with the owners, who hired me to work here in exchange for this cabin at the Haven." Delta waved his arms around the cabin, which consisted of a single bath, two small bedrooms, and the open living space where they were talking.

"So is the whole place surrounded by fences and armed guards?" asked Ethan before adding, "It's kinda like a prison."

Delta grimaced, not sure how to take Ethan's statement. "Well, fences and guards can have two purposes, depending on how you look at it. When you go to jail, they're designed to keep the prisoners in. At the Haven, the security has been created to keep people out."

"Why, Daddy?" asked Skylar.

Delta sat down next to his daughter and took her hands in his. "Well, baby girl, depending on how bad things get out there, some people will be hungry and desperate, and they'll be looking everywhere for food, water, and shelter. At the Haven, we've taken steps to provide all of those things for the people who live here for a long time."

"How long, Daddy?"

"As long as it takes."

"As long as it takes to do what, Dad?" asked Ethan.

"Son, depending on what's happening, it could take weeks or months or maybe even years for the country to become normal and safe again."

The kids digested their father's words while he prepared two mugs of Nestlé instant hot chocolate. He topped their drinks with marshmallows and whipped cream. Delta opted for instant coffee, fully caffeinated. It had been a long night.

After he returned with the drinks, he got hit with a question from Ethan that he'd hoped to avoid.

"Dad, about these attacks. Did they hit Philadelphia too?"

Crap. He didn't want to lie, but he had a feeling where this was headed. "Maybe, son. They don't know for sure yet."

"What does that mean?" Ethan was skeptical of his father's response.

"Well, there was a large power outage in the area that included Philadelphia, plus New Jersey and parts of Maryland."

Skylar set her mug on the table and scooted to the front of the sofa. "Daddy, are you gonna get Mom? She should be safe, too."

"Baby girl, your mother's on a cruise ship and wasn't due to get back into port until tomorrow morning. You guys know how I feel about Frankie, but he is a cop and perfectly capable of keeping your mom safe."

Skylar vigorously shook her head in disagreement. "Not like you can, Daddy."

"Dad, if it's bad enough for the three of us to come here, it's bad enough for Mom to come too."

A chill came over Delta's body at the thought of his ex-wife staying with him. And, most likely, she was a package deal with that treacherous wife-stealing ex-partner of his.

"Guys, your mom has a new life now, one that doesn't include me. She'll be just fine up north."

"No, she won't, Daddy," protested Skylar.

Ethan agreed. "Come on, Dad. You can't just leave her up there. You have to go get her."

Delta took a deep breath and tried to keep his composure. "Son, honestly, your mother doesn't like me very much. I can't see how we could possibly live under the same roof."

"You have to try, Dad. We can't just leave her."

"Son, you don't understand," Delta interrupted him. "It's complicated."

"No, it's not. It's simple. Either you go get her, or I will. Or take us home."

Delta gulped down the last of his coffee and glanced down at his watch. He'd have to hurry to avoid being late.

"Okay, let me think about this and see what my options are. For now, you guys stay here. Keep the fire going, and when I get back, we'll talk about it some more."

Barely saying goodbye, Delta bolted out the door into the bright morning sun, with no clue as to how he was going to handle this.

CHAPTER 18

Hyatt Centric Times Square
New York City

As a couple, Tom and Donna Shelton had experienced the ups and downs of life. Their marriage had always been on solid footing despite Tom's devotion to the military and his country. This trip, intended to commemorate their fortieth wedding anniversary, had produced the greatest physical and emotional challenge of their lives together except for Donna's cancer scare.

When Donna had been diagnosed as having breast cancer years ago, the family drew closer together, and the crisis forced Tom to reevaluate his life. He'd always put his duties as the commanding officer of the Naval Weapons Station at Joint Base Charleston above his family, and they understood because of the importance of his position. Donna's breast cancer diagnosis changed everything.

Tom planned his retirement from the Navy, and Donna fought the cancer. Her doctor had spotted a peanut-sized shadow on her left breast and immediately performed a biopsy. The test confirmed their worst nightmare—the mass was cancer.

Donna was in shock. Consumed with the possibility of dying before she turned sixty, terror overcame her. Spending countless hours at the infusion center, followed by a lumpectomy and chemotherapy, Donna's emotions ranged from sad, angry and worried to, at times, completely unpredictable. Then there were the side effects of the chemo. Hair loss, exhaustion, and nausea. But the couple persevered.

Tom's retirement was a blessing to the family. Outwardly, he put on a good face to assuage any guilt Donna might have for causing him to exit the Navy before he'd planned to. Inwardly, Tom still felt a sense of duty, and as a result, he secretly maintained lines of communication with the military to keep him in the loop by receiving classified information and, based upon his years of experience, lending advice when called upon.

The family declared a miracle when Donna's cancer was defeated after a year of chemo. She followed up with the doctor, and her scans had continued to read clean for the last four years. This anniversary celebration at Times Square for New Year's Eve was the start of a countdown of another sort for Tom and Donna. For many cancer survivors, reaching five years without recurrence means a much higher probability of survival. In the coming year, without any hiccups, Donna could declare herself cancer-free and put the ordeal out of her mind.

For those who haven't experienced a loved one with cancer, using the term *journey* to describe what the cancer patient goes through was not entirely accurate. The term *journey* implied a stress-free, almost zen-like experience. What cancer patients and their families actually experienced was fear and sheer exhaustion.

It was a level of stress that surpassed what Tom and Donna had just been through. When he and Donna made it back inside the hotel room, they breathed a collective sigh of relief. The chaos on the streets below their upper-level room in the Hyatt Centric Hotel in Times Square had begun to dissipate somewhat. The stampede of hundreds of thousands of New Year's Eve revelers had evacuated Broadway and scampered through the streets of Midtown like mice fleeing a cat in a maze.

Then Tom's phone had buzzed. The message was ominous, but it also evoked memories of a former life, one in which he'd performed admirably for his country and for those in power who didn't wear the uniform or a U.S. flag on their lapel.

He glanced down again at the text he'd received. A communication from a part of his life he considered to be dead and buried. Yet, rising from the ashes like a phoenix, his secretive second job was regenerated and born again.

The real danger on the ocean, as well as the land, is people.
Fare thee well and Godspeed, Patriot!
MM

"Tom, is that from Willa?" Donna asked apprehensively. She'd found her way under the covers and had propped against the headboard as she flipped through the news channels with the volume turned down. Watching was one thing, hearing the details was another.

"Nah, wrong number," Tom lied.

"Dear, wasn't that a text message?"

"Yes, but it was still wrong," replied Tom before shoving the phone in his pocket. He worked to change the subject. "I need to charge my phone. Let's use yours to reach out to Willa, okay?"

Donna pointed to the chest of drawers, where her cell phone sat next to Tom's wallet. He retrieved it for her and then made his way into the living area to locate his phone charger. When he was out of Donna's sight, he deleted the text message.

He stood in the darkened living area for a moment before wandering into the kitchenette. He could use a stiff drink but opted for their celebratory bottle of champagne instead. Donna was chattering away with Willa, reassuring their youngest daughter that the old folks were okay.

The swelling of Donna's ankle persisted, and Tom noticed his wife hid the injury from Willa, just as she had hidden her breast cancer diagnosis from him at first. After the truth came out, Tom wasn't upset about the fact she'd withheld the truth. As he knew, being tight-lipped about certain subjects was a part of life, and among the secrets spouses keep from each other was the condition of their health.

For whatever reason, whether it was the fear of stigma, unwanted pity, or an attempt to not burden others, Donna, like so many women, had kept her husband in the dark about her cancer. It wasn't until she was told she needed surgery that she opened up to Tom and their daughters about her illness.

Now Tom was wrestling with an old secret of his own, one that didn't affect his marriage, but certainly weighed heavily on his soul. He mumbled to himself in the dark, with only the ambient light from the bedroom television dancing through the doorway.

He wasn't sure why he didn't turn the lights on. In the moment, he felt like remaining in the dark.

"Why are you texting me again?" he muttered to himself as he fumbled through the cabinets to find two glasses. He unscrewed the wire holding the cork in the champagne bottle and grimaced. He continued talking to himself, oblivious to Donna's conversation with Willa. "I don't wanna get sucked back in again. I can't help you anymore."

Tom sighed, retrieved a kitchen towel, and moistened it to gain a firm grip on the cork. Just as he was about to pop the cork, a fist pounded on their hotel room door.

"*Open up! Police!*"

CHAPTER 19

Hyatt Centric Times Square
New York City

The pounding on the door was relentless. It wasn't the polite knock of room service personnel or a neighbor. It was the *thump-thump-thump*, three pounding knocks on the door, that was adopted by every law enforcement officer in America. Without saying a word, the person on the other side knew a cop wanted you to open the door.

"Tom, who is it?" shouted Donna from the bedroom. She switched on the wall-mounted lights above the nightstand.

Tom ignored her question and turned his attention to the intrusion. "Just a moment," replied Tom, who was now dressed in his pajamas. He started toward the bedroom to retrieve one of the robes from the bathroom suite when the knocking persisted. Now Tom was aggravated. He turned around and put his eye to the peephole to view the hallway. What he saw was straight out of a pandemic novel.

He turned the bolt lock and the handle at the same time, allowing the door to open and the accompanying light to flood in. Three men and a woman stood in the hallway with a push cart ordinarily used by the housekeeping staff, but was now filled with white Tyvek hazmat suits, masks, goggles, and gloves.

"Sir, the mayor has ordered a mandatory evacuation of Midtown as a result of the attacks. All guests of the hotel must leave immediately."

"Mandatory?"

The officer replied, "Yes, sir. May we come in so we can get you outfitted with a Tyvek suit and other protective gear?"

"Um, my wife's in bed."

"I'm here, Tom," interrupted Donna, who had snuck in behind him, wrapped in her new robe. She flipped on the foyer light and hopped on one foot as she retreated into the living area to turn on additional lights.

"Come in," offered Tom as he stood out of the way. One male and one female officer entered the hotel room while the others remained in the hallway.

They questioned Tom and Donna about where they had been when the drone strikes hit and how long they might have been exposed to any radioactive fallout. Donna became frightened at the brusque questioning.

Tom tried to calm her by pushing back against the officer. "Officer, isn't it a little early to declare this to be a dirty-bomb attack? I mean, it's been less than two hours."

"The initial readings are conclusive, sir. We have to move quickly in order to—"

Tom interrupted with a question. "Wouldn't we better off staying in this sealed environment, you know, to allow the material to dissipate?"

The officer became agitated. "Sir, our orders come from the mayor's office with the added confirmation of the governor. Mandatory means mandatory. Now, where are the clothes you were wearing while outside?"

Tom pointed toward the closet in the master bedroom suite. "We stripped them off and wrapped them inside the comforter from the bed. We'd sat on it when we—"

The female officer interrupted Tom. Pointing toward Donna's injured ankle, she asked, "Ma'am, do you need some assistance with getting into the Tyvek suit? I'd be glad to help."

"No, I can manage," replied Donna. "Where are we supposed to go?"

"Are the airports open?" asked Tom.

"No."

"What about Grand Central Station? It's not too far from us."

"No, sir. It was hit as well," replied the lead officer. "The City of New York has an evacuation plan in place. You are in evacuation zone six."

New York was one of the most densely populated cities in America, both from a permanent resident standpoint, as well as visitors and workers. The New York City Emergency Management office had created a website called *Know Your Zone.* During any type of crisis, ranging from a major hurricane to a mass evacuation due to pandemic or nuclear attack, anyone could access the website, input their location, and be given directions to the nearest evacuation center.

"What does that mean?" asked Donna.

"You are to report to Norman Thomas High School at 111 East Thirty-Third Street between Park and Lexington Avenues. They'll be able to explain your options."

"Options?" asked Donna.

"Yes, ma'am. You'll be evacuated from the city using a combination of school buses and chartered transportation. There are many destinations. They'll be able to tell you more at the evacuation center."

"Who's going to drive us?" asked Tom.

The officers rudely chuckled at his inquiry. "Sir, there's never been gridlock in the city like this in its history. You'll have to walk."

"I can do the math, Officer. That's more than ten blocks. My wife has a sprained ankle. She can't go anywhere on foot."

"Bailey!" the officer shouted to one of the men in the hallway. "Get a wheelchair up here for this woman."

"Yes, sir!"

Tom was incredulous. "You want us to push a wheelchair ten blocks or more in this madness? That'll be impossible."

"Sir, the evacuation order is mandatory. You'll be fine."

Tom and Donna felt helpless as they were being forced out of their hotel room. While they donned their Tyvek suits and associated gear, the officers stepped across the hall to contact another hotel guest.

Donna whispered to Tom, "Do we really have to leave? Maybe they'll get distracted and we could wait, you know, at least until morning."

"That might be worth a try," he replied. "Let's gather our things and try to stuff it all in a duffle. We'll make it look like we're cooperating."

"Good idea."

Tom retrieved their bags, and they picked through the essentials to take home with them. Donna was willing to leave behind the majority of her outfits in order to keep the plush robe Tom had purchased for her the night before.

They had just finished packing when Officer Bailey pushed the wheelchair into the room and waited.

The lead officer poked his head in to address the Sheltons. "Okay, are you two squared away? Do you know where you're supposed to go?"

"Um, yes, we do," replied Tom hesitantly. He was puzzled at the continued presence of Officer Bailey.

"Good," said the officer in charge. He turned to the remaining officer. "Bailey, escort these folks down to the east side emergency exit. Remember, 111 East Thirty-Third Street. You head east about four blocks to Park Avenue, and then south a dozen blocks to the high school. Good luck."

Tom closed his eyes and shook his head, as their plan had been thwarted. Donna reluctantly sat in the wheelchair, and Officer Bailey piled the two duffle bags in her lap. After an extended wait for the elevator, they arrived in the service hallways of the hotel, where a line waited to exit the Hyatt. The refugees were all dressed in Tyvek suits and were carrying suitcases and blankets.

Once they reached the exit door, a hotel security officer handed them two bottles of water and a printed map with the route to the evacuation center highlighted. He thanked them for staying at the Hyatt Centric Hotel, apologized for the inconvenience, and directed them out into the chaotic streets of Manhattan.

CHAPTER 20

Midtown Manhattan
New York City

Tom wheeled Donna into the middle of a dark alley amidst the dozens of hotel guests, who milled about in their white Tyvek suits like ghosts looking for a house to haunt. Most were confused at the suddenness of their eviction from the hotel, while others were frightened at being thrust into the mayhem occurring on the streets.

"We stayed in our room for a reason," began one man. "My wife and I didn't want any part of this, and that was before the attack."

"Do you think they're telling us the truth?" asked another man. "You know the government. You can't trust them. This could be some kind of false flag?"

"A what?" asked a lady in response.

"You know, that's when the government manufactures a crisis in order to—"

Tom had heard enough and began pushing Donna through the confused guests toward where the alley opened up onto West Forty-Fifth Street. He put Donna in charge of navigation, and she used her pocket reading light to illuminate the map.

"Tom, let's go with the flow of people whenever possible," she suggested. "If we see a street that turns south that is less crowded, we'll take advantage of it."

"I agree, dear," said Tom. Then he leaned down and kissed his wife on the cheek. "I'm proud of you."

She touched his cheek and kissed him back. "Well, thank you, Mr. Shelton, but for what?"

He smiled. "For not falling apart, now or earlier. For being a great soldier during, you know, the last four years. For loving me for the last forty."

"It's because I love you and trust you that I can do all of those things. So, as the heroes always say, let's roll!"

Tom laughed as he pushed her to the edge of the sidewalk. The mass exodus from Times Square had lessened considerably since they had fought their way back into the hotel hours ago. The pain and suffering, however, had not.

Revelers who'd been trampled sat against the walls of tall buildings or had sought shelter in doorways of businesses, complaining of injuries or crying because they were distraught. As Tom pushed Donna down the middle of the street between stranded vehicles, an occasional body could be seen—eyes open, heart stopped.

They both turned their heads to avoid seeing the dead, opting to put it out of their minds rather than dwell on the senselessness of what had happened. On one occasion, as they made their way past Bryant Park near the New York Public Library, a body blocked their narrow path between the parked vehicles. Tom gently pulled the older woman by both feet until she was out of the way. He knelt down next to her battered body, shut her eyelids, and said a prayer for her.

The solemn moment was a reminder of how lucky they were under the circumstances, and it gave Tom a newfound vigor as he pushed a little harder to get his wife to safety.

It took them an hour and a half to traverse the New York City streets toward the Norman Thomas High School. They knew they were close when they observed a military presence at the intersection of Park Avenue and East Thirty-Third Street. A roadblock consisting of two Humvees greeted refugees as the line wrapped around the tall office building that housed Houghton Mifflin Harcourt Publishing.

After forty-five minutes, they turned the corner and were able to see the evacuation effort. Dozens of school buses, New York Metro Transit buses, and private charter buses were lined up on West

Thirty-Third Street, facing in the direction of the East River and Queens.

The refugees standing in line were orderly, unlike the pushing and shoving of those fleeing Times Square. Tom surmised that the people in line were familiar with the city's emergency plan, and he now considered the early, mandatory evacuation of the hotel to be a blessing. After these buses pulled out for destinations far away from Manhattan, it would take a lot longer to remove those who remained.

"We're next in line, Tom," said Donna in an attempt to get her husband's attention. Exhausted from the mile-long trek through the madness, Tom had momentarily checked out from reality.

He pushed Donna forward through one of five rope lines that led to the buses. A woman with a clipboard, a communications headset in her ear and a sidearm on her hip, motioned them forward.

"Destination?" she asked in a curt manner. Her eyes darted from Tom's face to Donna in the wheelchair. "No, first, I have to ask, ma'am, are you confined to a wheelchair? This doesn't look like—"

"No," Donna quickly replied. "I twisted my ankle, and the hotel provided us this for transportation. We had to travel fifteen—"

"Okay, good. Destination?"

"We're from Charleston, South Carolina," Tom responded.

"Here are your options," the woman continued. "Let me warn you that all air travel in and out of LaGuardia and JFK has been cancelled indefinitely. These buses can take you east to MacArthur on Long Island, but the flights are booked up for six days. For that matter, flights are booked up everywhere at this point a minimum of five to seven days, depending on airport location."

"What about bus travel?" asked Tom.

"The Port Authority bus terminals are located in the middle of the attack zone near Forty-Second Street and Eighth Avenue. Not an option."

"Um, what are our options?"

"Long Island, as I mentioned. Then there's Allentown or Scranton in Pennsylvania, Poughkeepsie or Albany in New York, or New Haven, Connecticut."

Donna turned in the wheelchair and looked up to Tom. "None of the options are good for going home. Let's just go to Long Island. It's probably the closest, right?"

The officer nodded.

Tom's mind raced. He wasn't sure if it was feasible, but there were markers to be called in. Sure, it had been years, but it was worth a try.

"Sir?" The officer impatiently insisted on an answer.

Tom quickly replied, "We'll go to New Haven."

Donna studied his face. "Tom, why there?"

"I'll explain on the bus. Let's go."

CHAPTER 21

New Year's Day
Six Flags Great Adventure
Jackson, New Jersey

Tyler Rankin made sure the kids were buckled up in the backseat of his Bronco and confirmed that they'd locked their doors. While his family waited for him, he took another moment to walk toward the exit of the Six Flags parking lot to look for potential obstacles blocking their escape.

The other park-goers wandered around the parking lot, displaying a variety of emotions. Most were puzzled and bewildered as to what could have caused their vehicles to stop functioning en masse. The vast majority of Americans were oblivious to the term *electromagnetic pulse*. The concept of an EMP destroying the power grid and the small electronics they relied upon never crossed their minds.

The emotions of the people standing around, comparing theories and speculating about what was going on, ranged from distress to agitation. Tyler had studied the devastating effects of an EMP enough to know Americans were not prepared for life without electricity, or vehicles without power. Soon panic would set in, immediately followed by anger.

It was time to go.

Fortunately, very few vehicles were departing Six Flags at the moment the EMP struck. The exits were clear, and the only potential obstacles were people standing in the way. He made his way back to the truck, where Angela gave him a smile of encouragement.

"Okay, babe, what's the plan?" she asked as he settled in his seat.

Tyler glanced in the backseat. In the short few minutes that he'd stepped away, their exhausted children had nuzzled against their pillows and fallen asleep.

"Good work." He pointed in the backseat with his right thumb.

Angela chuckled as she snapped open the gun case and removed their handgun. She seemed to weigh the weapon in her hand before she expertly pulled the slide and confirmed the chamber was empty. Then she examined one of three magazines stored within the eggcrate foam of the case's interior, all loaded with .45-caliber bullets. She slapped one of the magazines into the bottom of the pistol's grip and loaded a round into the chamber.

"It was easy, actually," she explained. "The kids asked me what happened to all the cars, and I started explaining to them about pulses of energy and how electronics can't take the short powerful bursts. I was barely into the how's and why's when I noticed they were both out."

"Well, I hope they stay that way for a while," said Tyler. "Listen, we've got a lot to talk about, including how we're gonna get home. But first, we need to get away from all of these people."

"I'm ready. Are you gonna just plow through them?" asked Angela as she pointed toward the groups of people standing in the way of the exit.

"Pretty much. Hopefully, they'll be surprised when our truck starts and heads toward them. It's about half a mile to the exit. Under the circumstances, that's a long way. If I'm right, they'll move out of the way, shocked at a working vehicle. If I'm wrong, they'll block our exit in an attempt to catch a ride or worse."

"Worse?" asked Angela.

"Yeah, steal our truck."

Angela looked ahead and nodded. She slowly slid her hand onto the gun and cradled it in her lap.

Tyler noticed the subtle movement and smiled. "It's gonna be fine. Just hold on."

Nervous with anticipation, he wiped his sweaty palms on his jeans. He glanced into the backseat one more time to check on their sleeping beauties. Then he turned the key in the ignition just enough to see if the dashboard lights and gauges responded.

"We're in business," said Angela as the vehicle started.

"Okay, here goes." Tyler tried to start the motor, but it wouldn't turn over.

"Ty, what's wrong?"

"Um, it's cold. The truck always has a hard time with a cold start in the winter."

"Dammit, Tyler, people have already noticed the sound. Keep trying!"

The engine groaned but wouldn't fire.

"They're coming!" Angela raised her voice, causing Kaycee to stir in the backseat.

"Mom?"

"It's all right, honey. Lie down. The truck's being stubborn."

"Hey, does your truck run?" a woman shouted from their left. Both Tyler and Angela whipped their heads around to see how close she was.

A man shouted from behind them, "Hold up, buddy! I need a ride to the hotel. Come on, kids!"

Tyler looked in the rearview mirror and saw a man running toward the Bronco with three teens in tow.

He tried the ignition again, and this time the motor started. He didn't hesitate as he pushed the manual stick shift into first gear and let the clutch out. The truck lurched forward toward a group of women, who shrieked and jumped out of the way.

"Let's go!" Tyler said excitedly as he pushed the gas pedal to the floor. He quickly shifted gears as he picked up speed.

As predicted, most of the people on the exit road were in shock to see him coming, but a few attempted to wave him down. Tyler didn't hesitate. He laid on the horn and kept going for them, assuming they would jump out of the way. It was a game of chicken he was willing to play to win.

"Oh, crap!" shouted Angela. "Another car just pulled out of a parking space." A vintage Chevy pickup from the sixties pulled out of a space ahead of them. The truck was struggling to run, most likely due to the cold weather.

"I'm gonna shoot the gap through the cars. Hold on!"

Tyler slowed and found an opening between the parked cars. This sent them to a different parking row and a whole new set of obstacles in the form of people standing in the way.

He slammed the palm of his hand on the horn as he approached, sending them scampering for cover.

"Go! Go! Go!" shouted J.C. from the backseat. Both kids were awake and leaning forward to observe the action.

Angela turned around and instructed them to sit back, which they did, for all of ten seconds. Then their curious faces were back to see their father play demolition derby with the stranded motorists.

"Almost, babe," Tyler said calmly.

"Oh my god!" exclaimed Angela, pointing to their right. "They swarmed the pickup truck, and they're pulling the driver out of the front seat."

"This is why we aren't slowing down," mumbled Tyler, who gripped the steering wheel until his knuckles turned white. He leaned forward in his seat and bore down on a large group blocking the final turn before they were out of the park.

"They're not moving!" shouted Angela.

"They will." Tyler slammed his fist on the horn as he roared toward them at nearly sixty miles an hour.

"Move, you idiots!" shouted Angela as she waved her arms across the inside of the windshield.

Tyler pressed forward, and several men stood in front of the crowd, defiant.

"Dammit!" shouted Tyler out of frustration as he let off the gas.

Angela looked over at him and said, "No, Ty. Keep going. I've got this."

He picked up speed again as Angela cranked the passenger-side window down. She hung her arm out the window, cocked the hammer on the forty-five, and fired a shot over the heads of the group blocking their exit.

They screamed and panicked in unison. Jumping out of the way or pushing their way to safety, the sound of gunfire created an opportunity for Tyler to roar past them, with the assistance of his wife's quick thinking.

Tyler glanced in the rearview mirror at the people who'd recovered from the scare, shaking their fists and giving him the middle finger. He didn't care about their hurt feelings. The Rankins had hundreds of miles to travel to get to safety, and this was just mile one.

CHAPTER 22

New Year's Day
Near Fort Dix
New Egypt, New Jersey

Tyler drove as fast as the forty-five-year-old truck could travel, leaving Six Flags and the throngs of stranded visitors chasing them down the road. Without a predetermined destination other than the New Jersey Turnpike, they found themselves approaching the small town of New Egypt, a small community of twenty-five hundred known for its wineries. Before they entered the quiet town, Tyler pulled into the Bible Baptist Church and drove around to the rear of the buildings, next to a softball field. He quickly turned off the engine and exhaled, the first time he'd done so since they'd escaped the parking lot.

"Way to go, Dad," said Kaycee with a thumbs-up. She and J.C. exchanged high fives. The youngsters were old enough to appreciate danger, but they were still at an age where any adventure generated an adrenaline rush, regardless of the circumstances.

Angela, who'd kept a death grip on their sidearm throughout, finally pried her fingers off the pistol's grip and set the weapon on the console between them. Tyler looked down at the gun and up to his wife's lovely face and smiled.

"You're an animal," he said jokingly. "When you shot over their heads, you scared the bejesus out of them. You talk about parting the Red Sea. Moses couldn't have done better, babe."

"Agreed. That's why I did it. They were challenging us, and I don't think those guys would've moved. Your horn wasn't working, so I used mine."

They laughed and reached across the console to hug one another. They looked into the backseat, and the kids were staring at them, smiling.

"What?" asked Tyler.

"Oh, nothing," began J.C. "Sometimes you two are gross."

"Gross?" asked Angela. "There's nothing gross about me loving your father."

"You guys are always hugging and kissing and stuff," said J.C.

"Good thing, buddy," said Tyler. "The day that stops, we've got big trouble. Let's get out of the truck and stretch our legs while I think. Everybody, keep your eyes open in case somebody saw us pull in here. We're surrounded by trees, so I think we're okay."

"I've gotta pee," announced J.C. innocently.

Angela chuckled. She looked around for their options. Near the baseball field were a few porta-potties. "Kaycee, why don't you guys use the bathroom over there. We have a long trip ahead of us."

"Okay, Mom," said Kaycee as she led her brother by the hand toward the toilets. She could be heard talking to J.C. as they left. "I almost peed my pants when I saw you fall out of the roller coaster."

"I was too scared to pee," replied J.C. "All I could see was the ground, and then I couldn't breathe. It was like my whole body froze, including my pee."

The two continued chatting as Angela and Tyler opened the rear hatch of the Bronco. He began rummaging through their bags, which consisted of clothing, snacks, a cooler of drinks, and two backpacks. The two identical black backpacks differed only in the gear attached using the MOLLE attachments on Tyler's. Pronounced *molly*, MOLLE was an acronym for modular lightweight load-carrying equipment. The system allowed for several attachments to be added to a backpack or military-style chest rig.

Tyler was capable of carrying more weight than Angela. He unzipped the main compartment and began to empty his gear onto the floor of the Bronco.

"What are you looking for?" she asked.

"Do you remember that tin of cookies Brett sent us last year for Christmas?"

"Yeah. They were terrible. Five different types of Fig Newtons? Ugh."

Tyler laughed as he found the tin in the bottom of the bag. "The kids liked them anyway, right?"

Angela shrugged. Tyler opened a side zipper pouch and pulled out his Morakniv Eldris firestarter/knife combo. The black knife with the short blade was perfect to store in their backpacks or tie around their necks when hiking. He removed the fixed blade from its hard plastic sheath and carefully cut the aluminum tape that sealed the tin.

"The cookies sucked, but the tin came in useful," Tyler said as he opened the lid to reveal a Kenwood TH-D74A triband radio. The Kenwood model enabled him to access ham channels, citizens bands, and emergency responder networks. Plus, it had built-in GPS capabilities.

"Is that from work?"

"Yeah. Richmond Fire-Rescue received upgraded handheld units three months ago. They offered the old units to us at a dime on the dollar. These originally sold for five hundred fifty dollars. I paid fifty bucks."

Angela took it from him and looked at the myriad of buttons on the front of the device. "How do you turn it on? Or, should I say, will it turn on?"

"I hope so," replied Tyler. "I created a small Faraday cage out of the cookie tin. I tested it when I loaded our packs before the trip. Let's see if it worked."

Tyler took the handheld radio back and pressed the power button. He beamed as the display lit up and a beep announced the Kenwood was fully operational.

"What's that, Dad?" asked Kaycee as she and her brother returned from their porta-potty break.

"Well, guys, I think this little radio may help us avoid a lot of aggravation on our way home. I know the logical, fastest way to get back to Richmond; however I-95 through Philly, Wilmington,

Baltimore, and DC doesn't sound like a very good idea under the circumstances."

J.C.'s chin dropped to his chest. "We're not gonna see the Liberty Bell or Independence Hall, are we?"

Tyler pulled his son close, draping his arm over his shoulder to give him a hug. "I'm afraid not, buddy. Not on this trip. That said, we're still going to have an exciting road trip on the way home. If my memory serves me, we'll drive through the countryside, maybe ride on a boat as we cross the Delaware, just like George Washington, and then, to top it off, we'll go in a tunnel under the Chesapeake. Whadya think about that?"

"Sooo cool!" exclaimed J.C., who jumped around on one foot, prompting Angela to look down at his feet.

"Joseph Charles! Did you go in those nasty porta-potties with one shoe on?"

"Um, yes, Mom. But I hopped in on one foot, right, Kaycee?"

"That's true, Mom. I watched him. But his sock is all wet from running through the wet grass."

Angela rolled her eyes and smiled at Tyler. "This is your son," she said with a laugh.

"Oh no, you created that monster. My child is the sweet one."

Angela playfully shoved Tyler, who, caught off guard, slid backwards and nearly fell on the wet grass where the snow had melted.

"Hey! Bad form!" shouted Tyler back and tried to catch Angela, who easily eluded his clutches as she raced around the Bronco.

"Can't catch me, pokey!" said the more athletic Angela, who kept the hood of the truck between them. Tyler was about to make another move when his radio squawked to life.

He could barely hear it because he had the volume turned down. He quickly adjusted the volume, but the transmission was lost. It was, however, a reminder they needed to make a decision and hit the road.

There were a number of factors to consider, the most important of which related to traffic and population centers. Tyler had already decided to avoid the interstate. Tens of thousands of vehicles traveled along that stretch of interstate in any given hour, almost all of which would've become disabled by the EMP.

Tyler knew it was best to avoid large areas of population and even small towns if possible. Their experience in the Six Flags parking lot confirmed that. He'd never driven the back roads from this area to Virginia before. From recollection, he knew the area was rural—a definite plus.

He was familiar with the ferry that ran between Cape May at the southernmost tip of New Jersey and across the mouth of the Delaware River into Delaware near Ocean City. About ten years ago, the ferry had run aground on a sandbar during an unusually low tide. The event had made the news and caught Tyler's attention.

After they crossed the Delaware, the ride down to Chesapeake Bay would also be fairly desolate compared to the alternate routes through Baltimore and Washington, DC. The final stretch into Virginia would be across Chesapeake Bay via U.S. Route 9, the Chesapeake Bay Bridge-Tunnel.

"That'll be a breeze," he mumbled to himself as he rooted around under the driver's seat in search of the atlas. The seven-year-old map book was a little out of date, but the roads hadn't changed any in this area. He studied the route and smiled. Roughly three hundred eighty miles of back roads and a straight shot to Richmond.

Now the only challenge they should face was fuel.

CHAPTER 23

USA Health University Trauma Center
Mobile, Alabama

Michael Cortland fought sleep. Despite being reprimanded on two occasions by the night nurses on duty, Cort continued to monitor the events around the country through the news. He desperately needed a cell phone. Not to reach to any members of his staff but, rather, to speak with his father-in-law, George Trowbridge. The words rang in his head, pounding out the throbbing pain resulting from his near-drowning experience.

Either you control destiny, or destiny controls you.

His rest was fitful at best. Initially, he'd fought sleep as he hungered for information and tried to create his own working theory as to who was behind the random attacks around the country. They were varied in their targets and methods, yet perfectly timed to occur just before midnight on the East Coast.

The coverage was riveting. The media lived for drama such as this, and every network, including ESPN, had some kind of coverage. Lost in all of the reports of terrorism was the crashing of Delta Flight 322 into the Gulf of Mexico at the mouth of Mobile Bay.

The local stations were on the scene, covering the rescue efforts. Thus far, no cause of the aircraft's total loss of power had been determined, nor was there a complete death count.

Cort knew one thing for certain. He was alive, and Congressman Johnson Pratt, the would-be prosecutor of the president, was not.

On the third visit by the floor nurse, Cort's lifeline to the outside world was cut off. She removed the remote function from his hospital bed, disconnected the power cord to the television from its outlet, and stood on a chair to toss the cord above the television. Cort followed her every movement, and as she finished, he quipped, "You don't trust me, do you?"

She didn't think it was funny and stormed out of his room.

Unplugged, Cort finally drifted off to sleep, if one could call it that. The images of death and destruction from around the country were quickly replaced with a vivid recollection of his own near-death experience. He tossed and turned as he re-created the nightmarish event in his mind.

Known as re-experiencing, having flashbacks to a traumatic event was a hallmark symptom of people suffering from posttraumatic stress syndrome. Some people had vivid nightmares that were exact replays of the trauma they experienced. Replicative nightmares, during which the brain replays the event over and over in a continuous loop, were the brain's effort to process what had happened. During sleep, Cort replayed the moment he left his seat to help Congressman Pratt. In his dream, he recalled how he swam past the dead bodies strapped into their seats until he reached into the darkness and touched the congressman's bloated body wedged into his seat. For nearly two minutes, Cort held his breath, fully in control of the situation, until he wasn't.

However, as the dream replayed, it became increasingly bizarre. His mind soon introduced a new twist to the events. His subconscious inserted a story he recalled learning as a child in Sunday school, the parable of the Good Samaritan as told by Jesus in the Gospel of Luke. Probably one of the most misinterpreted Gospels, it's the story of a man who comes across a traveler on the road from Jerusalem to Jericho who'd been beaten, robbed, and left for dead.

Other travelers, noticing the injured man, nonetheless passed him by. However, the Good Samaritan approached the victim, bandaged his wounds, loaded him onto his donkey, and rented him a room at the inn to recover.

Cort, however, had his own interpretation, one that instilled horror into an already emotionally shocking experience. He had been taught from an early age to help those around him, whether he was different from them or not. His family crossed his mind as he swam to check on the congressman. With each row of seats he passed, the drowning victims gradually lost their skin until they were nothing more than ghostly, shadowy skeletons lying limp in their seats.

The closer he got to the first-class section in his quest to save the congressman, he too began to lose hunks of flesh, floating off his skin into the water, only to be nabbed by fish that swam around the wreckage. Congressman Pratt, however, was not deteriorating in his dream. He was alive and well, breathing and laughing, as Cort transformed into a wraithlike apparition of his former self.

Cort's nightmare repeated, with each replay becoming more ghastly and frightening. Soon, the dream was so realistic that his body began to shiver from the cold depths of the Gulf of Mexico. His body shaking uncontrollably, Cort tried to force himself awake, reliving the precise moment when he took the last forced breath under water before he blacked out.

"Mr. Cortland. Mr. Cortland! Wake up, wake up." The nurse tried to awaken him, but Cort, in his deep sleep, heard the voice of the gate agent in Atlanta, paging him to enter the doomed aircraft. His brain rejected the request, screaming within itself to run from the gate, don't get on the plane.

Don't wake up!

The nurse repeated her plea to Cort. "Wake up, sir!"

"Huh. What?" Cort was forced out of his sleep through the gentle prodding of the morning nurse. He opened his eyes slightly to see the curtains open and a beautiful sunny day awaiting him outside. No dark, murky waters. No tiny bubbles floating past his eyes. No skeletons. No bloated congressman.

"Good morning, Mr. Cortland," the nurse began in her south Alabama drawl. She tenderly wiped the sweat off his forehead with a cool, wet cloth. "You were having quite the ornery dream. Try to calm down and take deep, level breaths."

Cort nodded and glanced around the room. After getting his bearings, he relaxed and his pulse returned to normal.

"Wow, that was awful," he said as he tried to push himself up in the bed.

"Let me help you." As she assisted Cort to get adjusted and more comfortable, she explained that his dreams might be vivid for a few days as his mind processed what had happened during the crash. "Perhaps I should find a psychologist on duty to come speak with you before you're discharged this morning."

"Wait? Discharged. Already?"

"Well, I know it seems sudden, but Dr. Wayne stopped by earlier and checked your vitals. You have recovered remarkably well, and most importantly, your breathing is excellent, as I just witnessed."

"So I get to go home this morning?" asked Cort, seemingly astonished at the good news. He wanted out of that hospital in the worst way, hoping he could leave the demons behind in the process.

"Absolutely," she replied. "A discharge nurse will stop by to provide you some instructions. Your wife has already called this morning to inquire about your condition. She has assured Dr. Wayne that she's capable of caring for you at home. Naturally, bed rest is essential. If you have any difficulties breathing, or side effects of the antibiotics we'll send you home with from the hospital pharmacy, you'll need to come back and see us. Okay?"

Even if he didn't agree, Cort wouldn't admit it. "Yes. I feel great. What time?"

"I believe your family is on their way to the hospital now. We have some paperwork to finish up, and then, as I said, the discharge nurse will speak with you and your wife. I said all that to say, um, probably by eleven?"

"Works for me," replied Cort with a big smile. He asked for some water, and she informed him a breakfast of liquids would be brought by shortly. He needed to avoid solid foods for a day or so until his throat healed. She also recommended he minimize his conversation, and by no means should he raise his voice.

Cort nodded and leaned his head back. He wasn't afraid of sleeping at this point. He was now contemplating his family's future.

CHAPTER 24

Interstate 95 Northbound
Near Sherwood Island, Connecticut

After they left the city, Donna and Tom speculated as to what would happen next around the country and whether the Times Square attacks were part of a much larger terrorism operation. The opinions of their fellow passengers varied and ranged from wild-eyed conspiracy involving the Illuminati to more conventional precursors to war as utilized by the Russians. Tom, who preferred to get all the facts before he rendered an opinion, listened to the conversation and occasionally joked with Donna as arguments broke out between the refugees over their respective theories.

When Donna finally dozed off, Tom was left alone with his thoughts. The text message troubled him, and it certainly influenced his analysis of the New Year's Eve attacks. He recalled the times he had been called upon to perform seemingly mundane tasks or provide innocuous information that appeared harmless on its face but might have been involved in some grander plan to which he was not privy.

He wasn't able to sleep, as everything he'd done for his clandestine friends was analyzed from different angles. His brain tried to reconcile his actions of the past with the events of last night. *Is there a connection?*

The turnpike turned toward the east at Sherwood Island, a Connecticut State Park overlooking Long Island Sound. The wheels created a series of tromping sounds as the fully loaded school bus crossed the bridge, stirring Donna in her seat. Her head bounced off the window slightly, jarring her fully awake to a rising sun.

"It's a new day," she mumbled. She reached over to grasp Tom's hand and smiled. "Happy New Year, dear."

"Happy New Year to you as well, Mrs. Shelton," he said with a smile and kissed his wife.

She probed his eyes and sensed he was troubled. "You haven't slept, have you?"

His response was curt. "No, just relaxing and thinking."

"About?" she asked, pushing herself up in the uncomfortable vinyl seat that was full of tears and holes. She didn't care. She was glad to be out of the Tyvek suit that had caused her to sweat while sitting in the wheelchair, despite the cold temperatures.

Tom waved his hand in front of him. "You know, all of this."

Donna pressed him. She knew her husband too well. Tom, like most men, usually had to have his thoughts dragged out of his mind, kicking and screaming. "Tom, please don't equivocate," implored Donna. "What's on your mind? Or perhaps you should explain why you jumped at the opportunity to come to New Haven. Do you know someone here? Somebody we can stay with while we wait for an available flight?"

"Um, yes and no. I mean, okay, I do know someone here. A man. A powerful, wealthy man whom I met once years ago while we were in port at nearby Groton. I was summoned, along with my commander at the time, to meet this man and his associates."

Donna warily twisted in her seat to avoid hitting her tender ankle. She gave it a slight wiggle to confirm the swelling had reduced somewhat thanks to the Advil she continued to take. Facing Tom, she asked, "You've never told me about this? You came here frequently before you assumed your duties at Charleston. You never mentioned meeting a man like this."

Tom sighed and glanced around to see if anyone was eavesdropping. He slowly leaned into his wife and lowered his voice as he responded, "This man, whose name I will tell you when we're off the bus, invited us to his home one afternoon. It was all very mysterious, you know, like in a movie. He made me an offer, Donna, one that I thought was harmless, but financially lucrative, all the same."

"He paid you to do a job?" she asked. The change in the tone of her voice indicated her concern about where the conversation was leading.

"Donna, don't worry. It wasn't anything illegal, at least I don't think it was. I was called upon from time to time to provide information about what I did for the Navy and, on rare occasions, delay implementation of an order. I never knew why, or how it impacted anything that I was responsible for. I just did it."

"They paid you for this?"

"Yes, a monthly stipend that I received until the time of my retirement. Dear, it paid for our daughters' college and our grandchildren's private school. It was the kind of money I didn't make in the Navy that allowed me to create a better life for our family."

"I never saw the money come through our accounts."

"I had a numbered account in the Turks and Caicos Islands."

Donna leaned back against the window and folded her arms. "How long did you hide this from me?"

"Eleven years, until now," he replied as he dropped his chin to his chest. "I opened it while we were in Providenciales for our anniversary trip." Tom was genuinely remorseful for keeping this secret life from his wife. He'd hoped it could remain buried, but the circumstances forced the skeletons out of the closet.

"I know you can't say his name, but who is he?" she asked as she leaned forward and whispered, "Is he in the military? A politician? What?"

"No, not really. He runs a firm in Washington. One of those think-tank, political-influencer operations that all the politicians hire to get what they want. He's one of the big movers and shakers in Washington who control which politicians get elected, which laws get passed, and who gains from it all financially."

"And you were associated with these men for over ten years?" Donna averted her eyes and stared out toward the sunrise. The bus was approaching New Haven, where they were to be dropped off at the local bus terminal.

"Yes, mostly through encrypted phone calls and text messages," replied Tom. He hesitated for a moment. He considered telling Donna about the text message he'd received in the hotel room. This was yet another secret, *a lie of omission*, that he had to keep to himself, for now.

That, plus the fact George Trowbridge was more than one of the movers and shakers. He was, in fact, *the man*. The tip of the spear. A maker of presidents. A builder, and destroyer, of nations.

CHAPTER 25

New Year's Day
HB-1
The Haven

The mood was solemn in the main barn of the Haven as Delta entered for the morning briefing. Ryan was speaking with Alpha while Echo got reacquainted with Bravo and Charlie. The four of them had known one another for over eighteen months. Echo, who was the fourth member of the security team, had rejected the Delta moniker because he had had a bad flight experience on a Delta Air Lines flight and therefore considered the name to be bad karma, at least as it applied to him. Thus he skipped to the next option in the military alphabet, Echo. Besides, with his last name being Echols, Echo simply made sense.

"Good morning, everyone," Delta announced his presence, as the group had turned their backs to the door while they discussed the news coming out of the northeastern United States.

"Welcome back, Delta," said Ryan, turning to approach and greet him with a hearty handshake. "How about some coffee? We're all operating on two hours of sleep combined."

"Yeah, that would be great," replied Delta. As Ryan made his way to the kitchenette to pour a mug for Delta, Echo was the next to say hello.

"Everybody, I want you to know Delta is one helluva woodchuck. Last summer, this guy practically gnawed the trees to the ground and chopped them up with his bare hands."

The two men exchanged handshakes and then bro-hugs. Delta

genuinely liked Echo and looked upon him as a fatherly figure. His own dad had passed away when he was a new recruit in the Philadelphia Police Department. Delta's father had spent seventeen years on the force, but the stresses of the job, coupled with the alcohol he used to cope, forced him into an unexpected heart attack way too early in life. His mother had never recovered and died herself soon thereafter from a stroke. The Hightower family had a history of coming apart at the seams.

"Thanks, Echo. I like working with my hands."

"Bravo, Charlie, you two haven't met Delta, am I right?"

Bravo stepped forward first and gave Delta a firm handgrip and chest bump. Charlie, tough, but still a woman, opted to wave from afar.

"Nice to meet you guys finally," said Delta. "It seems that every time I drove up from Atlanta, you'd just left or were scheduled to come in."

"True, true," added Bravo. "In our jobs, Charlie and I have to travel a lot. All of this stuff happening gives us both a chance to put down some roots."

Charlie chimed in. "Out of chaos came order, right, Bravo?"

"Damn straight!"

The two operators gave each other high fives. Will admired the comradery they shared. He'd had that once with the men and women of Philly SWAT. His partners might not have been military, but they certainly were on the front line of the war that had taken over the streets of America.

Ryan returned with Delta's coffee and the Mr. Coffee carafe, which he promptly emptied by topping off everyone's mugs. "Let's get started, shall we?"

"You got it, boss," replied Echo. The sounds of chairs scooting on the wooden floor of the foreman's office preceded the start of the meeting. The scene was reminiscent of any board meeting in a corporate office somewhere, except the members of the Haven security team were fully armed and dressed for battle.

Their backgrounds were diverse, which allowed for differences of opinion and due deference during the decision-making process when necessary.

Ryan had everyone's attention as he began. "We've all seen the news, so there's no need to rehash what's happening outside the Haven. Blair spent all night contacting off-property residents to advise them of our opinions concerning these events. Whether they choose to come is up to them. They are adults.

"With respect to our existing residents, everyone has a role to play. Not counting the people in this room and Blair, we have thirty-eight people on the property, plus four children."

"Six," interjected Alpha. "Delta's kids make six."

"Oh, yeah," said Ryan.

Delta spoke up. "Ryan, I can explain. You see—"

Ryan raised his hand and stopped Delta. "Not necessary. It is what it is, and we have the flexibility to deal with two young mouths to feed. We've finished construction on our church and the schoolhouse. We have at least two teachers on our roster. When Blair and I envisioned the Haven, we included children in the plan even though we didn't have any of our own."

"Um, thanks," said Delta. "I promise they'll pitch in any way they can."

"I have something in mind, by the way, but we can talk about it later," said Alpha.

Ryan nodded and continued. "Overnight, Alpha set up our perimeter security. We could use more warm bodies to fulfill that role. Based upon the responses Blair has received, we should have help coming. Although we're still missing the newest member of our security team, Foxtrot."

"When did you bring him on board?" asked Bravo.

"Well, he is a she, for starters," replied Ryan.

"Good! I didn't want to be the only female in this sausage-fest!" exclaimed Charlie.

Alpha, in his baritone voice, couldn't resist needling her. "Charlie, you're part dude anyway. My guess is you've got a sausage of your own packed away in there somewhere."

"You wish, big boy! If I did, it would be a Johnsonville and not a Vienna sausage!"

The group burst out in laughter as the two former Army veterans went at each other. After enjoying the lighthearted moment of locker-room talk, military style, Ryan brought the room back to order.

"Anyway, gentlemen, and lady, Foxtrot is MIA. She lives in DC, and the whole city is in chaos after the transportation system came to a standstill. She might be delayed anyway."

"Why's that, boss?" asked Echo.

"She's an attorney, and a dang good one too. In fact, she's on the legal team handling the president's case in front of the Supreme Court."

A few glances were exchanged between the military members of the team—Alpha, Bravo, and Charlie.

Ryan picked up on the skeptical attitude and nipped it in the bud. "Listen, Foxtrot isn't ex-military or law enforcement, but she certainly can hold her own. She's like a wolf in sheep's clothing."

Echo gave his opinion as the only other member of the team to have met her, as Alpha had been on National Guard duty when Foxtrot was interviewed. "Actually, boss, do not let appearances deceive you. She's more like a badass Barbie. This young woman can shoot, fight, and break you down with her good looks. I feel bad for the guy who assumes she's a pushover because of her appearance. They may not live to regret it."

Ryan added, "Not to mention the fact that you can throw her out in the woods with nothing but a knife and she'll find a way to live better than we do."

"Good enough for me," said Alpha. "I hope she gets here in time for the real fun. That time will be coming soon enough."

The security team discussed their protocols, any perceived weaknesses, and personnel holes they needed to fill. Ryan filled them in on X-Ray and the importance of his communications skills to the Haven. They also discussed preparing a space within HB-1 for his gunsmithing equipment and the bullet-manufacturing machinery.

Alpha was about to discuss their rotating shifts, which ensured one of the five security members on-property were always roaming the perimeter and conducting frequent gate checks, when Delta interrupted and asked to speak with Ryan first.

The two men walked out into the barn where they could talk.

Delta hesitated as he mustered up the courage to make the request. "Ryan, I don't know how to bring this up, but I've got a problem."

"What is it?"

"Well, as you've heard, I've got my son and daughter with me. It was my weekend to spend with them in Atlanta under our custody agreement. Um, all of this was totally unexpected, you know."

Ryan smiled and patted Delta on the back. "Hey, don't you worry about that. They're your kids, and we can manage. There are other children here and more on the way. We've planned for them, and trust me, two more children won't be noticed."

Delta took a deep breath and grimaced. "Um, it's not just that. Well, the kids are insisting I drive up north and find their mother. She's on a cruise with my ex-part—her boyfriend and they're due into port tomorrow morning in New Jersey."

Ryan walked away and rolled his neck on his shoulders. "I know about her from your file, Delta. I also seem to recall that you guys have a strained relationship at best. If I remember, she uses the kids as a club to get you to pay your support. Am I right?" Ryan didn't mince words.

"Well, yeah," Delta replied sheepishly.

Ryan thought for a moment. "I don't wanna come off as being a jerk, but you have to understand. Every personnel decision is carefully thought out. Make no mistake, the people we invited into the Haven have been approved using a process very much like filling a job in any major corporation. You're hand-selected by Blair and myself, carefully vetted, interviewed, and then, even if there is a modicum of baggage in your lives, you're still accepted based upon certain assumptions. Do you understand?"

"Of course. Ryan, I know this, and that's why I hesitated to bring this up. However, my kids are insistent, and I know how they can be, especially my oldest, Ethan. I have to find a way to deal with this."

Ryan was about to speak when his phone rang. He glanced down at the display and saw that it was Blair. "Hang on. I've gotta take this."

Delta stood there, staring at the ceiling of the barn, looking for divine guidance to get him out of this pickle. He needed to be a part of the Haven for the benefit of his children and himself. He firmly believed the country was on the verge of collapse, and neither Atlanta nor Philadelphia would be safe for his children.

Ryan returned from his call and approached Delta. "Listen, we'll take this up in a little while. I've got to deal with a situation at the front gate, and then I'll meet you back at your cabin. Okay?"

"Yeah, sure. But what do I tell—?"

Ryan cut off Delta's question. "We'll talk after I'm done," he replied before bellowing across the barn, "Alpha! Come with me!"

The two men rushed past Delta, leaving him wondering about his future.

CHAPTER 26

New Year's Day
The Haven

Ryan was perturbed as he drove the final stretch of driveway to the front gate. This was day one of what could be public unrest and panic exploding across the nation, and one member of his security team wanted to gallivant into the *dead zone*, as the media called the regions surrounding Philadelphia without power. Now a group he rejected was trying to beg their way inside the Haven. As he pulled the Ranger to a stop, he retrieved his cell phone from his pocket and read the mysterious message he'd received earlier.

This is just the beginning.

Truer words were never spoken, he thought to himself as he noticed the family of four huddled together under the watchful eye of his guards. He'd barely reached the gate when the holistic healer and his wife, the emergency room nurse, began to speak at him simultaneously.

The husband spoke first. "Have you seen the news?"

"We can't go home! There's no power," the distressed wife shouted.

Like a tennis match, the husband took his turn. "We have no other options, Mr. Smart."

"Please let us in!" The wife's volley was more forceful.

Ryan held both hands up and walked closer to the gate. "I'm sorry, but it doesn't work like that. We can't let you in."

The chair umpire had spoken. The husband's mouth fell open, and his distraught wife immediately gathered her children against her hips. She began to cry. Between sobs, she asked for an explanation. "But why? I don't understand. You brought us here to—"

"Ma'am, hold on. I didn't bring you here. This was part of a process, and you both knew that. During our interview yesterday, I got the distinct sense you have an issue with our use of weapons—"

The husband immediately interrupted. "She's over that, right, honey? Weapons aren't a problem. It's just, with everything in the news, we kinda agreed that there are too many guns. But now we get it."

"It's not just that, sir," continued Ryan. "Yesterday was the most important part of the process of bringing new residents into the Haven. My interview with you, and the feeling I get from it, is the determining factor. There can only be one decider, as they say, and that's me."

"Why did you exclude us?" asked the wife.

"Ma'am, with all due respect, you excluded yourselves," replied Ryan frankly. "Your most important role to the Haven was your medical training and expertise. You had no interest in seeing our medical facilities. You seemed more concerned with giving your children an opportunity to see the *Hunger Games* filming locations."

"I know, but the kids had traveled a long way and—" the woman began before Ryan cut her off.

"Listen, things could get ugly at some point when we're all called upon to defend these gates. The other men and women of the Haven need to have confidence that you're all in. I didn't get that sense from either one of you."

The wife continued to cry, and now the children were whimpering, staring at Ryan as if he were the evil man who'd just run over the family pet in the street. The husband separated himself from his family and approached Ryan at the gate. Instinctively, the guards raised their weapons slightly, prepared to open fire if the man tried something rash.

"Mr. Smart, you don't understand. We live in Trenton, New Jersey. There is no power. In fact, CNN reported the outage extends as far south as Wilmington in Delaware. That's a hundred and forty miles of mayhem according to the reports. We're unarmed. We'll never make it."

"Sir, I'm sure you can find a place to wait it out here in North Carolina. Do you have any friends or family that you could call on?"

"No, everybody we have is in Jersey," he replied as his voice trailed off. He was naturally dejected, and Ryan was feeling bad for the family.

"Wait here," Ryan instructed.

Ryan walked away from the gate and rubbed his temples. He called Blair and they discussed the pros and cons of allowing the family in despite their earlier decision. On the one hand, both parents had valuable skills needed in the Haven, and everything else about their background was positive. However, their apparent lack of seriousness yesterday, when the world wasn't collapsing around them, spoke volumes about their commitment as unrest escalated around them.

Blair, who was more levelheaded and unemotional in her decision-making, looked at it from an outside recruiter's perspective. She asked two simple questions.

Were you satisfied with your decision yesterday to reject them?

Is your reconsideration of their application based upon what's best for the Haven or your emotions?

Ryan couldn't argue with the conclusion. They would remain outside the gates. Now the compassionate side of the Smarts tried to find a solution. This was when Ryan dropped the bombshell that Delta wanted to retrieve his ex-wife.

Blair immediately objected. "Ryan, we don't need any soap-opera drama within the Haven, especially now that our worst fears have materialized. He just needs to explain to his kids that it's not gonna happen."

Ryan wanted to agree, but he'd talked with Delta directly and recognized the conflict that was brewing inside him. He was being forced to choose between his commitment to his children and the Haven.

After Ryan didn't speak for a moment, Blair continued. "Here's the thing," she began. "When Delta accepted his role here and the cabin we gave him, there was never any expectation that he'd have his kids here full-time. Heck, at the time he accepted our offer, his ex-wife was keeping the kids from him."

"I know," said Ryan sheepishly.

"My point being this. Like the family outside the gate, everyone we've dealt with knew what was expected coming in. Delta knew it was just him and not his children. So what's next? He goes and gets the ex-wife? What about her boyfriend, the wife-thief? Does he get to tag along?"

"Probably," replied Ryan.

"No. No way. This is a no-drama zone. We have excluded so many people for less than allowing a totally dysfunctional family unit within our gates. Tough love, Ryan. It's the only way."

"What do you suggest?" he asked.

"The family from Trenton can find their way home or get a hotel room somewhere until things settle down, which you and I both know isn't going to happen. It's up to them."

"And Delta?"

"He either stays put, with his kids respecting his authority as a father. If that's his choice, we'll allow an exception to our agreement because they are his children. Or he can deliver them home to their mother and then get himself back here ASAP."

Ryan agreed, and as part of the role he accepted within the Haven, he was charged with delivering the bad news to all involved.

CHAPTER 27

Congress Heights
Washington, DC

Prowler deserved to live in the wild. The Maine coon, considered the oldest breed of American domesticated cat, had a storied past. Distinctive in their physical appearance, the long-haired breed was frequently mistaken for raccoons when seen in the wilderness of Maine, their native state. Many theories existed as to this unique breed's ancestral origins.

One folk tale posited that before Marie Antoinette, the Queen of France, was executed in the late 1700s, she attempted to flee France aboard a ship captained by Samuel Clough. She loaded the ship with her most prized possessions, including her beloved Turkish Angora cats. Although she never made it to America, her pets reached the shores of Maine, where the Angoras bred with other cats to create the Maine coon.

A more interesting theory, one that scientists deemed to be genetically impossible, but then again, what do they know, was that long-haired feral cats mated with bobcats in the wild. This accounted for the combination of the large size, bushy tale, and unusual tufts of hair commonly seen on the tips of the Maine coon's ears.

Whatever the explanation was, Prowler, Hayden Blount's Maine coon, was as much a dog as he was cat. He weighed twenty pounds, the size of a beagle and larger than most terriers. Coupled with his long grayish-black hair, he was an imposing creature with eyes of steel. In the dark, he'd frighten the bejesus out of any burglar or invited guest, not that Hayden ever had either.

Looking into his golden-yellow eyes, it was clear Prowler

possessed an inner confidence and above-average intelligence. Fiercely loyal, the breed was known to be cautious, but not mean, around strangers. Prowler was different. Unlike most families who made a point to socialize their pets, Prowler had only known one human—Hayden.

He was independent and clingy, as many cat breeds could be, but he was hardly a lap cat. If one were to discuss the average Maine coon with a breeder, they'd describe them as a gentle giant, very vocal in their mannerisms, and an excellent pet for families.

They'd never met Prowler.

Hayden was not a drinker, but last night was the exception and not the rule. An empty bottle of cabernet sat on the coffee table between the television and the sofa, where she'd finally passed out after watching the news reports for hours. Hayden had slept until ten o'clock on New Year's Day, partly due to exhaustion from the ordeal she'd been through in the subway, but also aided by the wine.

Prowler, however, was not a patient cat. He'd grown accustomed to a schedule, one in which his mommy fed him at oh dark thirty, left for a dozen hours or more, and then returned well into the evening for a second feeding. While it was true that Prowler ate a hearty meal of Beneful wet dog food supplemented with a dose of taurine, an amino acid used in the metabolism of fat, late last night, his internal body clock was pissed that he hadn't been fed breakfast.

He began to let Hayden hear about his displeasure with a chorus of yowls and trills, a high-pitched, chirp-like sound usually made by songbirds, but one adopted by Prowler when he wanted attention.

The cacophony of vocalizations stirred Hayden, whose head immediately began to pound upon the ambient sunlight hitting her eyes. She had a few choice words for Prowler, who gave it right back to her in spades. The odd couple got their respective feelings out on the table, and then Hayden apologized to her bestest pal for a number of things, including drinking too much, sleeping on the couch instead of their comfy bed, and not feeding him on time.

Prowler indicated that all was right with the world again by rolling around on the floor, playfully swatting at the cork that had rolled off the coffee table, while emitting a gentle meow.

Hayden quickly fed Prowler before heading to the shower for the second time that day. The first was an absolute necessity to wash off the stench of the subway. The second was required to shock her body back to life after her self-pity wine party as she watched the nation collapse around her.

The attacks, and the potential impact they had on the political climate of the country, consumed her thoughts as she watched the news reports. In America, everything was politicized. The attacks could be blamed on the president for not maintaining his focus on the nation's defense amidst his various scandals. The president, on the other hand, could point the finger of blame on the other side of the aisle, arguing their past Defense Department budget cuts had resulted in a lack of resources to track terrorists.

Either way, the side with the best narrative would win, although the playing field was not exactly level. The president had made a mortal enemy of the mainstream media, and he rarely was the beneficiary of a favorable news report. As the chilly water poured over Hayden's head, she wondered if the finger-pointing blame game had already begun.

She toweled off, wrapped herself in a robe, and walked across the cold tile floors to the kitchen, where she popped a K-Cup pod of Death Wish coffee into her Keurig coffee maker. Known as the world's strongest coffee, Death Wish coffee was Hayden's choice for when she had to stay up late working on a legal matter at home.

Despite the high caffeine content, the smooth, never-bitter coffee had a hint of chocolate and cherry, her favorite combination in candies. Hayden, who took pride in her body and maintained a near-perfect, toned physique, had a weakness for chocolate-covered cherries. When she didn't have time to make her own, she opted for Cella's—America's oldest brand of chocolate-covered cherries, having been first produced at the end of the Civil War.

With her coffee made, Hayden took a deep breath and walked to her oversized windows and looked at the Potomac. More snow had fallen overnight, and a sudden chill overcame her as she experienced a déjà vu moment. She had stood in this exact spot, in her robe, overlooking the Potomac just hours before when she had learned of the attacks in New York City.

Since that time, she'd learned the terrorists had struck in many ways and in many places. Her mind raced as she wondered what that meant for her future.

CHAPTER 28

Congress Heights
Washington, DC

Hayden got settled on the couch with a three-day-old cheese Danish and her lap cat. Most of the CNN coverage showed a repeat of the images flashed across the screen from earlier that morning. Surfing the cable networks, she landed on the FoxNews channel, which featured a panel discussing the options available to the president if he deemed the attacks upon the nation were part of a larger, coordinated effort. The group debated whether the actions taken thus far constituted an act of war.

Judge Andrew Napolitano, one of the participants in the roundtable discussion and a renowned libertarian voice, recounted the words of a book he'd read years ago on the subject of American autonomy titled *Choose Freedom or Capitulation, America's Sovereignty Crisis.*

"*In that book, the author, a Harvard professor at the Kennedy School of Government, argued that by most definitions, an act of war, as established by accepted legal precedent, involved violent acts by an aggressor against a country or people who did not consider themselves to be formally at war with the attacker.*

"*However, with the advent of terrorism, and especially as a result of technologically advanced weaponry, the author proposed that any act dangerous to human life should constitute an act of terrorism, especially if it was intended to intimidate or coerce a nation, its government, and its civilian population.*"

"*Judge,*" began the panel's moderator, Bill Hemmer, "*based upon what we know at this point, the terrorists have employed several types of, as you called it, technologically advanced weaponry—cyber, electromagnetic pulse, and autonomous drone-delivered dirty bombs.*"

Napolitano interjected his opinion. "*And, Bill, let me throw in the prospect of the incidents in Atlanta, and quite possibly Mobile, as being connected as well. All totaled, six of our major cities have been attacked, all of which by what some might argue to be nonlethal weapons.*"

Bill Hemmer interrupted Napolitano's thought. "*Judge, are you saying that these attacks might not authorize the president to retaliate in kind or invoke some of the protections outlined in the Constitution or by past precedent?*"

"*There are many factors to consider, Bill. First off, any retaliatory strikes need to be approved by Congress, in my opinion. The practice of circumventing the War Powers Act by this president, and his predecessors, must stop. In the context of declaring an act of war, neither the Constitution nor any Act of Congress has stipulated what format a formal declaration of war must take, despite the fact they have the force of law. Once that declaration is made, the president's options widen considerably.*"

Hemmer asked, "*Martial law? Invoking continuity of government?*"

"*Yes to both, but under circumstances such as these, a formal declaration that the events constitute an act of war is probably not necessary, especially with full public support. Remember, Bill, in a political climate such as the one we live in today, I believe public opinion constitutes nine-tenths of the law, as the saying goes.*"

Hayden retrieved her laptop and began to research the practical impact a declaration of martial law or implementation of the government's continuity-of-government plan would have on the operation of the Supreme Court.

Her research began with Executive Directive 51 signed by President George W. Bush in 2007. Formally known as the National Security and Homeland Security Presidential Directive 51, the executive action replaced and expanded upon a similar directive signed by President Bill Clinton in 1998.

The directive provides that during a catastrophic emergency, in order to preserve the Constitution and the nation's government, the president may appoint a National Continuity Coordinator, whose task was to work between the three branches of government to protect and ensure the functionality of certain national essential functions, from critical infrastructure to law enforcement functions under a martial law declaration.

Hayden, who considered herself a very capable attorney, one whom the president trusted with the future of his presidency, read the actual verbiage in Directive 51 and shook her head in disbelief. This executive order granted the president complete control over both private and public sector activities, all in the name of national security.

From the definition of *catastrophic emergency*, determined solely by the president, to the specific tasks given the assistant to the president for Homeland Security and Counterterrorism who became the designated National Continuity Coordinator, this was a power grab that belied everything Hayden knew about constitutional law. Yet it was in place and Congress had done nothing for two decades to curtail its mandate.

The directive allowed the president broad powers once martial law had been declared, including the ability to seize and control all transportation and communication, regulate the operation of private enterprise, restrict travel, and suspend habeas corpus.

Hayden assumed the president would also suspend the operations of the Supreme Court during this period of *catastrophic emergency*, however he elected to define the term. Her mind began to process the ramifications of this on her supplemental brief to be argued on Friday. If the president were to declare martial law and invoke the powers granted to him by Directive 51, the justices would not consider their motion, and all hearings would be postponed.

However, Inauguration Day, January 20, was fast approaching. The law did not require a large public ceremony on the National Mall, which had become customary in the last century. As recently as Gerald Ford's inauguration, which took place within the White House, the president could formally take the oath of office anywhere that the chief justice of the Supreme Court was present, including an underground bunker.

Hayden was beginning to generate a theory, one awash in conspiracy, when her phone rang. It was her boss, Pat Cipollone.

CHAPTER 29

New Year's Day
Delta's Cabin
The Haven

In the front yard of Delta's cabin, Ryan and Delta spoke at length about the predicament they faced. With Delta nervously pushing the tire swing back and forth, Ryan relayed his concerns and the options he'd come up with, taking into account Blair's input. After ten minutes, Ryan received another call from the front gate, as the family from Trenton was becoming impatient. Delta was feeling the pressure to make a decision, so he asked to speak to his children alone. After Ryan departed, Delta went inside to sort things out.

Prior to the incident in Philadelphia, Delta had been a good father. Oftentimes, it was difficult for law enforcement officers to leave the stresses of their job back at the station when they called it a day. The constant pressure and fatigue of their careers caused by long shifts, dangerous assignments, inadequate gear, and, at times, mismanagement by superiors led to family problems as cops coped with the daily transition from the beat to their home.

Delta was one of the few who'd avoided the anxiety, depression, and even PTSD while he was assigned to Philly SWAT. As a result, he'd played an active role in Ethan and Skylar's upbringing until their close-knit family imploded.

During the tumultuous years following the incident in Fairhill Square, Delta lost control of the parenting aspect of his relationship with the kids. Tantrums, whining, and not listening all came with the territory. In the last year, Ethan had thrown a healthy dose of aggression and back talk into the mix.

Respect for authority was something ingrained in Delta's psyche. Like the military, a law enforcement officer understood that a hierarchy existed within their department, and giving deference to a commanding officer was paramount for their team to function when their lives were on the line.

A child's impudence, or back talk, was a form of challenging a parent's authority. It showed a lack of respect, especially if the child succeeded, or if the parent was over the top in their response.

From the moment Ethan arrived in Atlanta, he'd shown a level of disrespect for Delta that went relatively unchecked. A noncustodial parent, especially in a hostile divorce, had a difficult row to hoe. Delta only had his children's ear for a few days, while his ex-wife, Karen, could manipulate them for weeks and months on end.

This family dynamic made Delta's decision even more difficult. It would be one thing if he had a decent working relationship with Karen as they attempted to lead their children to adulthood. However, the opposite had been the case since the day she had been discovered cheating on him.

Everything that went wrong in their lives was piled upon his shoulders, and the blame was laid at his feet. The tone had been set during the last two years, and taking a firm hand with Ethan now would serve to push the teen even further away.

Against that backdrop, Delta decided to employ a tactic he hadn't used in his tenure as a dad. He was going to lie.

Not a big lie, at least not in his mind. He preferred to look at it as a *little white.*

"Hey, kids," Delta began, trying to adopt an upbeat tone. *Little white #1.* "Mr. Smart and I just had a long conversation about your mom, and we've come up with something that will work out perfectly."

"Okay, Daddy," said Skylar, who sat up straight on the sofa and gave her father an adoring smile. *Ugh. I will get zero father-of-the-year votes.*

"As you guys know, your mother is out on the cruise, and most likely they've been made aware of the situation on the East Coast."

"The power outage," interjected Ethan. "Is it going to be fixed soon?"

"That's what we're hearing," replied Delta. "The crews are working overtime to restore power, and my bet is it's up and running before her ship arrives in the morning." *Little white #2.*

"Will you be able to meet her at the dock?" asked Skylar.

Delta walked away and added one more chunk of wood, which wasn't necessary, to the fire. He simply couldn't make eye contact as he lied to his children. "No, and here's why. The news is saying that cruise ships and airline traffic have been halted because of the uncertainty. All that means is your mom will have an extended vacation at sea. Lucky her, right?"

Lie was too strong a word for that statement. Delta considered that a fib coupled with a half-truth based upon supposition. He honestly believed the cruise line would know better than to drop their passengers off at a port with no electricity. It was more likely they'd leave them stranded somewhere else, like New York City or near Richmond.

"How will we know?" asked Ethan.

Delta had to be careful. Constant little white lies and fibs could become a crutch that ended up being exposed. He decided to tell the truth on this one. "I'm going to stay in contact with the cruise line and determine when and where they plan on dropping off their passengers. Plus, your mom has her cell phone on her, so we can stay in contact that way."

Ethan seemed to be buying Delta's approach. "I know, I've been trying to call her, but all I get is her voicemail. She'll call me back at some point, I hope."

"I'm sure she will, son. In the meantime, we're going to stay here at the Haven. I've got a job to do, and you guys will be a part of the action as well."

"Really, Daddy?" asked Skylar.

"Yes, ma'am. In about a week, they're going to get the school up and running, and they're looking to you kids for help. Because there are children of all ages at the Haven, we have to consolidate grades together, decide which schoolbooks to use from the library we have, and stuff like that. They might even ask some of you to help teach the younger kids. Would you like that?"

Skylar hopped off the sofa and hugged her father. "I would, Daddy. I think this is going to be a fun adventure."

"At some point, you'll bring Mom, right?" pressed Ethan.

Delta punted the question. "Let's take it one day at a time. After the cruise ship arrives and we're able to make contact with her, then the four of us will come up with the best plan of action."

Ethan appeared skeptical, but he eventually acquiesced by saying okay. Relieved that he'd bought a little time to avoid telling the kids he had no intention of bringing their mother and her boyfriend to the Haven, he quickly turned to the front door to send Ryan a text.

DELTA: We're staying here.

RYAN: Good choice. I'm sending these folks on their way.

DELTA: Thanks.

"Say, Dad?" asked Ethan.

Delta turned and faced his son, pleased that his demeanor had improved. "Yes, son."

Ethan held his phone up to show the display to his father. "My cell phone is dying, and I forgot my charger at your place in Atlanta. Do you have a charger?"

"Um, what kind of phone is that? Mine's an Apple."

"It's an Android by LG," Ethan quickly replied. "The Apple lightning cable won't work."

Here came the whopper of *little whites*. "Oh, no problem. I'll ask around and find you a charger, okay?" If his son's cell phone was inoperable, he couldn't contact his mother and determine that his dad had just filled the room with lie upon lie upon lie.

"Okay, thanks, Dad."

Ugh!

CHAPTER 30

Cortland Residence
Carlen-Midtown Neighborhood
Mobile, Alabama

The Cortlands lived in an historic part of downtown Mobile known as Carlen-Midtown. Named in part for the historic Carlen House, the neighborhood used to be on the westernmost edge of Mobile before expansion in the early 1900s encircled the area as the South recovered from the aftermath of the Civil War. The antebellum homes comprising the neighborhood were once referred to as *The Loop* because of the system of roads connecting it to the rest of the city. In the 1990s, some of the homes that had fallen into disrepair were purchased by savvy investors, renovated, and sold for a profit. The market value of the neighborhood tripled, and when Cort's mother passed away, he inherited the family residence.

"Daddy, does it hurt anywhere?" asked his seven-year-old daughter as she assisted him along the brick-paver walkway to their kitchen entry door.

Cort gave Hannah a little squeeze and attempted to hide the grimace on his face. "You know, it's a different kind of hurt. It's not like I was beaten or banged up any. Sure, my waist hurts from the seatbelt holding me in place, but the rest is like a dull ache. I feel like I just finished running to New Orleans and back without stopping."

"Like an elephant sat on you?" she asked innocently.

Cort nodded. "Yeah, kinda like that. I'm pretty sure if I could get Dumbo to sit somewhere else, I'd get better real quick-like."

His wife, Meredith, rushed up the steps and unlocked the kitchen door. She held the wood-framed screen door open as Hannah led

Cort inside. She leaned over and kissed her husband on the cheek as he passed.

"Maybe that'll make your boo-boo better, too."

Cort smiled, paused, and kissed her back. "Just being home with you guys is making a world of difference. Lots of kisses will have me up and running by tomorrow."

"No way, mister athlete," she said with a stern voice. "You're not going anywhere."

Cort furrowed his brow and walked into the kitchen. He mumbled, "We'll see."

Once inside, Meredith put the teapot on the stove and found some chamomile tea, Cort's favorite. The soothing effects of the flavonoids provide several medicinal benefits, including treating diabetes, reducing inflammation, and helping with sleep and relaxation.

"Isn't it a little early in the day for chamomile?" asked Cort.

"Not from what I understand," began Meredith in response. "The nurse told me about your dream episode. Do you wanna talk about it?"

Cort briskly shook his head without knowing it. The last thing he wanted to do was relive the nightmare. Ordinarily, he didn't remember his dreams when he woke up for the day. This time, it was different. The images were seared into his mind.

"No, but we do have lots to talk about. Obviously, my iPad was lost in the wreckage. I need to get some information off the one I use here at the house."

"No, Cort. You shouldn't be working. You're supposed to rest."

Cort closed his eyes and nodded. This was going to be difficult, but it had to be done. He tried to keep his voice calm—doctor's orders. "Honey, I know. But there are some calls I need to make, and the contact information is on iCloud." Cort was referring to the data storage service provided by Apple for users of their iPhones and computing devices.

"Like who? Who do you need to call that can't wait until tomorrow? It's a holiday, you know."

Meredith was justifiably upset with him. She'd almost lost her husband. They barely had a foot in the door and Cort wanted to phone his associates in the government.

"Honey, just a couple of calls, and then we can talk about what happened." A promise Cort intended to keep.

"And are you gonna explain to me what the Haven is?" she asked.

"What?"

"Last night, as we were leaving, you said something about the Haven. What does that mean?"

Cort wondered what else he might have said while dealing with the stress of almost dying. "Yes, we will talk about that." He began to leave the kitchen and head for his study when Meredith stopped him.

"Cort, I'll get it for you. Please just sit down."

He continued walking through the kitchen and headed across the living room, where Hannah had turned on their gas fireplace.

"Daddy, Mom said you probably won't be interested in watching the New Year's ball dropping in New York after what happened. I recorded the AKC dog show that came on this morning. I wanna see if any English bulldogs are gonna win."

"Speaking of which, where is Handsome Dan?"

Hannah pointed over her head as she got settled on the sofa. "He's probably asleep on my bed."

Cort grumbled as he left the room and entered his study. "Man's best friend, what a joke."

He shut the door behind him to prevent Hannah from walking in unannounced. He expected Meredith would bring his tea soon, so he hustled to remove the rare, antiquarian books from one of the upper shelves that only his six-foot-five frame could reach.

The void revealed a safe that was guarded with a biometric, fingerprint locking device to open it. The lock released with a slight click. As Cort opened the door, his mind wandered to his brush with death. How would Meredith access the safe? One that she had no knowledge of? Would they have to bring his right index finger from the morgue to retrieve the contents?

He shrugged and thought aloud, "Doesn't matter now."

He reached in and emptied the contents onto the cabinets below. Two handgun cases. A zippered deposit bag from First Community Bank full of cash. A GPS device and an old flip-style cell phone with a charger rounded out his stash that he jokingly referred to as the *break-glass-in-case-of-emergency* stuff.

Cort carried the items to his desk and set them on the leather inlay. Then he collapsed in his chair. He took a moment to examine the contents, which he hadn't touched in two years. He popped open the cases first and handled the two nine-millimeter handguns. One was a Glock 26 Gen 4 concealed-carry weapon, and the other was a full-sized Glock 17.

He set them aside and then unzipped the bag full of hundreds and twenties, neatly bundled in the bank's colored currency wraps, totaling ten thousand dollars. Finally, he plugged the cell phone charger in the wall outlet behind him and connected the phone. It would take a few minutes for the battery to charge sufficiently to make a call. This gave him an opportunity to retrieve his iPad and find the private, encrypted phone numbers he needed.

After Cort bent over to attach the phone to the charger, a twinge of pain in his abdomen jolted his body. He hoped the searing feeling was a result of the seat belt restraining him during the crash and nothing else. He shuddered as he shook off the pain, unaware that Meredith stood in front of his desk, staring at the guns and money covering the desk in front of her.

CHAPTER 31

Katonah, New York

The sprawling, sixty-three-acre estate located in the tiny community of Katonah, New York, was located ten miles from the Connecticut state line. It was barely forty miles north of Times Square, but the owner was very much in tune with the plight of those running for their lives. He had watched the multiple televisions in his study as the news reports flooded the networks. The attacks were brilliantly orchestrated for maximum effect—instilling fear. He couldn't have done it better himself, only it wasn't him this time.

"Father, have you slept?" asked his forty-eight-year-old son, Jonathan, the heir apparent to the family fortune and, more importantly, the reins to the various foundations and organizations created by his father, György Schwartz. For Schwartz, being one of the thirty richest and most powerful men in the world had been hard-earned through taking risks and engaging in shrewd financial dealings. However, his life had begun in poverty, a condition that shaped his life and world view.

"Some." The word was barely audible as the eighty-eight-year-old man had become increasingly tired, resulting in the sound of his voice reaching the level of a near whisper. "I am an old man, but I still have memories of the day the Nazis entered Budapest in '44. We ran for our lives, frightened of the unknown and the rumors of what the Nazis did to our fellow Jews. Those who didn't leave disappeared to a fate the world should never forget."

With nothing but the clothes on his back, Schwartz learned to survive in Nazi-occupied Hungary. He had an uncanny knack for manipulation and applying his creativity to fool the Germans. When the Nazis hired teenagers to hand out deportation notices to Jewish families in Budapest, Schwartz destroyed them all because his instincts told him that deportation was equated with death. He was right.

He began to pose as the Christian godson of a Nazi collaborator within the Hungarian government. This enabled him to go to school and avoid the Nazis' scrutiny. His ingenuity saved his life, but only subjected him to a more frightening period of time as World War II came to a close.

In 1945, Soviet and German forces fought house to house during the Siege of Budapest. Young Schwartz had become comfortable after creating the ruse that he was a Christian, only to be displaced by the horrors of war. It was a period of time that humbled him.

After the war, he emigrated to England and studied economics. Considering himself to be somewhat of a philosopher due to his childhood experiences, he obtained degrees in philosophy but found his position in life among economists and investors.

Drawing upon his vast experience in European economic affairs, Schwartz moved to New York and began his financial career on Wall Street. By age forty, he'd established his own hedge fund with a quarter of a million dollars, which grew to four hundred million in just ten years.

Today, through speculative currency trading and keen stock trading, Schwartz had amassed a fortune in the billions and, through his philanthropy, had created dozens of organizations with a singular goal—achieving human equality and a New World Order.

His hedge funds had generated profits considered to be extraordinary by any definition. His foundations had spent billions around the world assisting the plight of the poor. However, the end game for Schwartz and his family, led by his son, Jonathan, was a world without borders. Their prerogatives in the U.S. centered around reducing inmate populations, increasing government assistance to those in need, creating a pathway to citizenship for migrant workers, and taxing the wealthy entities, individuals and corporations alike, in order to lift people out of poverty.

His organizations were extremely complex by design. Transparency was their enemy, as many eyes, public and private, watched their every move. Despite this, Schwartz had learned as a young boy how to move through the shadows and how to survive.

With his vast financial resources, a loyal group of like-minded individuals, and an uncanny knack for reading political tea leaves, he was able to effectuate change by destabilizing nation-states, financial markets, and the psyches of the citizenry. He was only one man, but he commanded an army of political agitators.

"May I have the staff bring you some tea and biscuits?" Jonathan was concerned for his father, who'd aged considerably over the last several years. A joint DOJ and SEC investigation into the financial dealings of several of his organizations had made for several tirades and restless nights. The Department of Justice was focused on their funding of splinter groups around the country that were part of a newly created hate-group list by the president. In his opinion, the Securities and Exchange Commission inquiries were purely vindictive and retaliatory. Schwartz employed hundreds of attorneys and compliance auditors to ensure they didn't run afoul of the law. As far as he was concerned, the investigation was nothing more than political payback by the occupant of the White House.

"Yes, son, thank you," the old man said as he settled in his leather office chair. He pulled out a writing pad and began to scribble some notes.

His son made the request of the staff and took a seat in a Queen Anne chair situated on the other side of his father's desk. As his father appeared deep in thought, Jonathan politely sat quietly, allowing the brilliant analytical mind to work.

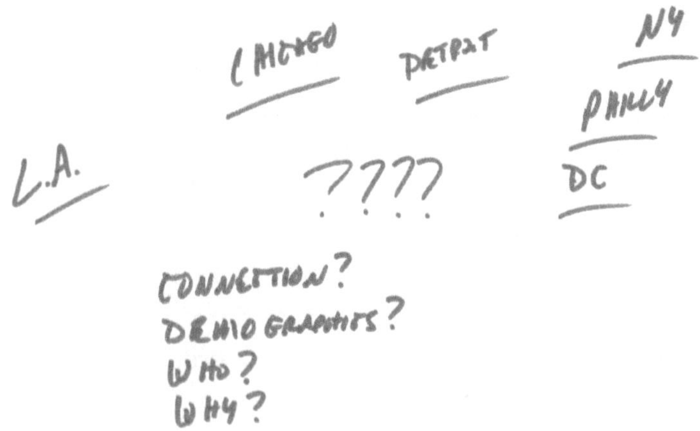

While he waited for his tea, he twirled his pen around on top of the notepad as if it were a compass looking for magnetic north, or pointing him in the direction to obtain answers.

After a few moments in which the two men sat across from one another in silence, Schwartz spoke. "Son, this is not the work of terrorists, at least not as they are defined by Washington. This is far more nefarious. It is a form of genocide I have not seen since my days in Budapest. It cannot continue."

"Father, the news media is already pointing fingers of blame at the Russians, who are ostensibly retaliating for the U.S. bombing raids of Tehran as this administration tries to spark a revolution. The other theory is China, partly because of the technology used in the attacks and also due to the escalating trade war initiated by the president."

"It is neither," said Schwartz. "The technology is irrelevant. The weapons of choice were ideal because of the lack of attribution. The perpetrators of these attacks knew this. They are also adept at media manipulation, as are we."

"Then who, Father, and why?"

"Specifically, I don't know, although I can speculate. The *why* is a matter of connecting the dots. Son, we have an opportunity that should not be squandered. I know this president as well as he thinks he knows me. He is about self-preservation. He knows how to swim with the sharks."

"What are you suggesting, Father?" his loyal son asked.

"I am suggesting the election is over. He believes he has won if he can just overcome this last hurdle before the Supreme Court."

"Do you believe the president is behind the attacks simply to avoid his potential ouster?"

"I believe that a delay benefits him. I don't know if he orchestrated the attacks. Regardless, a vacuum of power will be created when he invokes martial law. I intend to fill the void."

CHAPTER 32

Schwartz Estate
Katonah, New York

Schwartz paused the conversation with his son while their tea was served. After a brief conversation, he lay down to rest until lunchtime. His meals were carefully planned by an on-staff nutritionist. For health reasons, a general practitioner lived on the estate and was charged with the responsibility of extending the man's life. Money can buy influence, the best in medical care, and an estate protected by high-tech security, but it cannot buy you immortality. Schwartz knew this when he began grooming his son to take the reins, and the events of New Year's Eve presented a scenario in which he could accelerate his goals of destabilizing the U.S. dollar and the institutions of government that kept a thumb on its citizens.

"Son, have you reached out to our contacts?"

Jonathan wandered about the spacious private dining room while his father finished a simple lunch of organic field greens, a steamed vegetable medley, and a steaming bowl of quinoa splashed with a couple of tablespoons of vegetable broth for flavor. Quinoa, pronounced *keen-wah*, was a grain crop somewhat related to spinach, but was often ground into flour to be used as a rice and pasta substitute.

"Yes, sir, I have. Over the years, we have effectively diminished the argument of the right that claims Washington is full of deep-state boogeymen. Our sources in the media debunked the notion that there is some type of shadowy cabal of unelected bureaucrats that secretly runs the government. Little do they know, right, Father?"

Schwartz grinned and waggled his right index finger at his son while he ate. "Make no mistake, they have their own deep-state operatives."

"To be sure, sir, but not as many or as dedicated as ours."

"What do you have for me, son?" Schwartz was in no mood for an ideological conversation. Decisions had to be made. He carefully guided another spoonful of quinoa into his mouth.

"Sir, our sources in the White House tell me that the president had nothing to do with this. In fact, he was outraged that the intelligence community had no inkling of what happened."

His father interrupted him. "Which goes to my point from this morning. The bumbling fools in the Middle East, or even the Chinese or Russians, would not be able to keep an operation such as this one completely under wraps. Too many leaks. Too much incompetence."

"And the threat of retaliation, Father. Have you considered the possibility the president has orchestrated a false flag?"

A false-flag event occurred when a government undertook a secret operation in which it appeared to be attacked by a foreign enemy in order to justify going to war. It had been a favorite tool of government propagandists for centuries, primarily as an ideological weapon to control the citizenry with the fear of a manufactured enemy.

"Ah, a tool used by the greatest tyrants in our history," began Schwartz, suddenly becoming philosophical. "Herr Goebbels once said, the bigger the lie, the more it will be believed." Schwartz was referring to Nazi General Paul Joseph Goebbels, one of Chancellor Adolf Hitler's top advisors.

"Yes, sir. Stalin, too," added Jonathan.

"Oh my, yes. Josef Stalin. For him, the easiest way to gain control of a population was to carry out acts of terror. As he proved during his reign, the public clamored for laws because they feared for their safety from a foreign enemy."

"Not unlike this country after 9/11," interjected Jonathan. "If it is a false flag, what is their angle? Who is their boogeyman?"

Schwartz pushed his plate away, carefully dabbed the corners of his mouth with a white cloth napkin, and managed a chuckle. "Why, I am, of course, son."

"Father, you believe all of this has been planned and coordinated in an effort to come after you?"

"No, son, not me per se. But rather causes and ideals that I hold dear. Consider this. The president will have the opportunity to invoke provisions to ensure the continuity of his government. By declaring martial law, he will be able to postpone the Supreme Court proceedings indefinitely, or at least beyond his inauguration. In addition, in times of war, and arguably, the United States is at war with someone, the people rally around their leaders. They become very patriotic and nationalist-thinking."

"The opposite of our goals," added his son.

"Precisely. They are counting on the public to fall into line. Whether some type of extraordinary legislation comes out of this, or perhaps executive orders advancing the president's agenda, remains to be seen. My point is this. These attacks appear to be targeted, with a specific purpose of causing maximum damage to regions where the population consists of those who stand in opposition to the president and his political positions."

Jonathan stopped pacing the floor and sat down at the dining table on the opposite end from his father. He paused as a member of the staff gently knocked to announce her presence. While she cleared the dishes and offered the two men coffee, Jonathan scrolled through his iPad.

"The attacks are targeting the resistance movement," he said after they were alone again.

"Except for San Francisco, Portland, and Seattle," added Schwartz.

"I wonder why those areas were spared."

"They're waiting for a reaction, son. This is going to be a carefully played game of chess in which the winner will control the soul of America."

Jonathan nodded and then furrowed his brow. "How do you play a game, or fight a war, when you cannot identify your opponent?"

His father quickly answered, "You draw them out into the open. Make them reveal themselves."

"I'm listening."

"Son, heretofore, we have fought the battle on our own turf. We can no longer be satisfied with organized marches in Washington or occupations of Wall Street or even simple acts of defiance by blocking interstate highways. The broken windows and skirmishes of Portland must be expanded to America's heartland."

"The suburbs that are considered immune from activity," added Jonathan.

"Yes. In this ideological war, one that is now fought with advanced weaponry, we should expand the battlefield. I am tired of the inner cities burning in angst while suburban America sleeps safely in their four-bedroom home with two cars in the garage and a swing set in the backyard. They do not understand the plight of their fellow Americans because it doesn't directly affect their lives."

"We should encourage the resistance to rise up everywhere, not just in our typical, targeted enclaves."

Schwartz smiled. "Yes. The American South, for example. Midsize cities like Richmond, Charlotte, and Charleston. First, they must be made uncomfortable; then their eyes will be opened. While we destabilize society, I can finish my task of weakening the U.S. stranglehold on financial markets."

"Father, we have to work diligently to discover who initiated these attacks. If our theories are correct, the course of this nation will change drastically."

"Yes, son. I am tasking you with drawing upon all of our resources. Take the fight to the streets. I will expedite my financial activities, and if successful, it will cause an economic catastrophe that will turn everyone against this president."

"Unleash the hounds," said Jonathan matter-of-factly.

His father smiled and repeated his words. "Unleash the hounds with a storm never before seen on American soil."

CHAPTER 33

Cortland Residence
Carlen-Midtown Neighborhood
Mobile, Alabama

"Oh, I didn't hear you come in," he said nervously. He pushed off the arms of his chair and stood to face his bewildered wife.

"Obviously not," she said in a soft voice. "What's this all about, Michael?"

Ugh. She only called him by his given name when she was truly upset.

Cort fidgeted with his hands and then finally spread them out in defeat. "Honey, I can explain. Will you please sit down?"

She handed him his iPad and set the cup of tea that was still steeping between the two weapons. "Let me close the door. I don't want to frighten Hannah."

Cort was somewhat taken aback by her insinuation that the presence of the cash and weapons on his desk would frighten his daughter. The family had discussed the purpose of weapons many times, and Hannah appeared totally comfortable with them. Cort even took her to the gun range from time to time when he practiced.

He took a sip of tea and carefully sat back in his chair. He was beginning to regret rejecting the doctor's offer of pain medication. At the time, he was feeling okay because he was under the influence of the intravenous analgesics administered during his recovery. Cort didn't take any prescription drugs, and he was concerned pain medications might alter his state of mind during a time that required clear thinking.

She sat down, her gaze alternating between Cort's eyes and the contents spilled out on his desk. Just as he was about to speak, a short tone sounded on the cell phone, indicating it had powered up.

"What was that?" Meredith immediately asked.

"Um, it's a backup cell phone," he replied as he gestured over his shoulder. "I'm charging it because I need to place some calls."

"Why can't you use our phone? Or my cell?" she asked. Her hands had retreated inside her sweater sleeves, and her arms were folded in front of her, subconsciously wrapping her body as a protective mechanism.

"This phone is encrypted. When I make calls on it, nobody can listen in or trace its origin."

"And the guns? I didn't know you had them in the house. I thought we agreed that your weapons should be stored in the gun locker at the range."

Cort closed his eyes and nodded. "Yes, we did, and I'm sorry for not telling you about these two. I assure you, they've been kept locked in the safe until now."

Meredith leaned back in her chair and exhaled. She shook her head. "What safe? Cort, I don't understand any of this."

He pointed over her right shoulder toward the top of his ceiling-to-floor bookcases. She noticed the empty space and the wall safe door half open.

"How long has that been there?" she asked.

"I had it included when they installed my built-ins. I should've told you, but honestly, I thought I'd never have to open it under circumstances like these."

She reached forward and picked up a bundle of hundred-dollar bills. She used her thumb to flip through the cash to see if it was real. She set it down gently, as if it might explode if it wasn't handled properly.

"Cort, I hope you know how this looks. It looks sketchy, illegal, and more than anything, a lie. I don't know who you are. Are you a spy? A drug dealer? What?"

At first, Cort was apologetic for hiding this from his wife. He realized his job to sell her on the Haven would be that much more difficult now. He also knew what was best for his family. He might have gone about it the wrong way, but he had good intentions.

Like a Good Samaritan who almost died?

"Honey, let me explain this part, and then we have more important decisions to make," Cort began.

Meredith relaxed in her chair somewhat and listened intently to Cort as he told her about the safe, its contents, and how it was there in case of emergencies.

"Cort, I know you've been through a lot, and I empathize with how you feel. Hannah almost lost her daddy, and I love you more than life. Is it the plane crash or what's happening in the news that prompted you to run in here first thing, shut the door, and empty your emergency safe?"

"All of the above," replied Cort. He had to decide whether it was necessary to reveal his theories about the connection between the plane crash and the terrorist attacks around the country. He held that close to his vest, for now. "Something is happening, honey, and I believe last night's attacks were only the start."

"It's terrorists," she interjected. "It's always terrorists. You of all people should know that because of what you're privy to."

"That's true, but trust me when I say the Islamist groups aren't capable of what I've seen reported. There was advanced weaponry involved, including the possible use of dirty-bomb materials like uranium, strontium-90, or cobalt-60."

"I teach Sunday school and third graders, not high school science."

"Those are radioactive materials that, when coupled with conventional explosives, can disperse deadly radiation over a large area. That's what happened in New York and Detroit. I believe the mid-Atlantic states were hit with an EMP and …" Cort's voice trailed off before he posited his theory that his aircraft was struck with a radio frequency weapon. It was the only explanation he had that would result in a total blackout of the plane, and it had been planned to occur at the same time as the other incidents.

"I get it. We live in a dangerous world." Meredith spoke after Cort stopped. She was being very patient with him. "I still don't understand. You're home and safe. Are you just making sure this stuff is still here?"

Cort took a deep breath. It was time to drop the next hidden bombshell. He had so many, he wasn't sure where to start. "Let me tell you about the Haven."

"Yes, please do," she said with a hint of snark.

"A year or so ago, your father suggested that we have a place to go to, other than here in Mobile, in the event of a national emergency. You know, a safe place far away from population centers and where we could have others to help protect Hannah." Cort played the *protect-the-child* card and the *daddy-said* card in the same hand. It was if he held the ace through ten of spades in his bridge hand.

"Daddy suggested this?" Meredith asked.

"Yes. You've seen how the country seems to be descending into the abyss. We may not see it as much here in Mobile as in other parts of the country, but it's only getting worse."

"I know. Do you think these attacks are going to make it worse?"

"Very much so. Meredith, I have to make some calls and see what the intelligence agencies are saying. You know, the stuff that doesn't make it to the news. If I'm right, and you know I hate when I am, then we have to go."

"Go where? This Haven place? I don't even know where it is. And for how long? Hannah starts back to school a week from Monday."

Cort decided to avoid the second part of her questions. He didn't know how long either. It could just be a week, or it could be several months, or longer. He'd learn more after a couple of calls.

He stood and walked around the desk. He leaned against it and took Meredith by the hands, who had begun to cry. Despite the pain screaming through his chest, he assisted her out of the chair to hug her as she began to sob.

"This is not my world, Cort. This is yours and Daddy's. I live in Mobile, Alabama, with our gorgeous daughter. I teach third graders and Sunday school. I don't want any part of, um, whatever all of this is."

Cort felt bad for his wife for two reasons. While he had almost lost his life, she had gone through the trauma of uncertainty because of it. Her life had been on the brink of being shattered, and by God's miracle, Cort had survived the crash.

Also, he chastised himself. By insulating her from the real threats the nation faced from terrorist attacks and political unrest, he'd treated her like a porcelain doll that could easily be broken. Her father was guilty of that as well. As a result, Meredith was not fully prepared for a future that could include fighting for their lives.

CHAPTER 34

Cortland Residence
Carlen-Midtown Neighborhood
Mobile, Alabama

A scratching at the door caused Cort and Meredith to break their embrace and burst out laughing. She wiped the tears off her face and gave her husband a kiss on the cheek. Without saying another word, her smiling eyes told him she'd support whatever decision he thought was best for the family.

"That's your son," Meredith said with a chuckle as she gently ran her hands down his chest.

"Good thing. If it was Hannah, I'd think we'd have bigger problems than the apocalypse."

Meredith slowly opened the door, allowing Cort plenty of time to brace for the impact. If he thought getting body-slammed by the Gulf of Mexico at a couple of hundred miles an hour hurt, wait'll he got a load of the bruising English bulldog affectionately known as Handsome Dan.

The door had barely cracked when the big guy stuck his nose in and bulled past her, his four legs grabbing the area rug, propelling his seventy-pound frame toward Cort. With his tongue flopping from side to side and drool splattering in all directions, Handsome Dan greeted his favorite parent by virtue of gender.

It was a guy thing, Cort had surmised after the puppy had entered the Cortland home for the first time. A direct descendent of Handsome Dan XVII bred by Diane Judy of Johnson City, Tennessee, Cort, through contacts he had at Yale, had purchased the stout pup for Hannah when she was four years old. His sire, whose original name was Sherman, as in the Sherman tank, assumed the Yale mascot position in late 2006. English bulldogs had excellent dispositions with children and were sturdy enough to handle a child's roughhousing.

"Come here, Handsome," said Cort as he knelt down to the dog's level. They had taught Handsome, his shortened name, not to jump on people a long time ago as he continued to grow. By some standards, he was considered to be a dozen pounds overweight. However, his veterinarian gave him clean bills of health twice a year, so the Cortlands did their best to keep him around seventy pounds.

The wet, sloppy kisses covered Cort and he loved it. It helped him relieve the stress from the conversation with Meredith and allowed him to transition from loving husband back to being the chief of staff to a powerful senator.

"I'm gonna leave you boys alone," said Meredith as she admired the reunion. "I'll keep Hannah out of your hair while you make your calls."

"I love you, honey!" said Cort while he scruffed on Handsome's backside.

"I love you back, Cort." She playfully waved her fingers at him and then slowly closed the door. Cort exhaled. It was gonna be okay. Now he had to get to work.

The first call he placed was to his boss, Alabama Senator Hugh McNeil. When the voicemail picked up, he remembered that he wasn't using his regular phone. He left a detailed message. "Senator, this is Cort. You probably don't recognize this number, but it's a backup phone I have. You're also probably not aware of the fact that I was on Delta Flight 322 out of Atlanta. Sir, Congressman Pratt is dead. I don't think that is public knowledge. In any event, please call me back at this number."

Cort left the time and phone number. Within minutes, the senator had called back and expressed his shock that Cort had been on the flight. Then the two men talked about Congressman Pratt, shared a couple of stories, and naturally, the conversation turned to the political void left by his departure.

"Michael," said the senator, who always referred to Cort by his given name out of habit, "I don't know if Pratt's death will change the trajectory of the hearings regarding the president and any possible impeachment trial. I will say this, the woman who's next in line to Pratt on the House Judiciary Committee is from a red state. She's consistently in a reelection battle, especially after the Texas legislature redrew their districts. She doesn't have the same hankering for kicking the president out of office as most in her party."

"Sir, she has to know the trial would go nowhere in the senate," added Cort.

"That's right, young man. So why bother, in my opinion. They lost the election. They've got these traitorous RINOs running point on this Twenty-Fifth Amendment mess. She might just allow us to eat our own."

Cort chuckled. "Sir, Ronald Reagan would be rolling over in his grave if he were around to see this."

"He sure would, Michael. Before we hang up, let me mention something to you by way of a heads-up. Because of my status as ranking member on the Senate Intelligence Committee, I am on the short list of those who will be afforded protection by the Secret Service and the military in the event the president invokes the continuity-of-government provisions put into effect years ago."

"Do you think the president plans on declaring martial law?" asked Cort.

The senator paused before responding. He was a heavy breather, so Cort knew he was still on the line. "It's too early to tell, but I will say this. From what I've seen and, knowing the political advantage the president will enjoy if the government is shut down due to this terrorist crisis, I'd expect a declaration sooner rather than later."

"Makes sense."

"Again, I'm telling you this for a reason," the senator continued. "My wife and I will be moved to an undisclosed secure location like Raven Rock, Greenbrier, or Mount Weather. As much as I'm in disagreement with this policy, you do realize these protections aren't afforded to my staff, right?"

"Yes, sir. I understand. We've made our own arrangements."

"Good to know, Michael. Be safe, and I will contact you on this number once I know more."

The two men disconnected the call, and Cort leaned back in his chair. Handsome was sprawled out on the wood floor in front of the fireplace. Like the others in the home, they had been retrofitted to allow for natural gas burners and logs. The old chimneys and flues of the pre–Civil War home weren't considered safe for roaring wood-burning fires. He pulled the remote out of his desk drawer and turned the burners on low. Handsome enjoyed the heat on his back legs as arthritis began to take its toll on him.

Cort's next call was to Meredith's father, George Trowbridge. His bedroom had been transformed into a high-end hospital room with the finest equipment, and highly trained medical staff lived on the premises to help him cope with his failing kidneys.

It was hard for Cort to fathom that just yesterday morning, he'd been standing at the old man's bedside, discussing their favorite topic—Washington politics. It wasn't that his father-in-law didn't love his daughter and Hannah, but politics was his passion, and Washington was his playing field.

On this call, Cort intended to lead the conversation with a simple question, and he wanted a straightforward answer from the most powerful nonpolitician in Washington.

What did you mean when you said either you control your destiny, or destiny controls you?

He never got the chance to ask.

CHAPTER 35

George Trowbridge's Residence
Near Pine Orchard, Connecticut

Once they were dropped off at the bus station, shuttle buses were made available to take the refugees to the airport and hotels within walking distance of restaurants. Tom chose to hire an Uber driver to take him to the home of George Trowbridge. He didn't know the address, but he remembered how to get there from the Connecticut Turnpike. He directed the driver to the Leetes Island Road exit, and they headed due south toward Long Island Sound. Twenty minutes later, they approached the security gate manned by two armed guards at the Trowbridge Estate.

Tom got out of the vehicle and approached the guards, who quickly closed ranks and slowly raised their weapons, causing Tom to hesitate. He began to question his decision, but since they'd made their way out here, he followed through with his plan.

"State your business," the lead guard demanded.

"My name is Commander Thomas Shelton, Joint Base Charleston. My wife and I would like a moment to speak with Mr. Trowbridge if he's in residence."

Tom was intentionally formal in an effort to exude some form of authority and importance. At least, he hoped it would encourage the guards to call the house, with the possibility of gaining entry. It worked, as the lead guard immediately placed a call.

He stood there for ten minutes, aimlessly kicking at a few loose stones on the concrete driveway. The guards remained stoic as they awaited their orders. Tom noticed that two security cameras had adjusted their position to focus on him. One zoomed in several times before returning to its original line of sight surveilling the driveway and the open lawn.

A phone rang in the guardhouse and a third guard emerged. "Sir, you and your wife may enter. We'll send the car on its way."

"Thank you. Let me retrieve my wife and our things."

Tom quickly turned and helped Donna out of the backseat. She was able to walk on her bad ankle by placing her hand on his shoulder. The guards swiftly grabbed their bags and placed them on a stone ledge near the iron gate.

"Sir, with apologies," the lead guard began, "we need to search your things and perform a pat-down search. Ma'am, we'll call for a female—"

"That's quite all right, young man," Donna interrupted. "If it's okay with the commander, I'll allow one of you handsome gentlemen to do the honor."

The guards managed a smile and Tom laughed. "By all means, but don't get too frisky with my wife. I can still pack a punch."

"Understood, sir," the young man said with a smile.

Moments later, a black Cadillac Escalade approached the gate. The driver helped the Sheltons into the car, stowed their gear in the back, and roared up the driveway to the entrance of the stately home. With her husband's assistance, Donna was helped up the marble entry steps, where a female member of the Trowbridge staff welcomed them into the foyer.

"May I get you something to drink while you wait?" the young woman with a British accent politely asked.

"Miss, we would love something warm to drink, perhaps some tea," replied Donna.

"I'll have it brought to you." The young woman left them standing alone in the foyer as they took in the grandeur of the Trowbridge home.

"Was it like this the first time you came here?" Donna asked.

"I never got inside. Back then, there were no security guards at the front. The driver took us around the side of the house, where Mr. Trowbridge was sitting by his pool with a couple of his assistants.

The meeting was short, and then we were on our way."

Donna turned to her husband and asked, "What makes you think he'll remember you from such a short meeting?"

"Oh, he remembers. Otherwise, we wouldn't be standing here."

"Commander Shelton," a voice echoed through the marble entry. A man stood at the top of the wide, sweeping staircase against a large, fifteen-foot-tall window. "Please come with me. Mrs. Shelton, I presume?"

"Yes, Donna."

"I understand you have an injury," the man who was about their age began. "We have an elevator used by the staff if you'd prefer."

Donna smiled. "Thank you. I can make it with the assistance of Tom and the handrail. Besides, I'm dying to take in the view of the water."

The aide chuckled and turned around. "Oh, it is breathtaking. Sadly, over time, one takes it for granted. Please, we'll be seeing Mr. Trowbridge in his master suite, unfortunately."

Tom and Donna gave each other a puzzled look before starting up the stairs. She was hobbling slightly but moved significantly better than just a few hours ago. They were fortunate the ankle wasn't broken, or even more seriously sprained.

At the top of the stairs, the hallway revealed several bedroom doors, although the ornate double entry doors at the east end of the home obviously led to the master suite. They followed the aide into George Trowbridge's master bedroom and were astonished at what they saw.

The room was the size of a small home, with multiple sitting areas, a study complete with floor-to-ceiling bookcases, and furniture purchased from the finest antique stores in the world. The furnishings, however, stood in stark contrast to the myriad of modern medical equipment surrounding Trowbridge's bed. It resembled the equipment Donna had grown accustomed to while she was taking chemotherapy and recovering from her surgeries.

Tom immediately stopped and pulled on Donna's hand to halt her progress. He whispered to the aide, "I have to apologize. I had no idea Mr. Trowbridge was ill. This was a terrible mistake, and we shouldn't have intruded."

"Commander," Trowbridge's voice boomed across the room, "my kidneys may be failing me, but my hearing is just fine. Please come in."

Tom shrugged and followed the older man's instructions. He glanced over at the massive fireplace. The flames danced up and down, warming the room with both its heat and the orangish-yellow glow. His eyes followed the flames upward, where they became fixed on an astounding carving in the granite fascia. A skull and bones protruded out of the stone, in addition to the numbers 3-2-2 carved beneath. Tom was staring when Trowbridge interrupted his examination of the sculpture.

"May we have some privacy?" asked Trowbridge, and the medical staff quickly exited the bedroom. His aide remained, taking a seat on a settee near the fire.

"Sir, I sincerely apologize for the intrusion," began Tom as he slowly approached the bed. "I don't know if you recall when we met—"

Trowbridge waved his arm to dismiss the question. "Commander, I remember everybody I've met as well as the circumstances surrounding our relationship. My body may be failing me, but my mind is as good as it was decades ago when I graduated from Yale."

Tom smiled and reached for his wife's hand, encouraging her to stand by his side as he spoke. "Donna and I were in Times Square last night when the attacks occurred, and have been evacuated here until we can find a way home to Charleston. She sprained her ankle during the melee and is having some difficulty walking."

Trowbridge closed his eyes and grimaced as if a jolt of pain had gone through his body. Donna shot Tom a glance, as she knew he was aware that her ankle had become measurably better. She recognized her husband was seeking the old man's sympathy.

Tom continued. "I really need to get her home to Charleston, and I wondered if you might have a suggestion as to how we could do that?"

Trowbridge leaned forward in the bed and hollered for his aide. "Harris!"

"Yes, sir."

"Check on any available means of transport that will hasten my friend's trip to Charleston, or as close thereto as possible," ordered Trowbridge. Then he turned his attention back to Tom. "I assume if we can't deliver you to your front door, a nearby location would suffice."

"Yes, sir. Absolutely."

Harris left the room to make inquiries, allowing Trowbridge to explain his illness to Tom and Donna. Donna carried the conversation, telling the sickly man about her experiences with breast cancer and how it had changed her outlook on life. He, too, was philosophical.

"I've devoted my life to making our great nation a better place. Naturally, there are those who disagree with my devotion to the Constitution and the methods I employ to preserve America's ideals. Quite frankly, in this day and age, we can't even agree as to how those ideals should be defined."

Trowbridge paused and pointed toward a crystal glass of water with an ordinary plastic bendy straw. The contradiction was not lost on Donna, who retrieved the glass and assisted him as he took several sips of water.

Then he continued. "I've seen the political divide grow wider in our nation to the point it appears to be irreparable. You know, Tom, countries come and go. There's never been a nation-state or empire that hasn't collapsed. I fear America is doomed to that same fate."

"Is it too late, Mr. Trowbridge?" Tom asked.

"Maybe, maybe not. One will have—" He stopped speaking as Harris returned. Tom and Donna stood out of the way as the aide whispered in Trowbridge's ear.

"Ah, yes," said Trowbridge with a grave chuckle. "I know her well. What is her destination?"

Harris leaned in to whisper.

Trowbridge nodded his approval. "Very appropriate, I suppose."

Harris then added, "Sir, your son-in-law just called. I took the liberty of telling him you were unavailable."

"That's fine. I'll get back to him in due time. First, please make the arrangements for our friends so they can be on their way."

Tom and Donna's demeanor picked up considerably at the prospect of getting home soon.

Donna spoke first. "Sir, I can't thank you enough for seeing us like this and especially for your help."

"I'm glad to help. Commander, may I assume that your wife is aware of our relationship?"

Tom sheepishly nodded, honestly afraid that he would be rebuked for betraying the confidential association they'd established.

Donna spoke up. "Sir, my husband has kept a secret, your secret, for many years until about an hour ago. Even as he felt the need to explain how he knew you and why he felt like he could call upon you for help, Tom withheld all the details. I will never pry into his business, nor will I expect him to divulge anything to me."

Trowbridge chuckled. "You are a good soldier, Mrs. Shelton."

"And, sir, may I thank you for helping us put our daughters through college and our grandkids into private schools."

Trowbridge had a hearty laugh at Donna's candor. "Commander, you've married well. I hope you have the ability to take care of this fine woman during the times of turmoil that are headed our way."

"I do, Mr. Trowbridge. In fact, Donna and I have planned ahead for the type of collapse that you alluded to a moment ago. May I tell you about it?"

"By all means," said Trowbridge, who was genuinely enjoying his visit with the Sheltons.

Tom began to explain to Trowbridge the concept of the Haven and how it was designed to provide safety to people like them who wanted to avoid the social unrest that might spread across the nation during a time of crisis. During Tom's explanation, Trowbridge listened intently, and his smile grew bigger as Tom passionately explained his belief that the Haven was one of the best investments they'd ever made.

Harris returned and provided his boss a simple nod. Unexpectedly, Trowbridge asked Tom and Donna to leave the room for a moment and instructed Harris to close the door behind them.

Puzzled by the sudden change in demeanor, the Sheltons waited outside in the hallway, staring mindlessly at Long Island Sound, where boats traversed the water like it was any other day.

Several minutes later, the door to the bedroom opened, and Harris invited them in again. Trowbridge was sitting more upright now, with a Mont Blanc pen and a small lap desk with stationery spread across it.

Tom and Donna approached, their eyes searching for an answer as to why they had been dismissed.

Trowbridge adopted a more serious tone. "Tom, Harris has made the arrangements for you. They are unconventional, but they will solve your problem, mostly."

Tom was humble and apologetic. "Thank you, sir. I hope it wasn't any trouble."

"Nothing is trouble for me. There's only should I, or shouldn't I. You both will be guests of the USS *Virginia*, which leaves Groton at thirteen hundred hours."

"A nuclear submarine, sir?" questioned Tom. "With all due respect, the commander—"

Trowbridge cut him off. "Is within our employ. The matter is arranged, and your late addition to the ship's manifest allows less time to scrutinize your presence."

"Okay, thank you, sir," said Tom, who immediately felt guilty for questioning his benefactor.

"There is one more thing, Commander," said Trowbridge as he handed a letter to Tom, who maintained eye contact. "I have provided you an accommodation. I need something else from you in return."

"This letter?"

"Yes. Please deliver this letter for me. Its contents are eyes only for the recipient. Do you understand?"

"Yes, of course, sir." Tom turned over the letter to see a name scribbled on the front. "But, sir, how will I know this person and where to find her?"

"You'll know, Commander," replied Trowbridge. He appeared tired and he slowly slid down in his bed as Harris removed the writing tray. "Mrs. Shelton, it was a pleasure meeting you. Commander, thank you for your service to our country, and to me. Godspeed, Patriot."

Tom's face turned ashen as the parting words hit him like a hammer. "Um, to you as well, sir."

Harris didn't hesitate to intervene, and the Sheltons were hastily removed from Trowbridge's bedroom. Without saying another word, they were led down the staircase to the front door, where Harris gave them their instructions.

"Our driver will take you to NSB New London. The commanding officer of the *Virginia* will be waiting for you with your credentials. Safe travels."

Tom and Donna were hastily escorted out the door, and once in the cool, crisp air, they both exhaled from holding their breath during the whirlwind exit.

Alone for the first time, they waited as the Escalade returned to pick them up. Donna leaned over to Tom and asked, "Who's the letter addressed to?"

He read the name. "Meredith Cortland."

CHAPTER 36

New Year's Day
Cape May, New Jersey

Angela offered to drive the first leg of the trip back to Richmond, enabling Tyler to gather information from their Kenwood portable transceiver. The children had fallen asleep again, allowing Tyler and Angela to talk freely for the first time about what was happening around the country.

The stereo system Tyler had installed in the '74 model Bronco had been fried by the EMP. He lamented that he didn't have the original AM radio that was standard equipment in the truck. After his father's truck had been given to him as a teen, he'd naturally upgraded the sound system first. The upgrade was susceptible to the enormous pulse of energy generated by the EMP, ruining its components.

The truck, on the other hand, was running perfectly. As they started their trip, they had to drive around the perimeter of the massive military base at Fort Dix. The unusual sight of the orange-and-white Bronco making its way down the country roads was only surpassed by the groupings of military vehicles departing the base en route to the major population centers of Trenton and nearby Philadelphia.

Tyler explained the president had followed the advice of the Congressional EMP Commission led by Dr. Peter Pry, Admiral James Woolsey, and others. Since the 1980s, when Speaker Newt Gingrich began to warn Congress about the EMP threat, the nation's lawmakers only paid lip service to following the commission's recommendations but were unwilling to allocate the necessary funding to protect the power grid.

When the president took office, one of his first actions was to reconstitute the EMP Commission, and upon the recommendations of Dr. Pry and Admiral Woolsey, he ordered the nation's armed services to work diligently to harden their vehicles and equipment against the devastating effects of an electromagnetic pulse.

As a result, the troop carriers and armored personnel vehicles at Fort Dix were able to be dispatched to assist the National Guard in dealing with the social unrest that erupted in the major Atlantic Seaboard cities hit by the EMP.

Tyler was able to confirm that the localized EMP strike had had its greatest impact on a hundred-mile radius around Philadelphia that included the cities of Wilmington, Trenton, Reading, and Atlantic City.

Through careful monitoring of the emergency channels, they determined that the Cape May-Lewes Ferry was fully operational, although the wait times were significant. Travelers were trying to escape New Jersey and head farther south in an effort to avoid the chaos along the Wilmington-Trenton corridor along I-95.

"Tyler, if the EMP attack only effected this isolated area, maybe we won't have to leave our home," Angela said hopefully. "We love it there, and the kids are comfortable. We have great careers with promising opportunities."

"Babe, I wanna say that all of this doesn't have anything to do with Virginia, but I'm afraid these other events lead me to believe otherwise. All public transportation in DC was shut down simultaneously. New York is in chaos, and as we heard the first responders say, dirty bombs were likely detonated around Times Square and other key landmarks like Grand Central Station, the Empire State Building, and the new World Trade Center."

"It has to be terrorism, right? I mean, Russia or China wouldn't pull crap like this."

Tyler turned off the radio and stuffed it between his thigh and the console. "Agreed. Those guys wouldn't mess around with this little stuff. They'd fire nukes. This is definitely terrorism, and the attacks were widespread. It's not just where we are. Stuff happened across the country, both big and small."

"Like Atlanta?" asked Angela.

"Yeah, can you imagine what it was like trying to get out of that stadium? What about Mobile and the plane crash? Too coincidental."

Tyler glanced in the backseat to confirm the children were still sleeping. He leaned over to Angela and continued. "Babe, let's get home and reassess everything. We'll have access to the news networks, and we could even call the Haven to get their opinion. Ryan and Blair seemed like they'd provide us honest advice without sugarcoating the situation or unduly raising alarms, don't you think?"

"Yeah, I trust them," replied Angela. "It'll be a shock for the kids."

Tyler chuckled and looked at them again. "Nah, I don't think so. I think they'll look at it as a new adventure. It's like I read once in a novel. Every great adventure necessarily starts with running away from home."

Angela nodded and pointed ahead. "Check it out! Pretty impressive."

"Epic!" said J.C., whose little head had emerged from underneath a blanket so he could see.

"I thought you were asleep," said Angela as she scooted up and craned her neck to look at J.C. in the rearview mirror.

"Nope, been awake the whole time," said J.C. "And I'm not scared, are you, Kaycee?"

"Nope," she replied.

Tyler turned around in his seat and reached for the blankets to reveal both kids' faces. "You're awake, too?"

"Yup, the whole time," replied Kaycee. "I heard every word."

Angela continued to glance at J.C. as she slowed the truck at the Cape May terminal. "How about you?"

"Me too, every word." J.C. was grinning as if he'd just scored an extra Popsicle without his parents knowing it.

Angela started laughing. "That's it. You're both grounded."

"Why?" protested Kaycee.

"Um, for … for … for unauthorized eavesdropping, right, Dad?"

Tyler smiled and nodded. "Absolutely, a heinous offense, in my opinion. Unauthorized eavesdropping carries a grounding punishment of twelve hours."

"Sweet! I can handle that," said J.C. with a chuckle. Once again, the two peas in a pod exchanged high fives.

Angela shook her head as she inched the truck along toward the next ferry. "Wow, Tyler. You are brutal when it comes to doling out the discipline."

He smiled and sat back in his seat. "Yup, that's why I'm the beloved parent."

CHAPTER 37

Congress Heights
Washington, DC

They began the conversation with the customary New Year's well-wishes. Cipollone, the lead attorney fighting the attempt to oust the president via the Twenty-Fifth Amendment, never stopped working. Like Hayden, the man was dedicated to his profession and, most importantly, his clients. But the events of New Year's Eve changed the dynamic in their approach to the president's defense.

"Blount, I'll get right to the point," he bellowed into the phone. He was riding in a vehicle, and the traffic noise came through loud and clear. "I'm on my way to the White House now. The Chief of Staff has put out a 9-1-1 for an all hands on deck in the Oval, sans the president."

"Sir, I believe—" Hayden was about to caution her boss when he cut her off.

"Do you remember when Rahm Emanuel made the comment in '08 that one should never let a good crisis go to waste? Do you remember that?"

"Yes, sir, but—"

Cipollone interrupted, ignoring Hayden's attempt to speak, which was unlike him. The street-noise levels were at a fever pitch as horns blared and people were shouting in the background. "If the president chooses, and it's certainly his prerogative, to declare martial law, the Supreme Court would be forced into recess for a considerable amount of time, or at least beyond the inauguration. Blount? Can you hear this? It's chaos!"

Hayden raised her voice. "Sir! You can't advise the president on this. You have to be able to maintain a level of plausible deniability, or we might be conflicted off the case."

"Blount, the president is looking to us for advice. That's our job."

"But, sir, the implementation of the continuity-of-government plan is clearly within the president's purview. However, because a suspension of proceedings at the Supreme Court is a necessary result, we have to maintain a certain autonomy or independence from the decision-making process. Otherwise, opposing counsel will accuse our firm of suggesting the extraordinary action of declaring martial law as a means to protect the president legally."

"Look out!" Cipollone screamed into the phone. He regained his composure and returned to the call. "He would be delaying the case, not stopping it altogether."

"Yes, sir, legally speaking, that's true. However, as his political advisors pointed out, pushing the Court proceedings beyond the inauguration will have a profound impact on public opinion. Once he puts his hand on the Bible and raises his right hand, that imagery will send a message to the public that he was duly elected by the people. Support for the Twenty-Fifth Amendment attempt will wane, especially from those on the right who pushed it."

Cipollone didn't respond immediately, but Hayden knew he was still there by the noise being emitted through the phone line. Finally, he spoke. "I can't even go to the White House to explain my position. The mere fact my name appears on the White House visitors' log will raise questions. An exchange of phone calls is one thing, sitting in on a conference call with the president to debate invoking martial law is another."

"I agree, sir," said Hayden, with a sigh of relief. She admired her boss and his passion for protecting the president, but as was the case with most attorneys, he looked at things through the prism of the law. Whether a particular case impacted a business's operation, or the emotional toll a divorce took on a family, or the political machinations of a president, an attorney's job was to provide legal advice, and only an empathetic lawyer understood the case from the client's point of view.

Hayden, who disdained politics, understood people. She had also studied this president. While most politicians focused on re-election, the president had to focus on self-preservation. The average politician fought to win at the ballot box. This president had to fight the court of public opinion and a never-ending barrage of congressional investigations, many of which had criminal implications.

He wasn't an attorney, but he certainly was street-smart. The president didn't require her firm's advice to understand how he would benefit from invoking the powers afforded him by Directive 51 and an accompanying martial law declaration.

She disconnected the call and flopped backwards on the couch. The scenes on every major television network depicted major cities in chaos. Some people were frightened. Others were simply opportunistic thugs looking to take advantage of a weakness in the system when law enforcement was stretched too thin.

Hayden, however, was waiting for the third element to show themselves.

The anarchists.

CHAPTER 38

Cortland Residence
Carlen-Midtown Neighborhood
Mobile, Alabama

Cort led Handsome Dan into the living room to join Hannah on the sofa. He tried to keep his composure and not let on that there was any kind of problem. "Hey, ladies, did an English bulldog win this year's best in show?"

"No," replied a dejected Hannah. "It was some kind of dog called a fricassee."

Meredith laughed and wrapped her arm around her daughter's neck. Cort wasn't exactly sure what a fricassee was, but obviously it wasn't a dog.

"Hannah, a fricassee is a food dish. You know, like chicken fricassee. It's a stew with white wine and vegetables."

"What kind of dog won?" asked Cort.

"It was a *bichon frise*," replied Meredith in her best French accent. "It's a small breed in—"

Hannah interrupted her mother's explanation. "Daddy, it's a stupid poodle. A white fluff ball that shouldn't even count as a dog."

"I vote we fricassee the poodle!" shouted Cort as he raised his right arm in the air. Handsome was in agreement, letting out two hearty gruffs to join in the celebratory pronouncement.

Mommy buzzkill intervened. "Nobody's gonna fricassee a poodle, or a bichon frise."

After a few more jokes about poodles and stewpots, Cort looked back toward his study to encourage Meredith to go with him. She picked up on the nod of his head and left Hannah and Handsome on the sofa to discuss why he should enter next year's AKC beauty contest.

Meredith slowly closed the door behind her. "What did you find out?"

"Well, I spoke with Senator McNeill first. He said, but couldn't say, you know what I mean?"

"Yeah, it's the way Washington works."

"He expects the president to declare martial law at any moment. In fact, he's already been notified by the Secret Service to be ready to join other members of Congress in the facilities around the East Coast designed to protect the high-ranking officials of our government."

Meredith sat down and studied the guns and money, which remained in the same place as earlier. "I wish we all could be so lucky."

Cort leaned up against his desk again and patted her on the leg. "But, honey, we are. I've anticipated this day coming, and I've made arrangements to keep us safe at the Haven. It may not be an underground bunker with the military guarding it, but it is fenced, and it is guarded with some well-trained ex-soldiers and members of law enforcement."

"What would we do there? What about food? Hannah is just a child. How would we fit in?"

"Listen, you have to trust me," replied Cort. "The people who developed the Haven, Ryan and Blair Smart, have thought through every detail. There's a school and a church. It's located on hundreds of acres and along a river too. Hannah will have lots to do and so will you if you want. They need teachers and also somebody to lead Sunday school."

"Can we leave if we want?"

"Of course, honey. Anytime, although if things get bad and the martial law declaration goes into effect, I can't think of any place I'd rather be than the Haven."

Meredith wiped a tear from the corner of her eye. She looked outside at the beautifully manicured lawn and the stately oak trees that adorned their front yard. "We can come back, right?"

"As soon as it's safe. I promise."

She nodded and squeezed her husband's hand. "From what you're saying, I gather we have to leave soon. Am I correct?"

"Yes, tonight, in fact. I've already checked flights, and there's a nonstop out of Pensacola to Charlotte that leaves at nine. If we get our things packed, we can make it."

"I trust you, Cort. You've never been an alarmist, and I'm proud of you for thinking ahead like you did. I just wish you'd told me about it. I'm not that fragile, you know."

Cort bent over to kiss the love of his life. "I know and I am so sorry. It'll work out, you'll see. Now, would you like to help me break the news to our daughter?"

Meredith rolled her eyes and smiled. "It's all you, Daddy-O. I'll be here for moral support, but you're gonna have to sell her."

"But you're the mom," protested Cort. "Listen, it's a known fact that fathers don't understand preteen girls. There are so many factors to consider, most of which have nothing to do with what happens under this roof."

"Oh, you mean like friends at school, girls and boys alike? And band practice? And the history club?"

"Um, yeah. I guess all of those things."

"Yeah, good luck. I can't wait to see you use all of the political skills you've learned in Washington to deal with our twelve-year-old daughter."

CHAPTER 39

New Year's Day
Cape May, New Jersey

Tyler and Angela had just missed the 10:55 ferry departing for Lewes, Delaware, but were assured they'd be on the next available boat, which would leave an hour later. While they were in line, Tyler wandered around and struck up conversations with several travelers who'd packed their cars and trucks with more than just the customary suitcases to take a trip. Many of these people lived in New York City and had fled immediately after the drone attacks.

While the kids enjoyed running around the ferry and taking in the sights of the lighthouses and seagulls, the Rankins struck up conversations with as many people as they could to gather information about what had happened the night before.

The attack on New York was officially being labeled as terrorism by the Department of Homeland Security. The possible culprits ranged from radical Islamists to splinter groups funded by the North Koreans, both of whom had a perceived axe to grind with the U.S.

After Hamas rebels had fired over four hundred rockets into Jerusalem, the Israeli Defense Forces struck back with a vengeance. Working with the U.S. Navy, who remained a permanent fixture in the Mediterranean Sea, the IDF rained hellfire upon Gaza and Hamas strongholds, including compounds, observation posts and rocket-launching locations. Palestinians and their Iranian allies vowed revenge, assuring America that the fight would be taken to their homeland in retaliation.

The Kim regime in North Korea, officially known as the Democratic People's Republic of Korea, was anything but democratic. The Kim dynasty spent over half a century coalescing the North Korean people socially, ideologically, and with loyalty to their Dear Leaders.

The president made every effort to normalize relations with the rogue nation, but when the U.S. intelligence agencies determined that Kim Jong-un continued to hide nuclear missiles in more than a dozen hidden locations around the Hermit Kingdom, the president cut off talks and a war stance was adopted. Crippling sanctions and a massive military buildup threatened to bring the Kim regime to its knees. Many political analysts opined that the New Year's Eve attacks had been orchestrated by Kim using operatives embedded in America.

Tyler knew the world was a dangerous place and that America seemed to be the target of the bad actors' ire. He'd seen administrations try to make peace with the haters, to no avail. Then he watched as this administration took a get-tough stance. The result was the same. The United States was despised by many nations that vowed death to all Americans.

The eighty-minute ride across the Delaware was disheartening for Angela and Tyler. What could have been a momentous occasion for their children ended up being an eye-opening exercise that reminded them a war could be, and in fact had been, brought to America's doorstep. They were aware of this eventuality, which was why they prepped.

The ferry arrived across the Delaware, and the Bronco eased down the ramp onto firm ground. "Okay, you guys, that was pretty cool, right?" asked Angela as she relinquished the driving duties back to her husband.

"It was amazeballs!" exclaimed Kaycee.

"I wish our phone cameras worked," lamented J.C.

Angela allowed a pout, as her son enjoyed memorializing their trips through photographs and videos. The child even had his own Instagram account with a good-sized following.

"J.C., when we get home, we'll get us all new phones, how's that?" Angela tried to make it better. "Besides, you'll never forget this experience, right?"

"Yeah, I suppose. Um, how much longer?"

"We still have quite a way to go, guys," replied Tyler. He glanced down at his fuel gauge. He'd driven a hundred miles on this tank and would need to stop soon. "How about all of you help me find some gas, okay?"

The next twenty miles took nearly an hour as they stopped at one gas station after another, only to find out their pumps were empty. After the attacks, many residents of southern Delaware fled south in an attempt to avoid the anticipated masses of refugees out of Wilmington and Philadelphia.

With no luck at the gas stations and the fuel needle already on *E*, Tyler and Angela discussed alternative sources.

Tyler made his proposal. "Let's start down some of these side roads but continue to head south toward Chesapeake Bay. All we need is a can of fuel here and there to keep going."

"How much does it hold?"

"Twelve gallons," replied Tyler.

Angela shook her head. "I never even paid attention to how often we stopped on this trip."

"Every two to two and a half hours."

"Babe, I don't wanna get stuck in the middle of nowhere. I kinda lost track of where we are. Delaware? Maryland? New Jersey? It all looks alike over here."

Tyler looked around, searching for some kind of identifying marker, not that it mattered. "We just crossed into Delaware."

"That's right, Dad," said J.C. "Didn't you see the sign back there?"

Tyler rolled his eyes and reached for Angela's hand. "It'll be okay. Look for a friendly face who might help us. Or look for a lawnmower. Where there's a mower, there's—"

"Dad!" exclaimed Kaycee. "There! On your right. There are two gas cans in that shed by a riding lawn mower."

Tyler stepped on the brakes and slowed to a stop in front of a white farmhouse. A *for sale* sign was pressed into the ground near the gravel driveway entrance.

He and Angela made eye contact and he glanced at the gun. She slyly picked it up and placed it in her lap. Tyler slipped the gear into reverse and backed the car up the narrow, two-lane road until he had room to turn into the driveway.

He hesitated and then drove forward. As he did, Angela made a suggestion. "Let me go to the front door. They might be more receptive to a mother in need of assistance."

"Okay, gimme that." Tyler reached for the weapon, glancing in the backseat as he did. Both children were watching their every move. Sadly, they were growing up fast in this new year.

Angela left the truck and made her way to the front door. She rang the doorbell several times and waited while a man came to the front porch. His presence must have startled her because she took a couple of steps back.

The two spoke for a minute, and the remaining Rankins in the Bronco determined from the man's body language that he was not going to grant Angela's request.

Tyler, nervously fiddling with the pistol, was intently focused on the conversation between Angela and the man, as he was prepared to leap from the truck to rescue her if there was a problem. This was why he didn't notice Kaycee and J.C. slip out of the backseat and out the passenger side of the Bronco.

Tyler caught a glimpse of them out of the corner of his eye as the two kids raced along the back side of a hedgerow toward the small shed Kaycee had spotted earlier. Within seconds, they had each grabbed a red gas can and were scurrying back again to the truck.

They arrived at the door, and Tyler leaned through the bucket seats to help them load the gas cans behind him.

He shook his head and gritted his teeth to speak under his breath. "You two are in big trouble."

"We're already grounded," shot back Kaycee.

Insolence. But funny at the same time.

Tyler got them settled and started the truck as Angela made her way down the sidewalk to join her family. She was shaking her head side to side and then shrugged with her arms spread apart, indicating her disappointment.

Tyler mouthed the word *hurry*, causing Angela to pick up the pace. She was barely in the front seat when Tyler threw the Bronco into reverse and hurriedly backed out of the driveway.

"Where did that come from?" she questioned when the sloshing gas cans caused the odor to fill the Bronco.

"Um." Tyler began to explain before hesitating. He didn't want to condone what the kids did. It was, in fact, potentially dangerous. But, on the other hand, it was quick thinking and was absolutely what needed to be done. "Well, it appears these two are growing up to be gypsy kids."

Angela looked her children in the eyes, who immediately cowered under their mother's glare. "Guys, really? You stole the gas?"

Before the kids could respond, Tyler and Angela burst out laughing.

"Sorry, Mom," apologized J.C. first. "It's just that …" His voice trailed off.

Angela couldn't punish their kids for helping the family out, under the circumstances. "You two are now on double secret probation."

"On top of being grounded?" squalled Kaycee.

"Yes, ma'am," replied Tyler. "And after we stop to top off our tank, your mother and I will discuss what exactly *double secret probation* means."

Now the parents exchanged high fives.

CHAPTER 40

NSB New London
Groton, Connecticut

NSB New London, the Navy's first submarine base located at Groton, Connecticut, was known as the *Home of the Submarine Force.* Established as a naval yard and storage depot after the Civil War, the naval base was used sporadically until 1915 and the advent of submarine warfare. Over time, the facility was transformed into the U. S. Navy's primary submarine base and training school. Now, NSB New London occupies nearly seven hundred acres and was home to fifteen nuclear submarines. Almost every submariner in the Navy passes through Groton before deployment at sea around the world.

Tom and Donna barely spoke en route to the base. Both of them contemplated the encounter they'd had with George Trowbridge and agreed to wait until they were on board the USS *Virginia* before they dared to discuss their observations.

Despite the powerful man's assurances, Tom still had his doubts about their ability to board the *Virginia.* Nonetheless, their driver was able to sail through the security checkpoints, and within an hour, they were being escorted to the port commander's office to wait for the *Virginia*'s commanding officer for further instructions.

While they were alone, Donna opened up the conversation by discussing Trowbridge's health. "Tom, I'm somewhat familiar with kidney failure. Immediately following my diagnosis of breast cancer, as you recall, I became distraught and began researching the worst-case scenarios on the internet. One of the likely results of advanced cancer is kidney failure."

Tom whispered back, "Do you think Trowbridge has cancer?"

"No, not necessarily," replied Donna. "But this is what I wanted to tell you. I studied dialysis and it appears that Trowbridge is permanently hooked up. He's either been through several kidney transplant attempts, and his body rejected them, or he has something else going on that prevents a surgery. Either way, he's probably dying."

Tom subconsciously touched his coat where the letter to Meredith Cortland was held. "Do you think his mortality prompted the writing of this letter?"

"Considering the circumstances and our sudden appearance on his doorstep, I find it odd that he'd hastily pen a letter to be delivered by relative strangers."

Tom nodded in agreement as he stared mindlessly at the polished tile floor. "Not to mention the fact that I have no idea who this person is or where we'll meet her."

"Maybe she's on this ship?" asked Donna.

"I don't know. In case you missed that part of the conversation, we're traveling on a submarine."

"Under water, fabulous. Don't remind me."

A naval officer dressed in his blue and black camouflage fatigues approached the Sheltons and asked them to accompany him to meet the commanding officer. He motioned for them to take a seat in an office, where they waited. Several minutes later, a dapper man in his forties entered and closed the door behind him. He was carrying a manila envelope that he immediately handed to Tom before they had an opportunity to shake hands.

"Welcome to NSB New London. I'm Commander Jeffrey Anderson, the CO of the *Virginia*." Commander Anderson extended his hand to shake Donna's.

Tom immediately stood. "Commander Tom Shelton, USN, retired." He and Anderson saluted one another.

"Welcome, Commander Shelton," said Anderson. "I look forward to having both of you aboard the *Virginia* as my *official* honored guests." Anderson stressed the word *official* and added a smile as he did. He motioned for Tom to sit down and encouraged him to read through the dossier that had been created for them.

After a moment of thumbing through the paperwork, Tom looked up at Anderson. "The Discovery Channel?"

Donna shot him a puzzled glance and then turned her attention back to Anderson, who explained, "This is a cover I've used in the past when our mutual friend has needed an assist. The Discovery Channel produced a series titled *Submarine: Hidden Hunter* many years ago before the *Virginia* was commissioned. The series followed the pre-commission process as we put her through a battery of tests and sea trials. The advanced technology, which included, at the time, her air-independent propulsion system, was revealed. Finally, an inside look at raw recruits in Basic Sub School depicted the strenuous, regimented training our submariners have to endure to earn a spot on the *Virginia*."

"So, as the paperwork indicates, we're producers considering a follow-up series now that the *Virginia* has seen battle."

"Exactly. We're leaving in less than two hours, and your inclusion as my personal guests will not be scrutinized. Plus, it's a relatively quick trip for the *Virginia*. Although we're permanently based here as part of SUBRON 4, we're going to spend some time in Norfolk in preparation for our next mission. Classified, of course."

"Subron?" asked Donna.

"Um, sorry, ma'am. Submarine Squadron four."

"What if we're confronted while on board?" asked Tom.

"You won't be, but as a precaution, I'd like you to remain confined to quarters unless I accompany you. We'll be putting the *Virginia* through the paces, covering nearly seven hundred nautical miles at twenty-eight knots."

"Full throttle," commented Tom.

"That's correct, Commander. So, are you ready to come aboard? I've got work to do, and I'd like to get you settled while my crew is hustling around. And, ma'am, I understand your ankle needs some attention. I'll have a member of the medical team look in on you and get you squared away for your future travels. I understand you're from Charleston?"

"Yes, and thank you," replied Donna, who glanced over at Tom with a look of sadness. "It's our home port, for now."

They walked slowly so Donna could favor her leg. As they went, Anderson told them about the *Virginia.*

"Designated SSN 774, the *Virginia* is actually the tenth Navy vessel to be named for the Commonwealth. Our sub is nearly four hundred feet long and has a beam of thirty-four feet. The crew consists of fifteen officers, including myself, and a hundred seventeen enlisted personnel. We've traveled nearly a hundred thousand nautical miles on our last three deployments, and quite frankly, it never gets old. It's in our blood."

Donna laughed. "What is it with you sailor boys? You just can't get enough."

"I loved the open sea, Commander," said Tom. "However, it wasn't until I was permanently stationed at Joint Base Charleston that I learned to appreciate my family. Are you married?"

Commander Anderson stopped before they boarded and smiled. "I am. Her name is *Virginia.*"

CHAPTER 41

Congress Heights
Washington, DC

"Well, Prowler, I guess we're on hold until the president makes a move," said Hayden to her adoring cat. The beast of a feline had curled up on her lap to relax while she devoured the news and nursed her hangover. She hadn't heard back from Cipollone, so she assumed he'd followed her suggestion.

"I hate sitting here, doing nothing," she mumbled before picking up her cell phone. She saw the three calls placed to her from Blair Smart at the Haven.

She hadn't taken Blair's calls, not because she was necessarily avoiding her responsibilities to the Haven, but mainly because she didn't know whether going there was necessary yet. By all indications, the attacks had stopped by late afternoon on New Year's Day, allowing first responders to deal with the damage and state governments to restore order.

Plus, Ryan and Blair had looked to Hayden as a source of information, the type of insider stuff she could relay to them without necessarily betraying her confidential relationship to the president. Truthfully, anything she had at this point was only speculation, but at least she could advise them about the president's options.

Hayden scrolled through her phone to locate *recent calls*. Just as she was about to press Blair's number to return the call, a text message came through. She furrowed her brow as she read it aloud.

Luck can come from a tragic sequence of fortuitous events.
For one, everything in life is luck.
Godspeed, Patriot.
MM

Hayden stared at the display to determine who sent her the message. The sender didn't have a name, only a three-digit number followed by a two-digit number, separated by a hyphen.

322 - 04

"What the hell does this mean?" she asked Prowler, who squinted his mysterious golden-yellow eyes as he considered the question. Hayden studied her cat for a moment as if she were waiting for a response. One of these days, he'd speak and send her screaming into the night.

She read the message again, trying to discern its meaning. Then her phone dinged, announcing another message. It came from the same source.

Trust the plan.
MM

Hayden gave Prowler a gentle push off her lap and she jumped off the couch. She ran her fingers through her hair and reread the two messages.

"Seriously, people. Who are you, and what's with the cryptic messages? What plan? And who got lucky? It sure wasn't me!"

Hayden watched as a single boat puttered along the Potomac away from the city. Her mind drifted away as the words rattled in her head. *Luck. Plan. Patriot. Godspeed.*

She swung around and walked back toward Prowler, holding her outstretched arm with the text message screen displayed as if the farther away she held it from her body, the less it had an effect on her.

"Godspeed? Who talks like that anymore?" It was if she'd received a text from the seventeen hundreds. After considering the intent behind the text messages, she laughed it off as a prank or being sent to the wrong phone number.

Hayden thought maybe she had cabin fever, and despite the fact DC was out of control, her little corner in Congress Heights appeared to be relatively calm. She thought about calling Blair and decided to give it another couple of hours. Instead, she decided to prepare herself for the inevitable drive to the Haven by topping off her truck with gas and picking up some supplies at her favorite off-grid shopping destination, Walmart.

CHAPTER 42

West Clay Street
Jackson Ward neighborhood
Richmond, Virginia

The Jackson Ward neighborhood in Richmond was less than a mile from the Virginia State Capitol. The row houses that stretched from one end of West Clay Street to the other had been built at the time of the Civil War. Following the war, previously *free blacks*, as they were called during the era, from the north joined with freed slaves and their descendants to create a thriving community that became known as the *Black Wall Street of America*.

The neighborhood, initially called Jackson Ward at a time when political precincts were referred to as wards, also became known as a center for black entertainment. Dubbed the *Harlem of the South*, the venues were frequented by the likes of Ella Fitzgerald, Duke Ellington, and Nat King Cole.

Over time, however the community fell into disrepair. After the civil rights movement of the sixties, and the desegregation that accompanied it, the inner-city properties were abandoned. Jackson Ward became the target of redevelopment plans, severely disintegrating the historic community.

However, at the turn of the twenty-first century, at the urging of Virginia's governor, a push was made to preserve the historic neighborhood by placing the buildings on the National Register of Historic Places. Taking advantage of tax credits and favorable financing, investors came in and revitalized the neighborhood. One of those investors was the Schwartz family's charitable organizations.

Several homes in the five hundred block of West Clay Street were purchased and renovated. For a while, they were used as low-income residences. The close proximity to the state capitol soon found a better use for the homes—a staging ground for political protests against the Virginia state government.

Virginia was going through a period of political transition. More and more government employees chose to live in the state and undertake a lengthy commute to Washington, DC. Defense contractors flooded the Northern Virginia area, and their employees filled overbuilt neighborhoods left empty following the housing collapse of 2007 and 2008. The political demographics changed from red state to purple to leaning blue in the span of two decades.

Change takes time, and the Schwartz foundations were prepared to play the long game. New Year's Eve simply accelerated their timetable.

That afternoon, a group of forty-seven people assembled in the four row houses along West Clay Street. Prior to the New Year's Eve attacks, their activism was limited to coordinating astroturf political protests in Richmond and Washington, DC. Astroturfing, a term derived from the artificial grass used at indoor stadiums, was the practice of creating an illusion that the public outcry was spontaneous and supported by the grassroots of citizens.

In reality, the organizations behind these large gatherings paid the protestors, funded their expenses, and coordinated their efforts. They were a tool to manipulate the media into spreading the false premise that the entire populace was behind a measure when in reality the protestors were paid to vocally embrace the cause du jour.

On this evening, an actual grassroots protest, of sorts, was being planned. The men and women who attended the call to action weren't there to recruit protestors for fifteen dollars an hour to ride in a bus to Washington for the day. These people were the true believers in the cause. They called themselves the Resistance, although they identified with many different groups spread around the country.

Until now, they weren't organized as a collective. Operating on a regional basis, rarely were they called to perform a task outside their home states or a nearby large city. These were the hard-core few, often labeled as *anarchists*, a slur that many resented but others wore as a badge of honor.

Those on the right claimed anarchists were hell-bent on battling the police and destroying property, all in an attempt to voice their displeasure with the government. Meanwhile, these self-identified anarchists claimed to be on a quest for a just and equitable society, and that political labels were more than irrelevant. They were counterproductive and divisive.

Modern society looked upon the anarchists gathered on West Clay Street that evening as hoodlums and thugs who were trying to circumvent the ballot box to effectuate change. The gathering of young people saw themselves as something different and pointed to history to make their case.

They argued that throughout history, it has been necessary to shock the system in order to get people's attention. Riots and work stoppages were necessary in order to protect workers and to form labor unions in the early twentieth century.

The violence surrounding the civil rights movement was necessary to pass the critical legislation protecting the rights of all Americans regardless of race. Since the turbulent sixties, many Americans believe the times demanded a unified struggle to get the attention of those who were comfortable in their surroundings and oblivious to the plight of others.

They had bucked the system, shunned the government, and sometimes rioted to make their point. Now the battle would become much more personal. They wore black clothes and black bandanas to cover their mouths. Some wore the white Guy Fawkes masks used most recently by Anonymous, a loosely organized group of hacktivists known for their attacks on government and corporate computer systems.

Historically, the Guy Fawkes mask had been used by the Loyal Nine, the original Sons of Liberty, when organizing resistance to the British Crown during the years leading up to the American Revolution.

On one occasion, knowing they were going to need help organizing a resistance movement, the Loyal Nine turned to Bostonian Ebenezer Mackintosh and his gang of miscreants known as the South Enders.

Mackintosh was a poor shoemaker who was generally considered lower class in Boston at the time. After the death of his first wife, Mackintosh became involved in the militia and later joined the infamous Fire Engine Company No. 9 in South Boston. Over time, he became a fixture and a leader in the poor communities of Boston's South End.

As the head of the fast-growing South End gang, he coordinated activities of the annual Guy Fawkes Night held on the fifth of November. In 1605, Guy Fawkes was a member of the Gunpowder Plot to assassinate King James and several members of the House of Lords. The plot failed, but Fawkes became well known for his insurgent activities. Animated masks honoring Fawkes began to surface, featuring an oversized smile and red cheeks, a wide upturned moustache, and a thin vertical pointed beard.

Mackintosh used the occasion of Guy Fawkes Night to light an enormous bonfire and recruit more members into his gang. He orchestrated most activities in the south part of the city. Inciting public disturbance was not foreign to them. The insurgency became a thorn in the side of the British, enabling the Loyal Nine to sow the *seeds of liberty* and advance the cause of freedom.

Today, groups like Anonymous and others had to conceal their identities from the thousands of cameras that existed in the Orwellian state that was modern America. In the past they'd used a variety of tools ranging from megaphones to wooden poles to chunks of concrete so they could draw attention to poverty, racism, educational inequality, and gender bias.

Now the gloves were off. The restraints had been lifted. They had been given deadlier tools capable of fighting back against what was being perceived as a war against those who needed their protection the most.

This meeting on West Clay Street in Richmond, Virginia, was not the only one. Others like it were being held in Alexandria, Virginia; Charlotte, North Carolina; Memphis, Tennessee; and Atlanta, Georgia.

Their marching orders were the same—*make them feel uncomfortable. Take the fight to Main Street America. Leave your mark everywhere as a constant reminder of who we are.*

Resist!

CHAPTER 43

Walmart
Clinton, Maryland

Hayden had been raised by her family to be independent and self-reliant. Growing up, she hunted, fished, and enjoyed camping. She loved the outdoors and learned to live off the land, studying survival methods of foraging, trapping small game, and surviving in extreme temperatures.

Eventually school took over her life and she had to place her hobbies on the back burner. She still found ways to maintain her self-defense survival skills. Frequent trips to a gun range in Maryland were a part of her routine. Before the family farm was sold, she took trips back to Tennessee to camp and hike. Also, once she moved to Washington, she learned to defend herself physically through Krav Maga and verbally through the law.

Hayden prided herself on being a defender. Not necessarily of criminals, although she could. No, she was a defender against bullies. From childhood to the highest levels of power, Hayden defended those who were persecuted by mobs, whether it was kids in a schoolyard or an overbearing media.

She made her way through light traffic to nearby Clinton, Maryland, located just ten miles east of Alexandria, Virginia, where the closest Walmart was located. Hayden rarely went grocery shopping, taking the majority of her meals at her desk, except for the occasional working dinner with her associates at work or with a client.

Hayden went to Walmart for many reasons, including purchasing ammunition for the weapons she kept in her gun locker at the

Maryland Small Arms Range in nearby Meadows, Maryland. The range was frequented by military personnel stationed at Joint Base Andrews, some of whom she'd struck up friendships with.

The quick fifteen-minute trip was uneventful. Upon arrival at Walmart, however, she was surprised at how full the parking lot was considering it was a holiday. She'd assumed everyone had emptied their bank accounts and maxed their credit cards by Christmas or were assuredly tapped out from the after-Christmas sales.

Once inside, Hayden was astonished. The checkout lines were all open, and they were seven customers deep. Overflowing baskets of bottled water, canned goods, blankets, and other supplies could be seen.

She shook her head and turned to the left, where she found an abandoned grocery cart near the pharmacy. She commandeered it and set about filling it up. While she was in the pharmacy area, she stockpiled first-aid supplies, vitamins, and health supplements. She added at least three each of the toiletries she used.

She stopped in the camping supplies aisle and filled her cart with a variety of camping gear and off-grid cooking supplies. She didn't anticipate having to sleep in the woods overnight, but it was a part of her stored gear that needed backup supplies.

Making her way through the sporting goods aisles was more difficult. At her final stop, a crowd had amassed around the gun counter as customers, primarily men, waited on their purchases. Maryland did not preempt federal law regarding gun purchases. Most eligible buyers could make their purchase in the length of time it took to get a response on their background check.

Hayden didn't need any more weapons; eight was more than enough. However, as her father had told her once, you can never have enough ammo because without it, your gun is nothing more than an expensive club.

She politely pushed past the men and made her way to the counter. Two frenzied clerks stood waiting for the phone to ring. Their ammunition stock had dwindled, but it was far from empty. Hayden glanced around at the men who had the presence of mind to make their gun purchases quickly, considering the circumstances. The one thing they hadn't done yet, she surmised, was purchase ammunition. They were most likely waiting to pick up their weapon first.

All eyes were on Hayden, not just because she'd muscled her way into the all-men's club at the Walmart weapons counter, but even dressed-down in her Duke sweats, she was incredibly beautiful.

"Good afternoon, miss," the older clerk greeted her. "Are you here to purchase a gun?"

"Maybe she wants a pink Crosman air gun?" said one of the men at the rear of the crowd, which drew a hearty laugh from his fellow shoppers.

"No, ammo only, please," replied Hayden, ignoring the continuing snide remarks directed at her.

She focused on her arsenal rather than what she already had in her storage locker and in the condo. Everything she was about to purchase would supplement what she'd take to the Haven if it came to that.

"Okay, ma'am, tell me what you need," the friendly clerk offered.

Hayden thought for a moment. Had this been several years prior, she would've run up against Walmart's internal policy limiting ammunition purchases to three boxes per day. That restriction had been lifted, and now, unless a do-gooder salesclerk picked up the phone and contacted local law enforcement without cause, the sky was the limit for Hayden.

"I'll need five hundred rounds per weapon," she stated confidently. This drew gasps from the men behind her in line, and then several chuckled as more jokes were cracked about how BBs come packed in thousands.

The clerk retrieved a pen and a pad of paper to begin making notes. Hayden reeled off her firearms, some of which were duplicated, like her handguns.

"A thousand rounds of nine millimeter, Luger, one hundred fifteen grain. Give me the PMC Bronze."

"Okay."

"A thousand rounds NATO five-five-six. Make them Federal, American Eagles. Sixty-two grain."

The clerk nodded. Hayden heard some whispers coming from behind her. "She's got two AR-15s. Who is this chick?"

"A hundred rounds of Remington sluggers. A hundred rounds of bird. And three hundred rounds of double-ought buck. All Remington, please."

The clerk wrote down her request. "Um, ma'am, I'm glad to accommodate you. But, um, how much more do you need? Do you realize how much this ammo will weigh? We can't help you to your car with it all."

"I appreciate your concern, but I can handle it."

"I'd be glad to help the little lady," muttered the man directly behind her, who continued to crowd Hayden at the counter. She didn't consider the men to be a threat to her safety. They were just jerks to be ignored unless they crossed her boundaries. Then they'd get taught a lesson.

"Okay, what else?" asked the clerk.

Hayden rounded out the ammunition she needed for her hunting rifles and her AR-10. Although her weapons varied due to their specific uses, she tried to maintain common, interchangeable calibers.

She took her time, paid for all of her purchases, totaling almost fifteen hundred dollars, and walked out of the store feeling better prepared. The parking lot had filled to its maximum capacity now, and customers were making their way through the rows of cars looking for an available space. An older woman was trailing Hayden as she pushed the overloaded shopping cart to her Range Rover. She waved to the woman to let her know where her car was, and the driver waved back in appreciation.

As Hayden finished unloading, she noticed another car had arrived and was waiting for her space, continuously inching forward in an attempt to take the spot before the older woman. Hayden was about to walk toward the car to tell the male driver the space was already promised when she noticed there were two other males sitting in the backseat. It struck Hayden as odd that nobody was in the passenger seat, but it didn't matter. She turned around and got in her own vehicle.

When she backed out, she deliberately backed into the direction of the male driver, effectively preventing him from taking the space. Then, once the old woman was parked, Hayden pulled out of the way of the man, who revealed his irritation with a honk of the horn and the display of his middle finger.

The gesture caused Hayden to laugh. "Another bully defeated," she said aloud as she pulled forward again and idled directly behind the older woman's car. Her instincts told her that the irate man might take out his anger on the woman who won the spot.

He whipped the wheel to the left and jetted past her, shooting her the bird a second time. Hayden had adopted an idiom many years ago when dealing with an unreasonable temper tantrum. *Let them stew in their own madness.* Engaging the person never ended well. Instead, she decided to let their anger ruin their own day, not hers.

The older lady exited her vehicle, waved to Hayden, and gave her a smile in appreciation. Hayden considered what she did to be a small gesture, a random act of kindness that the world needed more of. However, the encounter inside the store with the rude men, and now with the driver in the parking lot, was a reminder that emotions such as anger and resentment could fester into bigger problems. In fact, the unrest she'd observed in the news reports was testament to that.

Hayden stopped by the gun range and emptied her gun locker. If circumstances required her to leave for the Haven on short notice, she wouldn't have the luxury of gallivanting around town. She planned on getting ready to leave.

She approached a highway overpass as she crossed from Maryland back into the District of Columbia. Three young men dressed in black had gathered around the bridge abutments and were spraying the pillars with black spray paint. They weren't graffiti artists whom she'd seen work in the past. No, these men had an agenda.

They were each in various stages of completing the same image—a rose held in a man's fist. Hayden thought for a moment and reached for her iPhone. She found the camera app and slowly approached the overpass. Without the artists' noticing, she snapped a picture.

A single black rose held high in the air. It had to be symbolic of something, Hayden just didn't know what.

CHAPTER 44

New Year's Day
Capeville, Virginia

"Thirteen dollars a gallon? You're joking, right?" Angela was incredulous. Tyler had pulled into the Lankford Truck Plaza on Virginia's Eastern Shore, excited about the prospects of replenishing their near empty gasoline tank. The cans pilfered by the children had topped off the Bronco's tank and left some to spare, gaining them an extra forty miles before stopping. With a fill-up, they could easily make it to their home in Richmond.

"I'm sorry, ma'am, but we simply pass on the cost of the fuel we get from our jobber," the assistant manager explained. "Fuel is scarce all over, with most stations along the Eastern Seaboard closing up as a result. The only reason we have any to sell is because we're the first station on this side of Chesapeake Bay. And, as the sign outside reads, we're the last stop for fuel as well."

Angela was still stewing when she noticed a line was forming behind her of angry travelers, likely frustrated by the exorbitant cost, but exasperated by Angela's quibbling with the manager.

She rolled her eyes and reached into her pocket to provide the man her debit card. "We need to fill up on pump four."

"Cash only. Credit card machines are down due to what happened in New York."

"What?"

The man rudely rapped the palm of his hand on the counter. A piece of copy paper with the words CASH ONLY scribbled in ballpoint ink had been taped to the counter next to the advertisement for Marlboro cigarettes on sale.

Angela rooted around in her pocket and retrieved all of her crumpled-up cash. She flattened out the bills one at a time and spread the money out on the counter. "Give me ninety-four dollars' worth on pump four."

The man scooped up her cash, and without saying a word to acknowledge her purchase, he shoved the money in his pocket and looked to the next person in line.

Angela was about to leave and then decided against it. "Hey, I need a receipt for that. You know, for tax reasons."

The assistant manager glared at her, retrieved the cash from his pocket, and promptly rung the transaction up on the register. He angrily tore the receipt off the machine, ripping it in two, and dropped it on the counter.

She scooped up the receipt and smiled as she walked out of the truck stop, knowing that she'd made the probable thief's day a little less pleasant.

Tyler had already started pumping the gas when she returned to the truck. "Babe, we can only get ninety-four dollars' worth of gas. The thirteen-a-gallon price was correct."

"That's nuts," Tyler grumbled.

"Well, this place is full of thieves, so let's forget about it. It's probably karma, anyway."

"Huh?"

"You know, for taking that man's gas back there."

Tyler finished pumping the gas and replaced the fuel nozzle. "Angela, please don't be upset with the kids. They were just trying to help. And, as it turned out, it made a difference. We wouldn't be standing here if they didn't."

"I get that, but at the same time, what's next? What kind of risks will they take down the road in an effort to be helpful? They're just kids."

Tyler nodded and opened the door for his wife. She was getting settled in when he bent over and kissed her on the cheek. He whispered in her ear, "You're right. I'll talk with them about it when we get home. For now, we've got a hundred miles of smooth sailing to the house. Let's regroup, get a good night's rest, and then address all of this tomorrow. Cool?"

Angela reached up to touch Tyler's face and kissed him back. "Cool."

A few minutes later they approached the Eastern Shore Welcome Center, where a number of travelers were parked on the side of the road near the toll booth. Tyler slowed down before going through the lanes to pay.

"What do you think the deal is?" he asked.

Angela studied the travelers, who turned in their direction as they drove by. "They're waving at us. Maybe their cars aren't running."

"That doesn't make sense," said Tyler. "I mean, how did they get here?"

Tyler slowly approached the four-lane toll booth marking the entry to the Chesapeake Bay Bridge-Tunnel. At nearly eighteen miles long, the bridge and tunnel combination was considered one of the engineering wonders of the world. Nicknamed *Chessie*, it stretched from Virginia's Eastern Shore to the mainland near Virginia Beach.

The bridge provided scenic, breathtaking views of Chesapeake Bay and the Atlantic Ocean. Along the route, the bridge dipped down below the water's surface at the Thimble Shoal Channel tunnel and later at the Chesapeake Channel tunnel built between two manmade islands. The tunnels allowed the shipping channels to remain open for oceangoing vessels traveling in and out of Chesapeake Bay.

As they sailed past the unmanned toll booth, the Rankins looked forward to yet another aspect of their adventure. This time, they would take in a spectacular sunset during their drive across the bridge.

When they emerged on the other side of Chessie's Thimble Shoal tunnel, it would be dark. Very dark.

CHAPTER 45

New Year's Day
Chesapeake Bay Bridge-Tunnel
Virginia

Tyler stopped the truck at the man-made island entering the Thimble Shoal tunnel in order to take in an incredible sunset. The family had been through an incomparable ordeal beginning with being stranded on Kingda Ka just eighteen hours ago, to almost losing J.C. in the process of getting rescued. Their drive home had been uneventful other than the issues surrounding gasoline. With the final leg of their journey coming up, Angela and Tyler looked forward to traveling through the familiar territory that was just ten miles ahead of them on Virginia's mainland.

"Okay, who's ready to go home?" asked Tyler, who, despite not having slept all night, was remarkably alert and in good spirits. Their children had slept plenty, and Angela had even managed a catnap here and there. Tyler was functioning on adrenaline and a sense of purpose, plus an occasional bottle of Angela's Starbucks Cold Brew.

"We are!" Kaycee and J.C. responded in unison.

"I've got shotgun!" yelled Angela, and she broke in a sprint to return to the Bronco.

"I'm taking the wheel this time!" said J.C., who pushed off his sister to get a head start. He was almost on his mother's heels when Kaycee caught him.

"No way, I'm almost sixteen. Let me drive!" shouted eleven-year-old Kaycee.

She and J.C. jockeyed for the lead as they raced each other to the truck. When they arrived, the two youngsters pulled and tugged at one another to open the driver's door and slide behind the wheel.

Tyler, who thoroughly enjoyed the goofy kids he and Angela had raised, reached into his pocket to retrieve the keys. He held them high over his head with two fingers and dangled them just out of Kaycee's reach. "Hey, goobers. Nobody's going anywhere without these."

"No fair, Dad!" she protested, drawing a laugh from Tyler.

"We'll talk fairness when you turn sixteen and learn to ask *daddy dearest* for the keys then. How's that?"

Kaycee pretended a pout and then raced around the truck to enter the seat behind her mother.

"Hey! That's my side of the truck," said J.C. "I want to watch the sunset some more."

"We're going in a tunnel, dork," Kaycee shot back, teasing her younger brother.

Tyler shook his head and slid behind the wheel. He started the ignition and eased onto the road, which started its merge into two lanes. The tall concrete walls created a canyon effect that immediately blocked out the last remaining daylight and took them inside the cylindrical structure.

Rows upon rows of fluorescent lights lined both sides of U.S. 13 as the road took a noticeable drop below the surface of Chesapeake Bay. Angela studied the structure, periodically pointing out certain features to the kids. They'd traveled less than a mile when Tyler made an observation.

He leaned over and whispered to Angela, "Have you noticed we're the only car in here. I mean, nothing has passed us coming out, and I don't remember seeing anyone driving in while we were watching the sunset."

His wife shrugged and looked forward and then to their rear, as if to confirm what he was saying. "Um, maybe people have stopped for the night. Plus, gas is scarce and unaffordable, right? Traffic did die down the farther south we traveled."

Tyler seemed unconvinced. "Yeah, I guess."

With no traffic to contend with, Tyler stepped on the gas and quickly emerged on the other side of the Thimble Shoal tunnel. The sun had completely dropped below the horizon, and darkness had spread across the bay. They drove across an artificial island as the road narrowed to two lanes just before they entered the slightly longer Chesapeake Bay tunnel.

"Hey, Dad, somebody didn't pay the power bill for this tunnel," said Kaycee jokingly.

The fluorescent lights were not working, nor were the periodic yellow caution lights that had flashed continuously in the first tunnel.

"Still no traffic, babe," said Tyler. He took a long look in his rearview mirror, expecting to see headlights coming their way. Still nothing.

"Look out!" exclaimed Angela, causing Tyler to react by letting off the gas and slamming on the brakes.

The kids were thrown forward in their seats, and their stowed gear shifted around in the back. Tyler stopped just before running into the side of a pickup truck pulling a camper that had jackknifed, blocking both lanes.

"What's the deal?" asked Tyler, who allowed the engine to idle with the headlights illuminating the crash scene.

"Now I see why no cars were coming out," said Angela. "It would have been nice if they'd warned us back there about the accident."

"Maybe they tried," began Tyler. "Those people were trying to wave us down, remember?"

"Yeah, but they weren't cops or DOT workers," replied Angela. She began looking around the tunnel. "It's so narrow. Do you even have room to turn around?"

Before Tyler responded, he saw movement under the camper. "There! Did you see that? It looked like somebody was under the camper, waving their arm."

"They may be hurt," said Angela, her medically trained instincts kicking in.

Like most doctors, Angela was well-versed in the types of actions that could get her into legal trouble, especially malpractice matters. In order for a doctor to be liable for rendering medical treatment while off duty, they must owe a duty to the patient, such as a prior doctor-patient relationship. In most U.S. jurisdictions, a doctor has no affirmative duty to provide medical assistance to an injured stranger.

Angela, like most physicians, would never walk away from someone with a traumatic injury if she thought their life was in jeopardy.

She unbuckled her seat belt and reached for the door handle. "Let me check it out."

"No," said Tyler sternly. "You stay here with the kids. I'll be right back."

Before she could protest, Tyler jumped out of the Bronco and jogged to the jackknifed rig in front of them. He glanced inside the front seat and found it empty. He dropped to the ground and looked under the camper for the arm that he was certain had waved at him.

Nothing.

The whole situation bothered Tyler. Where were the emergency responders? Was Virginia Beach in the middle of something that prevented assistance from coming into the tunnel?

His mind raced as he stood and walked over the tongue of the camper's trailer to hop to the other side. That was when he found the source of the movement.

CHAPTER 46

New Year's Day
Chesapeake Bay Bridge-Tunnel
Virginia

Seven people were bound and gagged, tied together with electrical wiring and heavy-duty extension cords. Tyler stood in shock as he tried to see in the dim light provided by the Bronco's headlamps reflecting off the beige tiles lining the tunnel's walls.

He carefully approached a woman who'd fallen over near the bottom of the camper. It was her wiggling around that had caught Tyler's attention as he drove up on the jackknifed rig. He reached down to set her upright when her eyes grew wide. She grunted, trying to speak through the bandana that had been tied through her mouth and around the back of her head.

"Hold on, let me remove the—"

Tyler never finished the sentence as he was knocked across the back of his head with a two-by-four. The blow stunned him but didn't knock him out. He rolled across the concrete pavement and landed against the tile wall near a storm drain.

He tried to get on all fours and pick himself up, but the attacker was on him, kicking him in the side, knocking him down again.

"Don't get up," a man snarled at him in the dark. The man turned and spoke to another man. "Tie him up like the others. Check his pockets."

Tyler was still coherent, although his head was throbbing. The blow had caught him behind the right ear and just below the crown of his head. His head immediately began to swell, but his bigger issue at the moment was his inability to breathe due to the kicks in the ribs and stomach. The lack of oxygen and the still air in the tunnel prevented him from defending himself and shouting to Angela.

As the other attacker manhandled him onto his stomach and brusquely pulled Tyler's hands behind his back, he could make out his initial attacker speaking with a third person, a female.

"All right, it's the same as before. This time don't let them drive away."

"I won't," the woman replied. "We've got one of theirs. They ain't gonna just leave him behind."

"Either way, we've been workin' this deal for too long. We're lucky the po-pos ain't showed up."

Tyler could hear the woman kissing her partner, the ringleader of this trio of thugs. He was in pain but was fully aware of what was happening.

The three were opportunists, common criminals taking advantage of this car wreck in the tunnel. There was only one way out, and that was back toward Virginia Beach. He was still astonished that law enforcement hadn't arrived on the scene yet, but from the looks of the bodies piling up around him, perhaps nobody was able to reach out for help, or cell service was unavailable inside the tunnel.

Tyler stayed on the ground and pretended to be incapacitated as the other man rifled through his pockets. He took Tyler's license and credit card, together with the fifty dollars in cash out of his left pocket. He tossed aside the license before shoving the cash and credit card in his pocket.

"How'd we do?"

"He's the poorest one yet," the man replied in disgust. "Fifty bucks and some plastic."

The leader voiced his disappointment. "That sucks."

"I'm done with this crap, man. Let's get the hell outta here."

The woman agreed. "Yeah, we can burn through these credit cards on the other side and then head up to Wilmington. They're tearin' up the town, from what the news said."

"We'll take the new guy's car," began the leader. "If we see any cops, we'll tell 'em to hurry. Man, we'll be long gone before they figure it out."

Tyler's eyes grew wide as he tried to come up with a way to warn Angela. He wiggled around to get a better view of his surroundings, hoping to find some way to signal to her. There were no options and he was too late. The trio left the hostages and split up.

The woman left first, finding her way between the camper and the pickup as Tyler had done. The leader circled around the front of the pickup, his feet shuffling along as he squeezed between the bumper and the wall. The man who tied up Tyler walked around the back of the camper, kicking Tyler in the side one more time as he walked past.

Tyler closed his eyes and concentrated. He felt helpless. His only option was to try to be seen by Angela, so he forced himself to roll over in an attempt to reach the underside of the camper. Wedged against the tires, his progress was stopped, and all he could do was listen to what was happening.

"That's close enough!" Angela shouted. "Don't take another step."

"Or what, lady?"

"I'll drop you to the ground, as in dead!"

Tyler had never heard Angela like this. Her voice reflected a combination of anger and crazy.

The attacker's steps slowed but didn't stop. Each of them inched forward toward the Bronco, hesitating at first and then, emboldened by their numbers, pressed the attack.

"Come on, lady," the leader continued. "You got a gun or somethin'? You ain't gonna shoot it."

"Try me," snarled Angela.

The man nearest Tyler laughed and lowered his voice. "Give it up. You ain't shootin' nobody."

"Really?" Angela asked sarcastically. "Who wants to be first?"

"Step aside and give us your truck!" the woman shouted at Angela.

"No!"

"Lady, you ain't no killer," the leader shouted as he picked up the pace and approached the truck.

"No, I'm a mother!"

Angela quickly fired two rounds into the man's torso, the explosive report of the powerful .45-caliber weapon echoed off the tunnel's walls.

"Billy!" exclaimed the woman as she could be heard rushing to the leader's side.

"Damn you!" shouted the other man as he dashed toward Angela.

Two more shots rang out, and the sound of the large man's body crashing into the grille of the Bronco could be heard, indicating the second attacker had been hit.

Suddenly, the woman jumped between the camper and the pickup, dashing through the tied-up bodies, but she didn't escape. Two of the men tied together rolled over in unison and tripped her, causing her to stumble and crash to the pavement before striking her head on another car.

Tyler could hear her scrambling to get up, and the grunts of the hostages told the story. Working together, several of the tied-up pairs hopped on their butts until they were on top of the woman, pinning her down so she couldn't get away.

Seconds later, Angela emerged around the wrecked camper, swinging the gun from side to side, searching for a target.

"Tyler!" she shouted.

He grunted his response and tried to wiggle out of the restraints. She rushed to his side and loosened the cloth used to gag him.

"Are they dead?" he asked.

"Oh, yeah," she replied. "How many more?"

Still gasping for air, Tyler said, "Just her. Make sure that one doesn't get away."

Angela made her way around the tied-up bodies and only stumbled once as she found the men sitting on the injured woman who'd been part of the attack. The woman was struggling to get up, but the more she did, the more the men pushed the weight of their bodies down on her back.

Angela removed their gags so they could speak. "Are you guys okay?"

"Sure," replied the younger of the two. "Can you untie us?"

"Hang on," she replied. She swung around and ran back to the Bronco. As she cleared the camper, she found the kids, who'd left the Bronco. They were staring at the dead man who'd collapsed against the truck's grille.

"Kids, I said stay down in the backseat." She used her arms to herd them away from the dead body.

"Sorry, Mom, but we knew they were dead."

"Yes, Kaycee, they are. And I really didn't want you to see this. Please get back in the truck."

"Okay," said a dejected J.C.

Angela made sure they were secure, and then she retrieved Tyler's knife from his backpack. She returned to the hostages, and despite her concern for her husband, she untied the two men holding the woman down first. They immediately returned the favor and trussed the woman up, facedown on the concrete highway.

After she untied Tyler, she checked on everyone to see if anyone had more serious injuries. While she checked her husband's protruding knot on the back of his head and his tender ribs, sirens could be heard in the tunnel, although the echo effect obscured the direction they were coming from.

She helped Tyler to his feet, and they made their way back to the Bronco. In her backpack, she kept several instant ice compresses. The single-use packets provided pain relief from sprains to bee stings to nasty bumps on the head. She simply squeezed the packet and shook it vigorously, resulting in an icy cold method of reducing the swollen knot on Tyler's head.

"Okay, your ribs aren't broken, but they are bruised."

Tyler nodded and said, "It hurts to breathe, especially when I inhale."

"Understandable. Until you heal, you'll be taking more shallow breaths. I'm gonna give you some Advil for your pain. You really need another ice packet, but both injuries are on your right side. I've got some KT Tape in my bag. I'm gonna wrap it around your midsection and then add two more ice compresses. I'll wrap them in place until we can get you to a hospital."

"No," said Tyler, taking shallow breaths in between sentences. "Home. Let's get home."

"Okay, okay," she said with a laugh. She pulled out the Kinesio tape, an elastic cotton strip with an acrylic adhesive used to create a snug fit. "Hold still while I get you taped up. Then I'm gonna check with the police who just showed up."

Tyler nodded and allowed his wife, the ER doctor, to patch him up. Before she could get him into the truck, two police officers emerged between the pickup and camper with their weapons drawn. They immediately checked the pulse of the two dead attackers and cautiously approached the Bronco.

"Are you folks all right?" the female officer asked.

"Yes, my husband's banged up, but we're better than those two. I'm Dr. Angela Rankin."

The male officer addressed Angela. "Dr. Rankin, I'm Officer Francis, and this is my partner, Officer Wilson. Um, ma'am, did you shoot these two men?"

"I did," she quickly replied.

"We're gonna need the gun, please, ma'am. It's just procedure."

"Sure, I understand," replied Angela as she reached behind her back and pulled the handgun from the waistband of her jeans. She held the barrel with her fingers and handed it to the officer like she was holding a dead rat by the tail.

"Thank you." The female officer led the conversation while the other officer placed the weapon in a plastic baggie he retrieved out of his rear pocket. "Please stay with your vehicle while we process the scene. Detectives are on their way and will need to take your statements. Do you understand?"

"Yes, of course," replied Angela.

"Do you folks have ID?"

Angela retrieved her license from her pocket and handed it to the officer. She looked at it in the truck's headlights. Tyler explained that his was on the ground behind the camper. After a few more instructions, Angela got Tyler settled in the passenger seat. She walked around the back of the Bronco to avoid stepping on the dead man who was bleeding out on the pavement.

For a minute, the family sat in the truck before Angela found the presence of mind to shut off the ignition. After the police officers established temporary lighting in the tunnel, she turned off the headlights as well.

An ambulance arrived together with an investigative unit that would undertake the hours-long, arduous task of processing this crime scene. Ten minutes had passed, and none of the Rankins spoke a word until J.C. broke the silence.

His innocent words saddened Angela, who never wanted her children exposed to something like this.

"Mom, dead people don't really look like they're sleeping."

He was right. There was nothing peaceful about being dead.

CHAPTER 47

Naval Station Norfolk
Norfolk, Virginia

It was late evening when the USS *Virginia* arrived at the Naval Station in Norfolk, Virginia. The base was the home port of four carrier strike groups and their assigned ships. In addition, the six submarines of the Atlantic Fleet, now supplemented with the *Virginia*, occupied what was generally recognized as the world's largest naval station.

While on board, Donna was seen by one of the specially designated doctors who'd been awarded the Submarine Medical Insignia. He'd been through medical exercises and qualification measures in submarine warfare. The additional training required for the special designation included radiation health, diving medicine, and submarine medicine.

Life aboard a submarine has been described as raunchy, cramped, and occasionally, the underwater vessel literally smells like a porta-potty. It took a psychological toll on the submariners. There were additional risks, however.

Every day at sea brings with it a certain amount of risk, including exposure to radiation. Nearly one-third of the *Virginia*'s interior was made up of nuclear components related to powering the vessel and its payload of armaments.

Tom, who was invited to spend some time with Commander Anderson, enjoyed a tour of the *Virginia* and hung out for a while in the submarine's control room and attack center.

The doctor bandaged Donna's ankle to immobilize it, allowing Donna to put more weight on it as she walked. As he cared for her, they discussed her cancer and the effect radiation exposure might have on her remission status.

Since Donna was alone with the doctor, she told him about being in Times Square. The doctor confided in her that the Department of Defense believed the drones were equipped with dirty bombs. He went on to explain the impact that might have on her remission from the breast cancer and what signs to watch for in the future.

Donna was initially distraught, but the doctor quickly reassured her that the chances of her body ingesting enough of the radiological material to set her back were slim. He provided her a sedative and suggested rest was absolutely necessary for her ankle, and her state of mind.

She eventually shook off the negative thoughts and allowed the sleeping aid to work its magic. When Tom awakened her, she'd slept the entire trip from Groton to Norfolk.

"Dear, Commander Anderson has a car waiting for us. All military installations in the country have been placed on their highest level of readiness."

"I slept like a baby," she mumbled as she sat upright in her bunk. "There's something to this sleeping while on the water."

Tom laughed and helped her get ready. She was able to put more weight on her ankle now, so moving about was much easier. Within ten minutes, they'd gathered their belongings and were escorted onto dry land, where a base police vehicle awaited.

It was late that evening as they drove from the naval base to the city of Norfolk. Their plan was to secure a hotel room, rent a car, and study the news reports so they could make a decision. The MP apologized for rushing them off the base. Naval Station Norfolk, like all military installations around the country, had been placed on the highest level of security alert.

After 9/11, the Department of Defense established a terrorist threat system known as Force Protection Condition, FPCON for short. The five levels of protection range from FPCON Normal, which applies to a situation of no terrorist activity, up to FPCON Delta, describing a situation when a terrorist attack had taken place or was occurring in the immediate area of the base.

This was a red flag to Tom as to the position the DOD had taken following the New Year's Eve attacks. Their intelligence must have indicated future terrorist attacks were imminent for them to place all military facilities on FPCON Delta—the highest state of alert. In fact, if this designation had been made before they boarded the *Virginia*, even Trowbridge's connections couldn't have gained the Sheltons passage on the submarine.

As they drove down the Hampton Roads Beltway toward town, half a dozen police cars and emergency vehicles raced past them with their sirens and emergency lights fully operational.

"Wow!" exclaimed Donna, fully recovered from her Ambien-induced deep sleep. "Something big must've happened."

The military police officer provided an explanation. "We constantly monitor local law enforcement frequencies in case something outside the base develops into a threat to our security. That's especially true since last night."

"Makes sense," interjected Tom, who'd had the same procedures established for Joint Base Charleston.

"Yes, sir. Anyway, the locals kicked it into high gear a little while ago. Apparently, there was a multicar collision in Chessie that escalated into something far worse."

"Chessie?" asked Donna.

"Oh, sorry, ma'am. Chessie is the nickname for the Chesapeake Bay Bridge-Tunnel. The accident blocked both lanes of the tunnel, but that's only part of it. There have been reports of hostages and shots fired inside. SWAT teams have been dispatched and also ambulances, as injuries, even fatalities, are presumed."

"Great," began Tom. "It seems to be a sign of the times."

"Yes, sir," said the driver. "I have to say, this is nothing compared to the reports coming out of DC and my hometown of Philly. The city of brotherly love is anything but that. It's like a war zone up there. Washington has major problems, too. In DC, with transportation at a standstill, together with panic spreading down from New York into the capital, the National Guard had to step up in an effort to restore order."

"This happened tonight?" asked Tom.

"No, that's the thing about it," replied the officer. "These savages began burning the city during the daytime, totally different from what we've seen in the past. Usually, once nightfall hits, the torches are lit. Not on this New Year's Day. Cities are burning round the clock."

Tom leaned back against the headrest and closed his eyes, wishing this nightmare would end.

CHAPTER 48

DoubleTree Hotel
Norfolk, Virginia

While Donna checked in at the DoubleTree Hotel near the Norfolk Airport, Tom rented a car at the twenty-four-hour kiosk operated by Payless Car Rentals. It was midnight when they were finally able to crash on top of their bed and stare at the ceiling.

Tom spoke first. "When we got married, I promised you our lives wouldn't be boring. I have to say, the last twenty-four hours has more than fulfilled my promise to you, Mrs. Shelton."

Donna laughed. "I've come to appreciate boring. Boring is good."

Tom's fingers found his wife's hand, and they lay there for a moment, holding one another. They joked about what they'd been through.

"Let's recap, shall we?" began Donna.

"Sure, go ahead. Let's recap then hit the minibar for a nightcap."

"You're a poet and didn't know it," said Donna as she raised his hand up and down, rhythmically pounding it on the mattress.

"Yeah, I guess so. Where do we start? Our fabulous hotel dinner for two, topped off with pricey champagne? Or should we go straight for the good stuff. You know, when we were in the middle of Times Square on New Year's Eve, waiting for the ball to drop."

Donna laughed. "It's a shame we can't stop there, because all of those things helped fulfill one of my dreams with you."

"Why don't we? Stop there, I mean. Let's remember the experience before the world went to hell."

"I wish I could," said Donna, turning suddenly serious. "We need to decide if we're going back to Charleston or to the Haven."

Tom let go of her hand and sat up in bed. He found the television remote on the nightstand and began to scan the cable news networks. There weren't any new attacks, so the reporting focused on the aftermath of the New Year's Eve incidents.

"It's all the same," said Donna. "People are looting, stealing, and acting out because they can. There aren't enough police officers to control the rioting."

"The good news is only certain cities are experiencing this. The large metropolitan areas that were the brunt of the attacks are the worst."

Donna propped up against the headboard too, using an extra pillow to elevate her ankle. "Tom, should you reach out to Tommie? I know you have to respect her job, especially at a time like this, but we need to decide if it's safe to go home."

"I could call Blair and Ryan at the Haven," countered Tom. "They keep a pretty good pulse on these things, and I consider them both to be levelheaded."

"Sure, but I know what they're gonna say," began Donna as Tom joined her and the two spoke in unison.

"*Come to the Haven. You can always go home if nothing happens.*"

They laughed together as they politely mocked the developers of the Haven. Tom finally regained his composure.

Tom directed the subject to the Smarts. "You know, I never got the sense those two were trying to sell us property. It was more like, I don't know, an interview. It's as if they were trying to surround themselves with people they could trust."

"And get along with," interjected Donna. "They didn't seem to need our money. They needed *us* more."

"That's what sold me on the place, and it's the best insurance policy we've ever purchased. I could call Blair or Ryan, and even Tommie, but I think I know what we should do."

"Listen, Tom. The Haven is practically on our way home anyway. Why not stop there, ride out this storm, and decide whether it's necessary to stay or not. Our cabin is stocked with food and drinks. The closets are full of clothes. You love to fish, and I'm sure I can hang out with some of the kids who are there. I just got an email from Blair the other day with pictures of the new schoolhouse. I'd love to put some of my old teaching skills to work."

"It's settled, then. Crack of dawn, we're up and at 'em, headed to the Haven."

CHAPTER 49

New Year's Day
Richmond, Virginia

It was three hours before the CSI unit had adequately processed the crime scene, cleared the crashed vehicles, and removed the dead bodies. Although Tyler and Angela had been cleared to leave, they were cautioned against backtracking up to the interstate. Wilmington's streets were out of control, and social unrest had spread into Baltimore and Washington, DC. Despite the anticipated delay, the Rankins were still better off waiting for the tunnel to be cleared. So they napped until they were given the go-ahead.

It was almost midnight when they pulled into the driveway of their modest Richmond home near VCU Medical Center on East Clay Street, where Angela worked. Tyler insisted that he was fine to go home and argued repeatedly against going to the hospital for X-rays. Angela constantly felt his forehead and neck for signs of a fever. She gave him a pass on a hospital visit because he wasn't exhibiting any signs of a concussion or broken ribs.

The military bases around Virginia Beach, Norfolk, and Newport News were bustling with activity as they drove past. The National Guard had been called in to regain control of the cities from Washington, DC, to New York City, as well as those that had been attacked in other parts of the country.

Despite being exhausted, Angela and Tyler flipped through the news networks, gathering as much information as possible. The events of the last twenty-four hours had frightened them, and they feared for their family's safety.

"Tyler, even Richmond is in chaos as refugees are spilling into the city from the north. It's just a matter of time before the crap that we're seeing in Baltimore shows up at our doorstep."

"Agreed. We've got to go. It's like we've said, we can always come back. I mean, look at the trouble we had getting home. In another few days, we may have trouble getting out of town."

Angela wandered around the living room as she spoke. "I think you're good to travel. I mean, at least from a medical perspective. But how do you feel?"

"I'll let you know in the morning. I've been banged up before. Remember the West End fire?"

Tyler had been in one of the first fire crews on the scene of a massive house fire in the city's West End neighborhood. During an effort to save a child trapped on an upper floor, a support beam fell on him, knocking him to the floor. He managed to get up and reach the child before they crawled onto the roof and were assisted to the ground. He suffered a back injury in the process that took weeks of recovery and rehabilitation.

"Is your pain as bad as that?" asked Angela.

"No, not even close. I swear, I'll be fine. Besides, we have no choice."

"Agreed," said Angela. She reached for the remote to turn off the television. "I've seen enough news, how about you?"

"No doubt. Plus, I'm tired of being part of the news. Between last night and this evening, it makes me wonder what tomorrow will bring."

Angela helped him off the sofa and stood in front of him. "I love you, Tyler Rankin. When I met you, I found me. I'll never forget the moment, and that day. We'd known each other for forty-seven days, practically living and working under the same roof. And then, all of a sudden, it struck me on day forty-seven. I really love this guy and I want to spend the rest of my life with him."

"Yeah." Tyler beamed. "I remember. Just out of nowhere, you told me that you loved me."

Angela teared up, a rare show of emotion. Then she laughed. "Trust me, I remember. And what did you say in response?"

"Um," Tyler hesitated.

Angela laughed as she wiped a few tears off her cheeks. "Yeah, exactly. Nothing. Nada. Crickets."

"No. Not really. I said—"

Angela was not gonna let him off the hook. "You said something like we share the same secret."

"That's right."

"Tyler, that was so lame. When a woman says she's in love with you, you say it back."

Tyler was in big trouble, and he knew it. "I did, eventually."

"But you left me hanging!"

"I know, I know. I mean, I couldn't believe it. You're beautiful, smart, and way better than I deserve. I thought for sure you'd change your mind after we got to know one another."

Angela led him into the bedroom. "Nope, and here we are, twelve years later. We have our beautiful kids, Kaycee and J.C. Our life is anything but boring. And the future is, well, if nothing else, gonna be interesting, right?"

"No doubt."

CHAPTER 50

Schwartz Estate
Katonah, New York

Jonathan Schwartz finished up a phone call and joined his father standing in front of the fire. Father and son had a nightly ritual in which they shared a glass of brandy and focused on their accomplishments in order to finish the day on a positive note. Tonight, as midnight approached, the mood was solemn. Millions weren't made. Hundreds weren't freed. Today, thousands weren't given an opportunity at a better life.

"The future is far from certain, son." The old man was philosophical. He took a sip of the brandy and grimaced as it soaked his throat going down.

Jonathan toasted him. "Lincoln once said the best way to predict your future is to create it."

"It is hard to disagree with that statement except there are so many uncertainties. One of my adversaries believes that either you control destiny, or destiny controls you."

"An adversary with one foot in the grave, Father. Unlike you."

"Do not underestimate him. He is tired, and his body may be ailing, but his wits are sharp. There is no more formidable adversary than he."

"Still, he's no longer a field general. He has an army, but how are they led?"

Schwartz finished his brandy and set the glass on a cocktail table near two leather chairs facing the fireplace. He gestured for his son to join him as he lowered himself onto the luxurious Italian leather.

Jonathan hovered near the fire for a moment, gently running his fingers along a blackish-bronze sculpture of a fist holding a black rose in the air. He adjusted it so the base lined up with the edge of the mantel. Then he joined his father, who responded to the question.

"He fights differently than I. I rely upon raw emotion and the will of the people. He is subtle. Even mysterious, as if form and sound doesn't exist in his actions. His forte is deception and sleight of hand."

Jonathan interrupted his father. "In that way, he determines his opponent's fate."

Schwartz laughed. "That, my son, is how he wins. Many consider fate and destiny to be interchangeable, but they are not. Fate is predetermined by the natural order of things. Regardless of what man does to alter their actions, their fate is the end result of the culmination of events in one's life." He took a deep breath and continued. "Destiny is much different. There is an element of choice in destiny. Qualities such as courage, compassion, willpower, and patience all have a profound impact on one's destiny. Fate is that which you cannot change."

Jonathan sat a little taller in his chair, always confident in his assertions. "I believe that destiny is on our side."

His father countered. "George Trowbridge believes it to be on his."

"We'll see," mumbled Jonathan as he finished his brandy and set it forcefully on the table between them. "The fuse has been lit."

THANK YOU FOR READING *DOOMSDAY: HAVEN*

If you enjoyed it, I'd be grateful if you'd take a moment to write a short review (just a few words are needed) and post it on Amazon. Amazon uses complicated algorithms to determine what books are recommended to readers. Sales are, of course, a factor, but so are the quantities of reviews my books get. By taking a few seconds to leave a review, you help me out and also help new readers learn about my work.

And before you go …

SIGN UP for Bobby Akart's mailing list to receive special offers, bonus content, and you'll be the first to receive news about new releases in the Doomsday series. Visit: www.BobbyAkart.com

VISIT Amazon.com/BobbyAkart for more information on the Doomsday series, the Yellowstone series, the Lone Star series, the Pandemic series, the Blackout series, the Boston Brahmin series and the Prepping for Tomorrow series, totaling thirty-plus novels, including over twenty Amazon #1 Bestsellers in forty-plus fiction and nonfiction genres. Visit Bobby Akart's website for informative blog entries on preparedness, writing, and a behind-the-scenes look into his novels.

www.ingramcontent.com/pod-product-compliance
Lightning Source LLC
Chambersburg PA
CBHW020936310726
48980CB00007B/795/J